IF I DISAPPEAR

IF I DISAPPEAR

ELIZA JANE BRAZIER

THORNDIKE PRESS
A part of Gale, a Cengage Company

LIBRARY OF CONGRESS CIP DATA ON FILE.
CATALOGUING IN PUBLICATION FOR THIS BOOK
IS AVAILABLE FROM THE LIBRARY OF CONGRESS.

ISBN-13: 978-1-4328-8362-1 (hardcover alk. paper)

Published in 2021 by arrangement with Berkley, an imprint of Penguin Publishing Group, a division of Penguin Random House LLC.

Printed in Mexico
Print Number: 01   Print Year: 2021

To Vanessa Wass. Don't disappear.

Every morning when I wake up to the cries of the baby next door, I turn you on. In the dark of a room that smells of the dog that lived here before, you tell the story of Asha Degree. Nine years old and she walked out of her home with a book bag, in the middle of the night, in the middle of a rainstorm. They forget but you remember. You are the hero of the heroless stories. You will save people; will they save you?

I listen to your podcast until three, four in the morning. I can't sleep. I miss work the next day. I lie in bed, and I turn you on again.

Together we travel through the depths of human depravity: the Manson murders, the Black Dahlia, Ted Bundy, all the murders of the Zodiac. We look because we have to. Because no one else will. You talked about the disappearance of Laci Peterson, and I thought, *You understand. You understand what it is to be a woman in a world that wants you to disappear.*

Your last episode goes out on March 27. It's almost spring break, and you tell the story of the murder of April Atkins, in a house filled with mannequins. It's dark and getting darker, but we know, we both know, that this story is important and has to be told. That this mystery is vital and has to be solved. The beaches are packed and the boardwalk is crowded and only we know.

There are no updates over Easter, so I go back and binge every episode, every word you ever told me. You have taught me the importance of details, and I make a note of every one. You grew up on a ranch near Happy Camp, California (population: 1,006), a town that was once known as "Murderer's Bar." You said it was preordained. You were destined for this job. In your worst moments, you also said, *I sometimes wonder if I'm destined to disappear.*

You said this on March 27, your final episode, and then you disappeared. No podcasts, no posts. Your Instagram and Twitter went inactive, no tweets about your cat, no filtered pictures of your yellow house with unfiltered posts about what it means to be alone and alive when everybody else isn't.

I'm destined to disappear, you said, and then you vanished. Your episodes stayed up, your pictures and your posts stayed up, but the updates stopped.

I still can't sleep. I relisten to every episode until I memorize the stories, know every turn by heart. *She crashed her car on a rural road. By the time the cops arrived, she was already gone.*

I know, the first forty-eight hours are crucial. And every hour you don't update, I think, *Something is wrong.* I think, *The case is going cold.*

I read every Instagram post, every tweet. I write down every detail.

Episode 57: You can never guess who will murder you, can you? Not until it happens. But you might have some idea. You might be suspicious, even before the fact.
Episode 37: Your best friend should carry a list of names, a list of people to question, if something happens to you.
Episode 49: I would want to leave a trail. I would want a good story, at least.

I leave the house to buy tea and realize it's been days since I've talked to another human being. My hair is unbrushed. My clothes don't match. I listen to your podcast

9

on my phone all the way to the supermarket.

I slip around the people in the aisles like I'm not even there. I find the tea, hurry toward the front. I feel this sense of panic, of dread, like not looking cute is a crime, and I don't want to get caught.

I hand the tea to the clerk. He says, "How are you?" and my first impulse is to tell him about you. I want to tell him you're missing. I want to ask if he thinks you might be dead. But that is crazy, sounds crazy, looks crazy. But isn't that what they want us to think? Isn't that why cases go unsolved? Because no one realizes there is evil around us all the time.

I turn your podcast on as soon as I get back to the car. I shut the door, and your voice fills the space.

". . . She swerved to avoid rocks and the car spun out, landed sideways in a copse of trees above the river. . . ."

I grip the steering wheel as I drive.

". . . She staggered out into the dark. An eyewitness passed her on the road. 'I told the police when they asked me,' the witness later said. 'I don't care to comment beyond that.' If she had stopped to help her, this might have been a very different story."

I pull into my space in the underground parking lot. The tea is gone. I recall putting it on top of my car when I went to unlock the door; then I turned on your podcast and forgot it was there. It must have slipped off when I drove away. I could go back and look for it, but the tea mystery is not worth solving.

"What would you do?" you ask as I exit my car, take the stairs up to my apartment. "If you saw a woman alone on the road after dark?" I pass along the hallway, all the doors of the neighbors I don't know. "Would you help her? Would you stop? Or would you just. Keep. Driving?"

I stand outside my door. I slip my hands into my pockets, where my keys should be.

". . . Sometimes I wonder . . ."

My pockets are empty. I left my keys inside the apartment. I try to turn the knob, but I have set the door to lock automatically. You told me to, in case of break-ins.

". . . would anyone look for me?"

I catch my own reflection in the mirror down the hall and think it's you.

". . . Would anyone care?"

The timer on the overhead light buzzes. The lights go out. In the dark, your voice expands, grips me like a chill.

". . . If I disappeared."

Your voice cuts out. I am alone in the dark, and I know, deep in my bones, you want me to find you.

You have prepared me. You have taught me everything I need to know. You always knew you would disappear. And you knew I would find you. I know you better than anyone. I know to ask questions and — most important — I know not to give up. I will solve your mystery. I will save you. It was meant to be me.

EPISODE 1:
ON THE MURDER LINE

San Quentin Prison is located eight hours south of the Siskiyou Forest. There is one bus route that travels through this wilderness, into the dead space between Eureka and Yreka. The locals call it the Murder Line. Recently released convicts, prison escapees and drifters hop on this line and vanish into the forest.

One blue-skied summer day, four teenage girls in tank tops and cutoff jeans hopped on the eleven thirty bus from Happy Camp, headed north. One was never seen again.

The road to your parents' ranch coils up from Eureka, a port city in Northern California. You warned me that the road was winding, but I didn't expect the way it bends and twists, collapsing in and out like an accordion, offering one lonely vista. Spin. Offering another. The mountains above, crowded with trees. The snaking river. The falling rocks on the flexing road. My mind flexes with it, in and out, in and out. And then another bend in the road.

Trucks start to stack up behind me, and I search frantically for a place to pull over. A pale sliver of a turnout appears, on the edge of the cliff above the river. I glance at the line of cars behind me. I jerk the wheel, and my car drops off the road, juddering on the dirt. My hands are sticky with sweat. My heart pulses.

I stop the car, yank up the parking brake. I flinch as I envision the brake snapping, the inevitable slide to the river below. Even on flat ground, I picture the land giving way. And I race headlong into the river. I know about the Klamath River from Episode 15: *a muddy brown color;* Episode 43: *so strong that when people drown, their bodies are swept all the way to the ocean.* My body will wash up along the shore, hundreds of miles away from here.

I wait for my heart to stop racing, give up and check the parking brake again.

I stick one white, chalky Dramamine between my teeth. In Episode 13, you said you took two Dramamine a day just to get to and from high school. But still you got dizzy; you still felt sick. *Eventually,* you said,

I realized it wasn't worth leaving the ranch.

Fountain Creek Guest Ranch, the place you grew up. They offer fishing, horseback riding, breathtaking vistas, but most of all, they offer isolation. You grew up in a place where no one else lived.

Episode 18: I could hear myself think, which wasn't always a good thing.

Episode 34: I will never not know what it's like to enjoy my own company.

Your life was idyllic, until a local girl — a girl just like you — disappeared.

Episode 1: When bad things happen in a small town — I don't mean to say it's worse. I don't mean to diminish anyone's experience. But there were twenty-three kids in my entire school. And then there were twenty-two.

Nothing truly bad has ever happened to me, and I envy you this, a clear reason: my life changed when, things fell apart when. I break a sweat and think it must be my fault.

You became fascinated, first by her disappearance, and then by the disappearances of others: local, national, global. You researched, you became a part of the true-crime community and then you started your own podcast. You wanted to make a difference. You wanted to save someone. You wanted to save everyone.

Episode 14: When I think someone somewhere might hear this . . . when I think anyone anywhere can access it . . . Yes, I don't have the audience of *Dateline* or even *My Favorite Murder,* but the thing about a podcast is, anyone anywhere can listen. And maybe you will be the one to find someone who is missing. Maybe you hold the key to the evidence that will solve a murder. Maybe I can be the reason someone is saved.

You broadcast from your house on your parents' land: a yellow house with a red roof drawn in lines so idealized, it could be a Disneyland attraction.

I found the ranch website online. It bragged that it was a "family-run business." I saw your picture, you for the first time, and you looked exactly like I thought you would. You looked like me.

Below me the Klamath River is fast and brown. Above me the mountains are piled with trees. From Episode 1, I know that they are firs, pines, oaks, maples, madrones, spruce and manzanitas. I recognize this

16

world from your pictures, but I am not prepared for the sheer majesty of it, the car-commercial, Reese Witherspoon–in–*Wild,* Instagram-is-not-enough expanse. I've never been anywhere like this. If it weren't for you, I wouldn't even know it existed.

I think, oddly, how excited you would be, if you were here with me, diving into your own disappearance, solving your own mystery. I take a deep breath, and I plug in my phone and press play. Your voice fills my car, gravelly but discreet, breathing mystery.

I release the parking brake, start the engine and pull back onto the road. I pass a strip of highway dedicated to Dear Mad'm, and I remember you told me her story (Episode 19). Dear Mad'm was an eighty-year-old woman who moved to a primitive cabin on the Klamath in the nineteen fifties to garden, hide from cougars and write a book. She decided her life wasn't over, but to do that, she had to leave behind the world that told her it was. She had to come here.

I am sailing, inspired, when the road curves and I don't slow fast enough and the car slides and my stomach lurches. And suddenly I'm absolutely sure I am wrong about everything.

You're not missing; you just logged off. I will arrive at your yellow house and find you there, and I will say, *Hey, I was just in the area, longtime listener.* And you will stumble backward, afraid. And when your next episode goes out you will say:

Episode 85:
This morning my psycho stalker showed up at my house, as if she was in the neighborhood. I think she wants to kill me. If something happens to me, her name is Sera Fleece.

She is your typical loser/burnout. You know the type. She thought that if she hit certain markers, made the right achievements, her life would pedal itself, would speed off so she could just relax, satisfied, achieved. But instead it kept asking her to drive it; it kept sputtering, breaking down, falling apart. She dropped out of college when she got married. Then she was pregnant; then she wasn't. Her husband left. And she had to start over again. So she got a job but it didn't pay enough. She found another guy but he didn't love her enough. So she got another job that paid less, an apartment that charged more. She found a guy who loved her less, and another one who loved her even less after that. Every year was less, so she cared less and less.

18

And then she stopped caring completely. And then she came looking for me.

My hands are shaking as I pull into another turnout. It's like you can hear my thoughts, wherever you are. It's like you are watching me. I see vultures circling up ahead, in the space between two mountains. And I wonder if they are here for you or me. I wonder how you would tell my story, if I disappeared.

I have gone too far. I missed the turnoff for the ranch, somewhere between the spins and the trees. I have the mile marker (63), but the numbers don't match, and now my phone screen is a wheel, circling around a lost signal.

You warned me about the phone service. Per Episode 7: There is no cell phone service, *none,* from Eureka to Yreka except for one huge turnout above the Klamath, just south of Happy Camp, where one network (Verizon) gets service some of the time. On any given day there is at least one car parked out there on the edge of the cliff, with the sky overhead, and the signal invisible, somewhere above, so the seeker holds their phone up to the sky.

I was prepared. I took screenshots of the

directions on Google Maps. I wrote down the mile marker number, but I still missed your parents' ranch. I know this when I reach Happy Camp. There are low buildings scattered inside a wide river basin, a self-pump gas station, a bear with a dial that tells me there's always a chance of a fire. A sign reads *Welcome to Happy Camp: Home of Outdoor Family Recreation* above a picture of a silver steelhead the size of a shark.

I pull into a deserted parking lot and debate where I should go from here. I could turn around, focus harder, seek out the mile markers as the road twirls, or I could ask for directions.

I have to pee, so I get out of the car.

My head is still spinning. My legs are stiff and my knees wobble as I make my way to the center of town, one block away. I walk up Main Street (you used to call it "the rabbit hutch" because all the meth heads in their trailers stayed up all night, scurrying, scratching like animals in cages). I walk past the police station — per Episode 7, open only four hours a day — past the Happy Camp Arts Center, with the confusing signage on the door: *Don't come in — this is a house!!!*

The mill and the silver mine closed in the eighties; that's also when Happy Camp lost the second grocery store and the Evans Mercantile and the video store and the restaurant with the twenty-page menu.

I find the only coffee shop and head inside. It's narrow, with a kindergarten-classroom quality — clean but with too many amateur works of art. There are bookshelves along the wall, a rack of T-shirts in the corner. Six men in various stages of Hank Williams gather in one corner on foldout chairs, talking about lumber. I walk to the back and use the bathroom.

I wash my hands at the sink and ignore my face in the mirror. When I'm not wearing makeup, I generally feel that I don't deserve to exist. I decide that I don't need to ask for directions. What answer could anyone possibly give me? Twelfth tree on the fifth bend?

I duck out of the bathroom and rush across the floor as the men discuss wood infestations. A woman steps in front of me, an empty teacup in each hand. Long, thin dreads wrestle all the way down past her waist.

"All good," she says, no inflection. I duck toward the bookshelves.

"I just wanted to see your books." I lie, because I feel guilty for using the bathroom without asking. I want her to believe that I

21

am a customer and my bathroom use was just incidental. I want her to think that I am a serious buyer in the market for a good book.

"We do exchanges, or the price is on the cover."

I look at the books on the shelves. I am surprised by the selection, by the lack of religious books such shelves tend to collect. Instead they have Stephen King's *It,* well-worn but priced by size at three dollars, *A Room with a View* and *The Handmaid's Tale* for a buck fifty. I almost buy it just because I can't believe it's here.

The woman stands over me, watching, not saying anything.

I should ask her for directions; I know this, but it pings that I need to be careful. Anyone could be a suspect. Anyone could hold a clue. And I need to keep myself open. I need to hide my intentions until I find out whether you really have gone missing or you are actually here. I think of you, what you would do. How you would keep yourself aloof but innocuous, powered by righteousness.

"Do you know this area well?"

"I grew up here." She steadies her clattering teacup. "What brings you to Happy Camp?" I am sure she knows that I am here alone and that she is judging me for it. In my mind, in that moment, she knows everything about me, and she is smug and superior about it.

"A friend," I answer defensively, and immediately regret it.

"Who?"

"You probably don't know her." I cast my eyes around the store.

"I probably do."

The six in the circle quiet and tilt their heads in our direction. It's everybody's business. The population shrank, and I crossed the line into everybody's business.

"Dear Mad'm," I say like a crazy person. I see three copies of a slim yellow book on a bookshelf, a poster on the wall.

The woman steps back, satisfied that I am a psychopath. "No offense, but I'm pretty sure she's dead."

"I'm a writer." I straighten up. This is my official lie. I do write sometimes, journal entries about how I'm too depressed to write, mostly, but I like the idea of it. A traveling writer, always hunting for a story. "Like she was."

"What do you write?"

"Mystery." Mystery is what I write.

"Oh yeah? You gonna write about this place?" Whenever you tell people you're a writer, they always assume you are going to write about them. Whatever your plans were before, whatever genre or category, you will find them so sublimely interesting that you won't have a choice but to alter your angle.

"If I find a good story," I say. She nods once, efficiently, picks up her cups, starts to move away. "I'm actually looking for a place to stay." She stops. "Are there any guest ranches around here?"

She names a hotel and a ranch I read about online. She doesn't mention your parents' place, even though I know it's within ten miles of here.

"Anywhere else?" *Fountain Creek* — the name is on my tongue. *Just say it,* I wish. *Say it.*

"Nope. That's it. Small town. You're better off going to Eureka." I came from Eureka. Eureka is three hours and a few dozen hotels from here. It's like she doesn't want me anywhere near.

"I was hoping to find a place with horses." I know your parents' ranch is the only place with horses.

"No, there's not any horse riding around here. You could go out to Yreka, probably."

"I thought I heard about a guest ranch that had horses and fishing or something."

Her eyes stiffen, drop darker. The group

24

in the corner goes quiet again. They are mulling over their cold coffee cups. It's noon at the OK Corral, and I expect a cowboy to stride through the front door at any second and shoot me dead.

"I don't know the place you're talking about," she says, blank eyes, like I'm crazy, like I'm the crazy one, and I hate that. There is nothing I hate or fear more than someone else thinking I'm crazy. I almost say the name just to stop her in her tracks.

Fountain Creek Ranch. It bleeds through my lips, makes bugs burst on my skin, crawl up in radiating waves. "No? I must have heard wrong."

"Probably." She moves carefully away, like I've shat myself and she's politely excusing herself from the smell.

I scan the room, but the men have their eyes trained on their cups and their callused hands.

I want to stay. I want to force someone to tell me the truth. Minutes in and I already feel like a failure and I came here to escape that feeling.

I want to scream your name. I want to shout *Rachel Bard!* at the top of my lungs until they quiver and tremble with guilt and with their lies, and I want them to know I'm your friend, you're my friend and I came here to save you and I will. Because something has happened to you and everyone knows but no one will do something about it. But I hold myself in, I hug myself close and I start toward the door.

Before I can get there, a man drives through it like I'm not even there. The back of his neck is molted chicken skin; his eyes are strangely dim.

"Where have you been?" the woman says, and suddenly, a teacup shatters on the floor near my feet, and I'm not sure if she threw it or if it just leapt out of her hands, and when I turn, they are embracing, almost a dancers' choke hold.

On the other side of the shop, the six men ignore them. No one says anything, like it's normal to drop everything the moment your man comes through the door.

I got fired, from my minimum-wage job, for allowing an old woman to shoplift. I saw her wandering around the store, ancient, invisible to everyone else. She put a pair of nail clippers in her purse, and I smiled. It made me smile. Then she took a silk scarf, a bottle of perfume. I imagined her at home alone, a glass of wine on the end table, scarf wrapped around her neck, spritzing perfume, clipping her toenails. I saw her gathering her spoils on a shelf like evidence, standing back and observing, cataloging, the evidence of her own disappearance.

My manager saw me watch her, but I don't know if he ever saw her. He saw me watching her, and he heard the screech of the alarm as she passed through the door. The funny thing was, he never went to catch her. He let her slink on through the mall like he owed it to her, like she wasn't even worth what she had taken. But he fired me.

I feel invisible now, as I do a lap around Happy Camp. As if I am blinking in and out of existence as I take in the abandoned storefronts and the trailers tucked behind brush and rough fences. One lone man has set up on a beach chair outside the Happy Camp Arts Center, where he sits as stiff as a corpse. His skin is so tight that his yellowed eyes seem to ooze in their sockets. If I had to choose a killer, it'd be him. He watches me walk past, and it's enough to make my bowels loosen. What am I doing out here? Am I trying to save you, or am I trying to get killed?

A stray cat approaches, hops onto the chair and walks over him like he's furniture. I'm afraid to look, afraid not to. Is it worse to look or not look? Still my eyes find his. He has an open hat in front of him, and I put a five-dollar bill in it. I try a smile; it's loose on my face and it falls and it doesn't matter. He doesn't smile back.

"You lost?" he calls out when I'm so far past him, it's unnatural to talk.

A shiver whips up my spine, and I turn around. The cat has burrowed into his lap. The man leans forward in one taut movement. "I said, you lost?"

I move toward him. I think he won't judge me. Not like the woman in the coffee shop. Not like ordinary people with ordinary lives. "Yes."

"You must be for Fountain Creek." I stop in my tracks. "You have the look about you." He draws his finger in an arc that could be a smile on my face or a noose around my neck. "You must be for the summer, the summer crew. That right?"

"Yes," I lie.

"Good job. Get to work."

"Do you know where Fountain Creek is? I couldn't find it on the road."

"Just look for the 'no trespassing' signs." He explodes into laughter like a car backfiring, and the cat curls and hops off his lap, peals out like he's caught fire. "Look for the 'no trespassing' signs! And make sure you use the bathroom before you go!" he says to his own private glee, and he whacks his leg,

28

coughs on laughter.

I hurry away from him, toward my car. "Thank you."

"Out here we take bets!" he shouts when I am too far away again. "On how long you all will last!"

Back on the road I feel anxious, like the town took me and shook me like a box of spare parts. And I know it's unearned and I need to get it together, need to find a way not to be shaken, especially if I want to find you. I need to keep myself together. I need to hold myself in. I need to be like everybody else, but better. I need to be like you.

I hit gravel in the road and I bounce on my seat and your voice makes me nervous, so I turn you off. I remember a glimmer of "no trespassing" signs just down the road. I remember being surprised by their abundance, thinking to myself, *That person really wants to be left alone.* What a strange way to mark a guest ranch.

As I drive, I make a plan. The man from Happy Camp gave me an idea. I will pretend to be a traveler looking for work. I will establish where you are. If you are there and safe, I will leave (unless you want me to stay). If you are missing, vanished, murdered, I will do everything I can to gain entry to your parents' ranch. I will use the things you told me to make myself indispensable. Luckily, I do know horses. I rode hunt seat as a kid, which isn't quite the cowboy rough your parents espouse, but it's close enough.

My hands grow waxy with sweat. My chest is so tight, has been so tight all day, that it aches, and I wonder, not for the first time, if heart attacks have an age requirement. I pass the Fata-Wan-Nun Karuk Spiritual Trails and Ishi Pishi Road. I swallow and I slow.

There are no trucks stacked behind me. The road has conspired to go quiet as I take that last bend. The turnoff lifts beside me, scattered with "no trespassing" signs like angry townsfolk carrying pitchforks. I lean forward and the sky grows bigger and I see the vultures circling overhead, the ones I noticed earlier. They were here all along, marking my destination. Are they here for you or me?

I almost duck out, drive on, back to Eureka like the woman in the coffee shop suggested. I grip the wheel and I allow myself to feel for a moment the freedom of turning away. Then I remember Episode 7 of your podcast, *The Last Dance*. Missy Schubert disappeared at a family camp in

30

the mountains. Her family reported the disappearance to the staff when she didn't come back to the cabin that night, but the staff refused to make an announcement; they refused to ask the other guests if they had seen her, if they could look for her. They said, to the parents of the missing girl, *People come here for vacation. We don't want to ruin anyone's trip.* And you said, *This is what ordinary people are like. They don't want to be bothered. They don't want to care. They would rather let a few people disappear, a few families suffer and never recover, than ruin everybody's vacation.*

I seize the wheel and swing hard to the left, just as a truck going the opposite direction appears. I narrowly miss it. The underside of my car bangs as I right myself on your drive. As I career up the road, the signs crowding my eyes:

No Trespassing
Private Property
No Public Restroom
Beware of Dog
And it's too late to turn back.

EPISODE 7:
THE LAST DANCE

It was the end of the summer dance. Missy Schubert arrived with her family, but she spent most of the night with the friends she had made at camp. She appears in a video taken by one of the campers, only shared with the family six months later, of her dancing with a member of staff. She throws her hands in the air. She shakes out her hair. Then he takes her hand.

I stop short of the mailbox and gaze out at the property. It's Sleeping Beauty's dude ranch: a low lodge, a row of cabins, a collection of horse pastures with cobbled fencing, all buried under a tangle of blackberry brambles. It doesn't look like the pictures from the website. The advertisements — *Your Wedding Here! A Fun Place for the Family!* It looks like it's been cast under a spell.

There is a small parking lot on the right. I can see your parents' house, deep brown clapboard with red accents. A single vine snakes up one side, pointing at a window where a golden telescope winks.

I shut off the engine when I see the hounds of the Baskervilles rushing toward me en masse. Behind them is a woman on a red ATV, kicking up dust, riding like a witch somewhere over a rainbow. The dogs surround the car, so I don't open the door. I just roll down the window as the ATV curves in front of me and I recognize your mother's face from the website.

I remember everything you said about her.

Episode 7: My mother has a tincture for every problem.
Episode 66: My mother is a "truther." She believes every fact is a lie spawned by the government to target her specifically.
Episode 54: The Murder of Dee Dee Blanchard: I get that. I get that so much.

She must be over sixty. She has winding dark hair with the kind of volume you only see in commercials. Her roots are gray and her eyebrows are blond and it surprises me that she chooses this matte, lifeless color.

The swarming dogs are rough and sickly, coarse fur full of burrs, bodies warped by uneven lumps like tumors. One is wheezing

33

so loudly, I think it should be read its last rites.

"What are *you* doing here?" she demands like we know each other personally.

I think of you, what you told me. *My mother likes strong people. Cold people, like her.*

I try to be strong and cold, but my lips are weak, my face collapses and my voice makes a plaintive whine when I say, "I heard you might have work?"

"Where did you hear that?" she says like that is more pertinent than whether or not she does.

"The store, um, just down the road."

"Where?"

"In Happy Camp."

"Don't talk to those people about us. Those people hate us. They've always hated us."

I glance around me, searching for clues. The air is different here, as if the pressure dropped and we are in our own separate universe, a bubble of life surrounded by trees. The highway is below us, but I can't hear it now. The sky is above us, but it looks pushed back. The air has a rich quality that makes me want to breathe deeply.

"Um, do you? Have work?" I want to ask about you. I want to ask about you right

34

away, but I can't. I have to play it safe. I have to keep my mouth shut and my eyes open.

She scoffs. Her head rocks slightly on the exhale. "What can you do?"

"Anything," I say. "I can do anything." I am qualified in almost nothing. I dropped out of college when I met my husband. I have never earned more than minimum wage. But this looks like a place where that might be a good thing.

You told me that your mother liked her people strong, but I can see she is drawn in by my weakness, like a shark by the scent of blood.

She leans in. "Work hard?"

"All I do is work." This is a lie. All I do is listen to murder podcasts and obsessively check my phone. I want to check it now, even though I don't have service.

"Where'd you come from? What about your family?"

"I'm thirty-three," I say like that explains it.

She jerks the key and shuts off the engine. My adrenaline is so high, I hadn't even noticed the sound, how loud we've been talking. We drop into the silence.

"Adelaide, but everyone calls me Addy."

I consider giving her a fake name, but it

35

crosses my mind that I want to get paid, even if I am here for you. "Sera."

"Well, Sera." She takes off her gloves and wipes her hands on her leg as if preparing to shake my hand, but she doesn't. Her hand stays on her knee. "Do you know anything about horses?"

"I've been riding since I was five."

"English, Western?"

"English."

"That's okay. If people know English, they can usually do Western," she says like she wants me to succeed. "Why don't you hop on back and I can show you the place?"

As I unbuckle my seat belt, I am slightly unmoored by how easy this is. Is it fate, or is it a red flag? I open my car door carefully, and the dogs swirl around my feet. I try to pet them as they pass, but they're lumpy and odd, like they have bones and body parts ordinary dogs don't.

She scoots forward and starts the engine as I climb awkwardly on behind her. The ATV jumps and I make a grab, grab her by mistake and she laughs, a solid bark. "You can hold on to the back." She means the basket behind us, but she jerks forward before I catch it. It is filled with cleaning products and potions that clatter together when we move. She laughs again and I scramble, wind my fingers through the bars and hold on tight as the ATV shoots forward.

We off-road across the overgrown lawn, over bumps and dips that jar my carsick head. It strikes me suddenly that this is *too* easy, that there is something wrong with being so desperate for workers that they hire people off the street, with no family or friends to recommend them. And then I think of the woman at the coffee shop, how she didn't mention this place. That must have been intentional. This is a small town and you went to Happy Camp High School and there is no way that woman didn't know this place existed, but she didn't mention it. And your mother said the people in Happy Camp hate them.

We break free of the lawn, and we sail down a dirt road, a cloud of dust roaring up behind us, gravel spitting up from beneath the wheels, and your mother says, "We don't drive this fast when guests are here." I don't know why we have to drive this fast now.

And my wrists are twisted awkwardly and they wrench as we take a fast turn and I hiss and readjust them and your mother just laughs; she laughs like she can feel my pain and it tickles her.

We curve to a stop in front of an old tack room with antique farming equipment nailed to the wall: scythes, crooked axes, saws with thin, grated teeth. She bumps me back as she climbs off. I glance up.

"Why are those vultures circling?"

She narrows her eyes against the sun, peers up at the spot where they float in lazy circles. "That's normal out here," she assures me with a confidence that chips like a lie. "Things die all the time. This is the wilderness."

I think: *Evidence.* I can almost hear your voice in my mind, telling the story of my own disappearance.

Sera Fleece arrived at the ranch at three thirty-seven p.m. on May 12. She immediately noticed the vultures circling overhead. But when she asked, her question was dismissed. Adelaide Bard told her it was normal, in the wilderness, for vultures to circle. And Sera believed her.

The audience groans. How stupid can you be?

"Off," your mother says.

I climb down. Now that I am out of the

38

car, now that I am no longer driving, the exhaustion creeps in, pleads with me, *You want to go home. You want to put on a podcast and zone out.* I have to remind myself that I am nowhere near home. I pull back the wings of my shoulders, trying to stretch, but lumps rise from either shoulder blade, tender and weak. I want to burst into tears, and it shocks me, the way my emotions always do. I have a feeling your mother wouldn't be impressed.

The dogs have followed us, but they are mellow now. They stretch out on the over-long grass and gnaw at their tumors.

"What we need," your mother says, standing in front of the barn with her hands on her hips, "is a new head wrangler, someone to look after the horses."

My heart contracts. "Where's the old head wrangler?"

She scowls. Her face has aged, but her eyes stayed young, lit like she's swallowed a candle. "Don't worry about the old wrangler."

"I just mean, to teach me the job. It might help if I knew who they were?" My every sentence becomes a question around your mother. I feel like I'm at a disadvantage, and I don't know if it's exhaustion from the drive or if it is just a quality of hers, to make others feel weak, inferior.

"I'll tell you what you need to know."

Suddenly I can't hold you in any longer. "Do you have family here? Kids?" My voice curves in desperation. I am not good at this. I'm not good at going undercover. I'm not good at wearing my heart anyplace but my sleeve. Neither are you. We share this DNA.

She wheezes like the rasping dogs. "I have a son, and I have a daughter."

"Where are they?"

Her eyes expand and contract. "I don't like to talk about personal things."

"Does anyone else work here? Is there anyone else here?" The quiet has set in, taut in my joints. A horse nickers, but I can't trace the sound. We are in the bowl of the mountains, where sound curls and ricochets, so it could be right behind me; it could be a mile away. It comes from every and no direction.

"Jed," your mother says. "But he's on vacation. Been here six months and he's already on vacation. That oughta tell you everything you need to know about him."

With no preamble she moves toward a large barn. It's painted light blue on one side, but they forgot to prime the wood, so it's uneven, riddled with splinters and unfinished. I follow her inside, where alfalfa hay is piled high.

"How many horses do you have?"

"Twenty-one. They come and go. Mostly rescues." Does she mean they come as rescues or they leave as rescues?

She plucks a rusted machete off a bale, then presses it into the baling twine. The twine snaps and the bale spreads. "This Jed came out here from Texas, moved up with his wife. They didn't last a week!" I am momentarily lost, thinking she has just said they were here six months. "His wife just up and left in the middle of the night. Not a word to me, although this woman was supposed to work for me. She never worked for me. She just left and he stayed here." As she speaks, she drops the machete, bends over and picks up sections of alfalfa, carries them into the tractor loader and slots them in tight. "That's what happens out here. This place is a proving ground. You got any problems in your relationship — you'll see! You can't hide from anything out here."

I come to life, gathering alfalfa, helping her load the tractor, trying to prove my worth. But the harder I try, the more I seem to fumble. I shiver and drop hay. I stagger with what she lifts easily. I stuff flakes in the wrong way, so she has to go back and fix them.

"I need someone who can work with the horses and get them ready for the summer. You can do that, *right*?" She talks like we have a long and storied history, like she goes from conversation to conversation with strangers, thinking they are all the same person following the same thread.

She breaks the twine on another bale and we load that too.

"That's enough." She claps her hands together. "You need gloves." She indicates my arms, which are riddled with tiny, angry red scratches from the alfalfa stalks. I hadn't even noticed. As I look at them, they start to burn.

"How long have you been here?"

"Too long." She rushes toward the tractor seat. "You can stand here." She pounds the step with her foot as she sits up tall in the driver's seat. "I'll introduce you to the horses."

I scurry up onto the step and hold on tight. The tractor is a big green machine with grease in the creases. It throbs to life, and she drives it like she has something to prove.

She laughs at me when she sees how I grip the handles. "It only goes twelve miles an hour."

I try to smile, but it's not every day I scam

a suspect, walk into a job that I'm not qualified for with a perfect stranger in the middle of nowhere. Lately I feel wrong everywhere. I feel wrong in the world. I laugh when I'm supposed to frown, and I cry when I'm supposed to smile. I'm wearing a mask all the time, and it should be easy to wear one now, for you, but I also feel shaky, listless and limitless. It's like I've fallen into a fantasy world, like I've dropped into a podcast.

She should have known right from the start that something was off. She DID know. She knew but she ignored it. She was afraid, but she kept playing, closer and closer to the fire. There's the threat you can't see and the threat you CAN see and sometimes the threat you can see seems safer.

We pull up outside the first pasture. She stands and I hop to the ground to get out of her way.

"They each get one flake. Spread them far apart, or they'll fight."

Four horses approach the fence, snapping their teeth. They are all different shapes and sizes — a fine-boned Arabian, a sturdy draft mix, a pinto and a small Morgan pony with a flaxen mane and tail. She names them, but in such a jumble, it's like she's naming them on the spot.

"Angel Two, Jewel, Kevin and Belle Star." She separates the flakes, hurling them over the fence so they spin, spitting stalks.

The horses fight for who will be fed first. I remember reading somewhere that horses have a pecking order so detailed that they know which horse is number six, number thirty-six, in any given herd. This pecking order comes out when they are fed. They take the flakes in turns. I hurry to help before she finishes without me. I throw the last flake at the fourth horse, which stays well away from the others, nervously prancing back and forth. This is the flaxen pony, Belle Star, and she paws and tosses her golden mane.

"Should I move it?" I say, thinking if I move it closer to her, farther from the other horses, she might take it.

Your mother sniffs. "She'll figure it out." She swings back up onto the tractor, and I scamper to follow. Belle Star keeps dancing, as if penned by an invisible fence, tossing her mane, flicking her tail.

We stop at three fields, feed all twenty-one horses — paints and drafts and quarter horses. We roll from pasture to pasture in the tractor, and the landscape begins to take shape. The ranch is cut into the bottom of a mountain. There is a narrow plateau where the cabins rest, a curling chain of white boxes with red shutters. Your mother shows me the boating lake, the shooting range, a miniature train that winds around the property and the horse trails that climb in a sequence of switchbacks up the mountainside. The ranch has everything a guest could ask for, the perfect family vacation, and yet the lawn is overgrown, the cabins are clotted with spiderwebs, the outdoor games are rusted, the pool is mostly drained and the water that remains is the color of old piss. And blackberry bushes grow over everything.

"We're experimenting," she says, "with ways to kill them."

I observe the way your mother sits on the tractor, tethered forward always, tense in a way that makes me look back over my shoulder, shiver at shadows. I wonder what she is afraid of.

As we pass down the hill at the far side of the ranch, a pair of elk bursts through the trees. We watch them pass with a casualness born of confidence. Then your mother releases the brake, and we roll down the hill. We pass a burn pile, left running with quiet embers near the edge of a cliff. Beside it is a modern house painted a dark, deep purple. It stands in contrast with the others, the red-and-whites. It looks like it got lost on its way to San Francisco.

Your mother points. "That's where Jed is staying. Supposed to be here with 'his family'; that's why we gave him all that space. We built it for our son. It doesn't look big on the outside but it's big inside. We decorated it, everything exactly how he wanted it." The engine rumbles beneath her words. "And now Jed lives there." She jerks a lever and picks up speed.

"Where is your son?" I shout over the roar of the engine, but she doesn't hear or she ignores me. I remember what you said about your brother. Episode 8: *Everything came easily to him;* Episode 13: *My brother is one of the "good guys";* Episode 33: *He swallowed religion and now he's choking on it.*

She drives back into the barn and shuts off the engine. Twilight crept in while we weren't looking, and it holds everything in a heavenly light, at odds with the stifled atmosphere. Your mother points to her house, set high on the hill over everything. "In the summer we have dinners outside in the garden. We watch the sunset." She takes off her gloves. "I can give you forty hours a

46

week. Cleaning. Riding. Taking care of the animals."

"Where would I live?"

"We have a staff cabin. I'll show you it. It's nothing fancy, not like where Jed is staying." She slaps her gloves against her knee. "But we'll see if he ever comes back." She leans against the tractor. "You'll have to make your own food — there's a kitchen in there. You can't be expecting to eat with us every meal. We try to make as much of our own food as we can, but there's not enough to go around. Not yet. You'll have to take care of yourself when you're not working."

"That's fine."

"And don't buy your food in Happy Camp or anywhere around here."

On cue, my stomach heats with hunger. "Where else can I go?"

"We buy all our food in Ashland."

"Ashland? Where's that?"

"Oregon." Her eyes are fixed.

". . . Isn't that kind of far away?"

"It's only three hours. We go up once a week for supplies. That's where Emmett is now, visiting friends; he'll be back in a few days." Emmett is your father. "I wouldn't give my money to the people around here or the California government. And you don't want to hang around Happy Camp.

You don't want to talk to the people there."

"Why not?"

"Would you want to hang around a bunch of liars?"

"I guess not."

"We have everything you need here."

All I have in my car is half a bag of Flamin' Hot Cheetos. I will need food sooner rather than later, but I am afraid to say anything, afraid to lose my tenuous grasp on this job I am not at all qualified for (if there is any qualification beyond a willingness to disappear).

We take the ATV back to my car, and then I follow her to the staff cabin. It's a dim, boxed cabin set crookedly on a bright green patch of poison ivy. It reeks of rat shit; I can smell it as I exit the car.

"Obviously we weren't expecting you." She opens the screen door and it falls off the hinges. "We don't lock doors here. There's no point. If someone wants to get in out here, a lock won't stop them." She has left the motor running on the ATV. The cabin opens on a front room, crowded by an old-fashioned pipe stove. "Don't try to use it, unless you want to burn yourself alive." She flicks a light switch and nothing happens. "I'll get Emmett to look into that." The sunset seems to have exhausted her, and there is a crabbiness as she shows me the various rooms, directs me where to stay. "You should choose this room. The bathroom's just next door." She shows me the kitchen and the quilts in the closet. "No heating." Everything is coated with a thick layer of dust. The floor is a sea of dirty boot prints. "You can clean it yourself. Unpaid, of course."

The window runners are stuffed with dead flies and black and red beetles. There are spiderwebs draped in every corner; they even wind around the broom. As we move through the house, there is a persistent scratching overhead that I recognize as mice, or rats, and that your mother does not acknowledge.

"That's it." She stops back at the door. "Well, I'll see you tomorrow. Seven o'clock start." She hops down to the ground because the porch is missing; then she tears off on the ATV, leaving a cloud of dirt behind her.

The lock is broken. In the windowpane there is a crack that looks like it was made by a bullet. The cabin is cold. Although she told me there is no heating, I fiddle with a large wall grate before realizing there is nothing underneath. I pull one of the quilts from the closet and pile it on the slim single mattress. I climb into bed to keep warm, pulling the quilt tight around myself. I have nothing to eat and no time to drive to Oregon. My head is still spinning from the road. I wouldn't even want to drive to Happy Camp if I could (which I can, I remind myself; your mother doesn't control me).

I'm here now, like I tripped through the looking glass. I can't go back. I lost my job, and I haven't paid rent. They are probably in the process of evicting me. I could go to my parents' place, but they would put up with me for only a week or two. And it never solves anything; it just keeps me on an endless reset loop.

Out in the world, I am lost. I am less and less every year, but inside your voice, inside your stories, I am a hero, I am a solver of problems, I am a saver of women everywhere. I am a saver of myself. I am home. You *are* my home.

I have every episode of your podcast downloaded on my phone, and I fall asleep to the sound of your voice, Episode 7: *The trees out here feel like they're alive. I can't really explain it. You have to experience it for yourself. This place is just . . .* You sigh. *Crazy.*

And then you tell me about the missing

Missy Schubert. How she danced. Where is she dancing now?

EPISODE 9:
THE WRONG PLACE
AT THE WRONG TIME

Daisy Queen showed up at the main house at twelve forty-five for a one o'clock appointment, to sell LuLaRoe. Samples of her blood were found on six pairs of leggings and eight perfect tanks.

I wake up in the middle of the night to the sound of voices arguing. They could be miles away or right behind me. The voices could have filtered out from my dreams, which are amplified by the unnatural dark. I grasp for my phone, forgetting I'm not on my bed and then remembering, when the uneven springs coil and retract beneath me. The stink of the place is so full in my nostrils that my temples ache. I try to concentrate on the words but I can't decipher them. I hear a feral whoop, like someone challenging the dark; then a motor roars and zooms away. I finally find my phone trapped in a tangle of quilt between my legs.

3:37 a.m.

I make a note of it like it might come into play later. *She heard a car stop outside at three thirty-seven a.m. She arrived at three thirty-seven p.m., and she heard arguing at three thirty-seven a.m.* Like life is a pattern that can be mapped.

I lie on my back in the dark; the only sound is the rodents tickling the wood. I was dreaming about an argument too. Me and my ex-husband. What was it about? My muscles seize as I remember.

I feel like I have no purpose.

If you'd had the baby, you'd have a purpose.

The baby died. In the dream. Why do I have to dream about that? Isn't it bad enough that it really happened?

The ranch goes quiet — the rodents even stop tickling the wood — and I'm left wondering if the voices were ever really there to begin with.

It's just after six. The morning light reveals that the quilt is dirty, the mattress stained. The stink of rat shit is so strong that as soon as I fight my way out of the covers, I open every window, shredding the spiderwebs, mowing down the bug carcasses trapped in the runners.

53

It's cold but I'm driven out by hunger. I have half a bag of Cheetos in my car and another jacket, a pair of gloves. I couldn't bring anything else with me. I didn't plan ahead. Even as I got into my car early yesterday morning, I thought I would turn back around, realize all this was crazy, that I belonged somewhere, after all.

I spent most of the past year in my bedroom. I was tired. Tired of going out. Tired of Tinder dates once I realized it was a sex app. Tired of meeting up with old friends who couldn't get babysitters, so it was me watching their kids or me watching them watch their kids, phone calls for which they couldn't get away, so they actually seemed *annoyed* that I wanted to talk to them. So we had nothing in common anymore, so the person I once knew was now just so *relieved* to have escaped themselves, to have moved on to something better, the magnitude of which I could never imagine, the power they feel in looking at a small version of themselves that they made.

You never wanted kids. Never. You just didn't understand it. *How could you bring kids into a world like this?* you said. *Where there is evil everywhere?*

I spent the past year obsessively checking my favorite true-crime forums for six, eight, ten (fourteen?) hours a day, watching unsolved-crime episodes on YouTube, reading case files and finally listening to you over and over until I was hypnotized, pulled by your magnetism into your world, so immersed that it seemed only natural, it felt only right, that I should cross over into it, into the place that you swore I couldn't understand unless I experienced it.

I had always wondered what would happen if I disappeared. If I just kept driving. What if it was my choice? Instead of just allowing myself to vanish, day by day, year by year, what if I drove toward it, into the vanishing point at the end of the world, to a place where people went to disappear?

I stepped on the gas, and I drove onto the twisty roads, into the isolation, the loneliness of my greatest, most inevitable fear. I drove toward you.

The air outside the cabin has the exquisite, uncontained cold of the true outdoors. There are no warm pockets, no artificial respite. It soothes my aching fingers. I open my car door with care, even though your mother's house is on the other side of the ranch. I know that sound travels mysteriously out here. I wrestle a fleece-lined denim jacket from the back of my car. It was my ex-husband's, and it's roomy and smells of nothing, the way he did. I find hiking gloves and the bag of Cheetos. A horse nickers.

I have less than an hour before I'm supposed to meet your mother, and I plan to use it. I will find your yellow house. I start down the main thoroughfare, moving away from your mother's house, away from the entrance, toward Jed's house and the far edge of the ranch. A thin wisp of trail shoots off through the trees past the miniature train tracks, and I take that, thinking I will not be seen.

The trail is overgrown, scattered with rocks and wet with dew. Beside me the land drops in a sheer cliff to the highway below. I pass by an empty field, and then I reach Jed's house. There the trail dives down the cliff in switchbacks.

I stop. There is a good sitting rock at the point of the cliff, the kind of place people go to think, gaze through the trees and across the highway, where the wide brown Klamath winds through the mountains. I sit down on the rock. There are cigarette butts scattered in a circle like a tribal stamp, glossed with spitting tobacco. I eat my Cheetos with my eyes fixed on the river.

Where is your yellow house?

I finish my Cheetos, stuff the empty bag

in my coat pocket to throw away later. Then I take a deep breath and head down the trail. A creek runs through the bottom of the valley, bringing a primordial greenness, so it looks Jurassic, Irish, always in bloom.

When I first notice the smell, I think I am imagining it. At first, it's an undercurrent, like a rat in a trap, but recognition is instinctual. It's a smell you know without anyone having to tell you what it is; it's the smell of death.

Episode 62: She walked into the kitchen and her sister was on the floor.
Episode 18: She found the body.
Episode 43: They were hidden in the walls, stuffed in garbage bags, hidden in the closet.
Episode 33: Their bones were buried in the garden.

I hear your story, in your voice: *She found her in the woods, like she was meant to find her all along.* Murder, she spoke. And I'm thrilled-attending-terror.

The flies come next; it's their turn. I hear the buzz, feel the warmth of the swarm, and then I see one, two zip, sail past, busy in their fly work. My muscles seize, tendons wind tight. It's harder than it looks, finding a body, stumbling upon a body. It's not all fun and games playing detective, and I cover my nose and my mouth with my gloves and I gasp into the worn leather and I wonder what I will do if I find your body. There's no cell service. The police station is open only four hours a day but which hours? Your mother is expecting me. She told me not to leave. How will I preserve the evidence? Or should I just run? Should I leave you behind?

I grip my phone, as if it might start working suddenly, if I really, really need it.

The flies collect. The body appears: small, hairy and dark. The vultures are circling overhead, but they're not here for you or me; they're here for the cat.

I stand over the body as the threads of bugs travel in and out of the caves its bones create. The cat is black with white spots, and I recognize it immediately. It's your cat. It's Bumby. I remember the pictures and videos: Bumby walking on the piano, Bumby watching you with his silvery yellow eyes, Bumby accidentally pooping on the wood floor, then scratching at nothing to bury it.

I feel a deep, impossible sadness. I feel the loss for you and for me, and I don't turn away until I know I'm a good person for looking.

I will tell your mother. I wish I could do more, and I hate to leave it there but I know better than to touch a crime scene, to tamper with evidence. There is nothing I can do to save him.

I pass Jed's house and I start to breathe again. But I feel guilty, complicit, as if by being here I am party to the crime, party to the act. As if your cat died because I came here looking for you.

I knock on the front door of your mother's house. The house is surrounded by crushed roses as if it was dropped on a garden by a tornado. No one answers the door. I step back and gaze up into the eaves. I see in one of the upper windows the gold telescope trained down at the ranch.

I hear the spit of a motor; then I see your mother speeding up a hillside trail on her ATV. She flies to another white house, smaller than the big house but with the same red accents, surrounded by a chicken wire pen.

I start up the hill toward her, past the cave of the miniature train station, past the swimming pool, which bleeds its chemical smell. I meet your mother at the door of the little white house.

"Follow me. I'll show you the animals."

"I have to tell you something," I say. She scowls, unimpressed by my earnestness, as I follow her into the little barn. "I found a cat, over by Jed's house. I found a dead cat. It was black with white spots."

"It's not Jed's house." She hands me a bucket. "These are the rabbits." She opens a door onto a pen with a hill of rabbits piled in the far corner. "We make their feed ourselves. It's all organic. Everything we give the animals and plants here, we make ourselves." She scatters it across the ground. The rabbits don't move. For a second, I think they're dead too. Then a whisker quivers. An eyelid flickers.

"Was it your cat? Was it Jed's?" *Was it Rachel's?* I want to say but don't.

She frowns a warning and leads me out another door, into the chicken coop. "These are the chickens." They peck around our feet and she reaches into the bucket and she spreads their food. "We have two goats." She points to their pen.

That is when I notice them, threading through the chickens and goats like grim illusions. They are all the same color: black with white patches. The same color as Bumby. They all move with the same jerky gait, an undomesticated crackle of energy. I

60

am used to seeing cats on the Internet: plump and spoiled. I have never seen them this way: wiry, feral, activated.

She sees me noticing, and she beckons me toward the chicken hutch. It's a narrow room lined with white egg-laying cabinets like tiny spaceships, and they are filled, the room is crawling, with cats. They drip down from the ceiling. They pool on the floor. They crowd in the cupboards, on top of tiny kittens, all that same patchy color, mewling like mice.

"They're supposed to keep the rats down." Your mother folds her arms.

"There must be a hundred of them."

"Yes, well." She moves away from the door and I step back. "They breed like crazy."

I am disgusted. She should have them neutered. It's cruel. It's creepy, the way they share the same color, the same unseeing glare.

"They're not pets," she says. "You can't pet them. Especially not the kittens. The mother will reject them. They're here to work, like everybody else. Where did you say the body was?"

"Over by . . . your son's house." The cats crisscross our path as we leave, like cloning errors in a video game.

"I'll take care of it. The trash collector

comes once a week — he's supposed to come once a week. Sometimes he misses a week in the summer and we end up buried in it."

"You're not going to put the cat in the trash?"

"Of course not." She smiles. "We have a pet cemetery, above the lake." I don't know if I believe burying the cat there was her intention, but I do believe I have shamed her into changing her mind.

"You should have the cats neutered."

Her smile drops. "Who's going to pay for that?"

I want to point out that there is clearly a lot of money going through this place, with the tractor and the ATVs and the pool and the miniature train, but I can see that I am skating on thin ice with your mother. I need to find you. Then I will call animal control.

She puts the bucket back in the little barn, and we walk out to the ATV. She claps imaginary dust from her hands. "We have horses and cleaning today. I'm guessing you want to start with horses?"

Your mother leads me to the tack room. It is dark and dank, and the big, cracked leather saddles are piled in rows with tarps over them.

"It's a mess in here." She lifts a tarp and sneers at the damp. "You'll organize it. Every horse has its own saddle and bridle. The names are stamped into the leather." She shows me the curved script carved into the leather. "My daughter thought of that. Isn't it cute?"

My breath whooshes in. "Your daughter?" Little sparks break out all over my skin. "Where is she?"

She turns abruptly toward the door, and her pupils expand and contract in the light. She sets her mouth in a frown.

But I can't turn back now; I can't let this stop. I have to get her talking. I have to talk about you. "Did she work with the horses?"

"I like quiet when I work." She likes *me* to be quiet. She selects a saddle. "We'll put you on Angel Two." I wonder what happened to Angel One. She nudges the saddle onto her hip and points at one for me to take.

"What about Belle Star?"

"No one rides Belle Star." It's like something out of a movie.

"If no one rides her, why do you keep her?" I say before I can stop myself.

Her eyes register surprise; then she smiles. "You ask a lot of questions." A pause. "I don't like it."

We catch the horses, brush and tack them up. I am nervous but it comes back to me. The way you currycomb in a circle, avoiding the legs and the face and the underbelly. The way you run your hand down the back of the horse's leg and squeeze to get them to pick up their hoof. When I go to pick up Angel Two's back hoof, she curls her leg and strikes suddenly. I jump back.

Your mother laughs. "I forgot to tell you; she does that."

"Is there anything else I should know?" I try again more gingerly. She strikes even quicker.

Your mom laughs again. "You have to whack her." She hands me a whip.

Angel Two offers her hoof up perfectly. She's smart.

We mount up and ride along the perimeter. The trail hasn't been cleared, so it's littered with piles of fallen wood, speckled with poison ivy. At one point, we pass under a widow-maker, a fallen tree suspended directly over our heads.

Your mother explains that there is only one guest trail. It goes up to Eagle Rock on one side and down to the Klamath on the other. "But don't tell the guests that! They like to think they're going somewhere new every day. Anyway, they never notice. It all looks the same out here."

"What about the trail by Jed's house?"

She pinches her nose. "What do you mean?"

"Where I found the cat. Where does that trail lead?"

"There's no trail there," she says like she can talk it out of existence. Suddenly I'm sure that trail is exactly where I want to start my search.

Angel Two moseys easily behind your mother's horse. I perch forward in my saddle. "You said Jed lives in your son's house?"

"Yes. We built it for his family."

"Why doesn't he live in it?"

She scowls. "You'd have to ask him that. Now this," she says, as if realizing she'll have to keep talking to keep me quiet, "is a mine shaft. Do you know what this area is famous for?"

I didn't know this area was famous. "Bigfoot?"

"And the gold rush. They came out here in eighteen fifty-one, and they found gold. A lot of gold rush towns vanished but this place survived." I think that's debatable.

"I heard it was called Murderer's Bar."

"Where did you hear that? That's a lie."

I don't tell her you told me. We drop down

into the valley of the mine shaft. The earth becomes a wall of clover, a palace of green. "It's beautiful."

She nods. "This is the showstopper. You always want to give the guests a little history — but not that Murderer's Bar stuff. You have to be careful what you tell people around here. Stories are contagious. Even the thoughts in your head can spread like a cold." She pauses, like she's lost her train of thought, then circles back. "The guests come out here and they say, 'I don't want to leave.' Every year they say, 'Addy, we never want to leave! We love it here!' They don't see the work. They don't see how hard it is. And that's what we want. We want them to come out here, see the beauty, sell the idea — we're the real wilderness family. We don't want them to see what it's *really* like."

"What is it really like?"

"It's work." We pass a row of blue tanks. "This is the water supply. Six cylinders. All of our water comes through here. There are separate lines: One runs to our house, another to the guest cabins — that's yours too — and the far ones go all the way out to my son's house and the ag lines in the pastures. In the summer, we have to space out the guest showers. If everyone showers at once, you know about it. I tell guests, 'Two minutes.' That's long enough. We're outdoors. You're gonna get dirty."

We ride down a low hill. "This is the shooting range." She points to an open swath of land with targets lined haphazardly at the far end. "We have just about every kind of gun you can imagine. Four hundred and twenty-seven." This number alarms me, and I immediately don't believe it. I feel this way about a lot of what your mother says; there is something performative in every word. "Some are a hundred years old; some are the latest and greatest, tricked out with lasers, the works. We want to give our guests a chance to try everything."

"I'm not really into guns."

She touches her lower back. "I'm always carrying. Twenty-four-seven. You should be too. Out here." Even though she has indicated it, I still can't make out her gun. She twists in her saddle. "I better tell you it's not too safe around. Especially down by the creek." She points way out across the ranch below us, past Jed's house. "You never want to go down there alone. And you oughta be armed. I can give you a gun if you don't have one."

"I don't need a gun. What's so dangerous about the creek?"

"There are gangs." I find it hard to imagine a lot of gang activity out here in the middle of nowhere. Perhaps she reads my disbelief, because she insists, "Sometimes we get messages from the police: 'Lock your doors and carry your guns. We just had another one leave San Quentin.' "

"Isn't San Quentin kind of far away?" I remember Episode 1, about the four girls on the Murder Line.

"It's close enough. And the police around here don't do anything about anything. We had a man once, decapitated his wife. The police put out a message, asking people to call in with any tips. Well, there must've been about a hundred people called in. And all the time he was walking along Main Street in Happy Camp like he owned it, drinking in the Snake Pit."

Her horse prances and she reins him in. She is a nervous rider, crouched, ready for anything. "I wouldn't go off this property alone. I wouldn't go anywhere for any reason. I wouldn't go past the perimeter trail. I don't want to get into a lot of talk, but you want to just stay here."

Only then does it occur to me that she may be alluding to you, to what happened to you. Were you attacked by a gang? Is that what she's afraid of? Are you the reason she is afraid?

"I have to go to Happy Camp. Today. I didn't bring food."

"Emmett can bring you food back from Ashland."

"I thought you said he wouldn't be back for a few days. I don't have *anything* here. I need to eat. And I don't have clothes. I only brought what I'm wearing." I also need to be able to leave the ranch. I need to look for you. I need to ask questions. In spite of what your mother claims, I need to talk to the police.

Her horse weaves and she yanks him back. "I might be able to give you a few things," she finally allows. "To get you through. And you tell me what Emmett can get for you in town." All this so she can keep me from Happy Camp — why? And why didn't the woman at the coffee shop mention this place? What would she say about your mother, about you? And most pressing, how will I leave when your mother is always watching?

My mother, you said. *She makes me feel like I'm wrong to ever want to leave. And I don't. Mostly I like it out here. Or else I don't think I would work anywhere else. Mostly I don't want to leave.* You sigh. *But sometimes I do want to get away from her.*

EPISODE 13:
OFF THE GRID

Elizabeth Lowe wanted to make a change. She cashed in her retirement. She bought a van and a backpack and an ultralight tent. She wanted to go off the grid. And she went so far, she never came back.

That afternoon your mother stations me in the lodge, where I am tasked with cleaning the floor-to-ceiling windows, the hard way. I have to take them apart: pop out the screens with a carefully applied butter knife because the tabs are broken, then tip and force out the sliding glass and remove the plastic runners. The vacuum your mother gave me doesn't work — the electricity is out here too, so I have to brush the dead box-elder bugs out of the window frames with a toothbrush. Sometimes when I'm not paying attention, I accidentally flick them in my face.

In spite of this, I find the afternoon oddly

70

peaceful. I have never really performed manual labor, and the physical effort is nourishing. The sun drops low through the windows, so the entire lobby catches the fire of its light. There's something magical about being (almost) alone, in knowing that I am in the middle of nowhere, that no one can see or hear or judge me.

I think about my past life like it was a show I binge-watched, both pulled in and amused by the character who didn't know she was on a streaming service, who didn't know she could escape, see herself at a distance. Will anyone be thinking of me? Will anyone miss me? No, I was no more than background noise. And now I've changed the program, and maybe someday, people will tune in to me.

I imagine with a small thrill the moment when I find you. In this vision, I pull you up from an underground bunker, the place they put you because they wanted you to disappear. The place they want to put me. You squint in the light. As you climb up from the ground. Your cheeks are dirty and your hair is gnarled, but you are smiling. You are smiling because I saved us.

I jump when your mother backs into the screen door with a box of food. "That's it for today; you can finish in here tomorrow."

She drops the box on the counter. "This should do you until Emmett comes back. He'll be in tomorrow morning." She goes to leave.

"I need to contact my family. Let them know where I am. Do you have Wi-Fi?"

She crinkles her nose. "We don't turn the Wi-Fi on until the guests come." I wonder how you broadcast your podcast without Wi-Fi. Maybe you went into town. Maybe you were working with someone else.

"When do the guests come?"

"Six weeks."

"Oh."

"There's a landline." She points to the back of the lodge where there is a service window looking into the kitchen. "Right there in the kitchen. You can call from there."

As soon as I hear the roar of her ATV, I rush to the phone. It's only when I pick up the receiver that I remember that I don't have anyone to call. I've only seen my friends in flickers. When I start to count back, I realize I haven't seen my closest friend in close to a year, others in nearly two. How did that happen? I watched a lot of YouTube. I listened to your podcast.

I pick up the phone. The only number I have memorized is my ex-husband's. I don't want to call him but someone has to know where I am. On *Murder, She Spoke,* you advised me to leave information with a trusted person — a close friend or family member — in case I disappeared. You called it an MMC Pack, a *Murder, Missing, Conspiracy* Pack. An MMC Pack can contain anything that may help in the event of your disappearance: a detailed physical description including any identifying marks, a complete medical history or a list of names of people to contact, people who knew you, people who cared about you, people who might know where you are. It's the first thing I plan to look for now that I am here and you are not. I don't have a trusted person, a friend to leave an MMC Pack with, but I have to let someone know where I am, even if it has to be him.

"Hello?" His voice surprises me even though I called him. "Hell-o?" he says when I don't respond. He probably thinks I'm a telemarketer he can harass.

"It's Sera."

"Whoa! What the fuck? I didn't think I'd hear from you again," he says like I'm a one-night stand that went wrong, which I might be.

I am unsure how much to tell him. My first impulse is to start with *I'm only calling*

73

you in case something bad happens to me, but I think that sounds insane, so instead I say, "I just wanted to check in. See how things are going."

"Yeah, great, Los Angeles, great. The house is good."

"That's nice."

". . . What have you been up to?"

"I got a job."

"A job? Who gave you a job?" Thanks.

"It's at a guest ranch, working with horses and . . . cleaning."

"I can barely hear you. Are you whispering?"

"I said, I got a job with horses."

"Oh. I didn't know you rode horses." He didn't know me at all.

"I'm at a place near *Happy Camp,* in *Northern California.* It's called *Fountain Creek Ranch.*" I want him to remember the names, but I don't want him to know I want him to remember them. "I haven't seen a fountain or a creek."

"Hey, that's funny." There is something so brusque and abrasive about him, so *LA,* and I remember the time we were together like it was a role I once played. A role I played so hard that there is nothing left, and now I am a shell of a person working with horses, cleaning windows like a head case between

74

nervous breakdowns. And I feel like I should tell him that I am here for you, I am looking for you, that I haven't lost my mind and I haven't lost my nerve; I am a hero of heroless stories. I am a champion of the forgotten. I am on the cutting edge, of something at least.

Instead I say, "Yeah, so random." "Random" used to be his favorite word, but I don't think people say it anymore.

And he snorts. "Sorry. This is so bizarre. Last I remember, you couldn't even cook your own dinner, and now you suddenly drive up the coast and get a job at a guest ranch? No offense, but this is like one of those psycho-podcast things you're obsessed with. Like, I'm wondering if you've been kidnapped or snapped."

"It is just like one of those podcasts."

"Oh. Okay."

My voice is hushed, rushed. I don't hear your mother's ATV, so I think (know?) I'm here alone, but I don't feel alone. There is something in the topography of this place that throws everything together, so every sound is an echo, so every light is refracted, and I'm trying to curb myself but I can't; it all comes rushing out of me in a wave of nervous delight. "I'm in the middle of nowhere. The town used to be called Murderer's Bar and it's — There's no cell service for two and a half hours in any direction. There's no police. It's only accessible by these windy roads on the edge of cliffs following a river, this big river, the Klamath River, and it moves so fast that bodies don't even wash up until they hit the ocean."

Long pause. "What the fuck, Sera?"

"It's amazing. Seriously, I've never seen anything like it."

"It sounds dangerous." A pause. "Especially for you." His voice has turned over, gone soft, and now I remember why we were more than a one-night stand gone wrong.

He doesn't love me — or he doesn't want to love me — but he does care about me, and I say, "It's a job. I have a job. This is a good thing." I don't ask him what other choice I have. I don't tell him I already feel more real here, more important looking for you than I ever did with him, losing myself. I don't tell him about you at all. I can tell that it would be too much. The chance that there might be a *Murder, Missing, Conspiracy,* that I might be walking willingly into a crime scene.

"You know, when people talk about changing their life, it's not supposed to happen overnight."

I want to tell him that he doesn't understand. I want to tell him this is something I'm supposed to do. This is something you would understand, but he doesn't. I can see now that last year, all that time when I couldn't leave the house, when I was lying in bed, listening to you, that was just preparation. You were preparing me, and it all means something — all that time I thought I was lost — it means something now because now I am here, and everything is coming together perfectly and it's like a dream; it's like the dreams I had when I fell asleep listening to your podcasts. It's a *Murder, Missing, Conspiracy,* and I'm the hero. I'm following the clues, and I'm going to find you. And I'm going to prove to him and to everyone that I am somebody, that all that time when I seemed like nobody and I felt like nothing, it was just preparation for this.

But I pull myself in. I don't tell him and I won't tell him, not yet. He doesn't trust me enough. He'll think I'm crazy, the crazy old lady getting in over her head, so I just pull myself in and I focus on the details. "I got to ride a horse today. And now I'm cleaning windows. I'm doing *something.* This is good."

The pause breeds many pauses. I can see

them all lined up in a row. He sighs. "Well, you could have cleaned our windows." I don't know why it stings, but it does. I chose a selfish man to love, and I asked him not to be selfish. And even now I want him to help me, to think about me, to understand what being a woman is when he's always and only ever been a man.

"I'll call you in a week," I say. "If I don't call you in a week . . ." I want to say something will have happened. I want to say to call the police. But it feels like I am manipulating him, like I am holding myself hostage to make him care. I have called the wrong person. So instead I just say, "I'm at *Fountain Creek Ranch* near *Happy Camp.*" And hope he will remember, if I disappear.

My parents are less demanding. They don't really do phone calls. They are the kind of people nothing ever happens to. The world could erupt and bombs could go off and the four horsemen could quiver into motion and they would be the same. My dad would watch Hallmark and my mom would watch *Dateline.* I end the call as I always do, wondering what kind of psychosis, what kind of to-the-core perversion, makes people that constant and ordinary.

I explore the lodge for a bit, unwilling to

go back to my cabin but nervous about continuing my search in the daylight. Maybe it would be better if I wait until the sun goes down. The mountains are high around us, and it will touch down early here. In another twenty minutes, I will be able to look for your house in the dark.

There is a bookshelf in the lobby, and I search for something to read: a few books on horseback riding, a lot of books about fishing and topography and four copies of *Dear Mad'm.* I take one and I put it in the box with my food and I carry it out.

Before I head back to my cabin, I circle the lodge. There is an old gift shop; T-shirts and zip-ups with the Fountain Creek emblem hang on wall racks, speckled with fly shit. Beyond it is a small greenhouse pulsing with the dying light.

I put the box down on the patio and walk toward it. I open the door and am hit with a wall of heat that burns my eyes. As the door shuts behind me, I realize it's not the heat. The shelves are stacked with potions in thick glass bottles. They carry no labels but are arranged neatly on the shelves, some threaded with ferns and flowers. In one, I spy a fish bone. My eyes sizzle around the edges and my nostrils sting. I can taste the earth at the back of my throat.

79

I grab the doorknob but the door sticks, making a strange sucking sound like it's sealed. My heart swells in my chest. My shoulders tense. I dig in my heels and throw all my weight behind me. The glass door flies back and I bump the shelf, setting off a chorus of rattling glass.

I try to shake the shivers from my shoulders. I pick up my box. But I can still taste the dirt. My eyes still burn.

I walk back to the staff cabin, the darkness like a salve as I blink the sting away. I use a worn, almost bristleless broom to attempt to clean, but I bring up so much dust and rat shit from under the furniture that my eyes flare up again.

I settle for clearing a circle around my bed. Then I go to the closet and pull another quilt from the top shelf. It flops to the floor and a book falls with it, a thin volume in a cream cloth cover. My nerves pop.

I pick the book up off the floor and bring it and the quilt to the swept circle around my bed. The spine cracks as I open it. I see the name Lizzie scrawled inside the cover with the year 2007. I am surprised her journal has survived this long in the closet, and then I start to read.

The first few passages are obviously Lizzie's. They maintain the same lyrical scrawl.

They start with how beautiful the ranch is, how free, how secret. And then a new passage begins.

This place is fucking nuts. That woman is a witch.

And then some details about Lizzie's life back home, a fight with her stepfather, a call from her ex. Three pages in, Lizzie vanishes and another author, this one unnamed, takes over, and as if in conversation with Lizzie.

I have never felt so WATCHED. I'll be talking to my family about something random, and the next day she mentions it. All the girls say the same thing. Either she's a fucking psychic or she's spying on EVERYONE.

She continues for four more pages. And then another author takes over.

She screamed at a guest today. She has no boundaries.
She is sick and obsessive.
She always tells us what to do.

It becomes a burn book for your mother, a list of all the wicked things she does. There are no names beyond Lizzie's, no dates. It seems to go beyond the normal employer-employee dynamic. They complain about the hours, the lack of breaks, the isolation, the hard labor, how many times a day she makes someone cry and the feeling, which everyone seems to have, that she is always watching.

She's a control freak.
She's a bitch.
She's EVIL.

I read every last word. When I finally shut the book, I think of what your mother told me, how thoughts out here can be contagious. Already, I think I don't like your mother.

I stash the journal under my mattress. I sit on the end of the bed in my swept circle, eyes fixed out the window, which faces the sun, which is drawing down toward the mountains. A horse nickers.

When it is dark enough, I stand. I know exactly where I'm going. I have learned from you how to solve a mystery, and I know exactly where I need to go. Exactly where your mother told me not to.

I take the same path skirting the perimeter,

where I found the dead cat this morning. The body has been removed, leaving a mark like scorched earth. I step around it. The trail ricochets down the steep mountainside, cut deep into the cliff.

At the bottom of the ridge, the trail is blocked by a neat pile of logs. I pause, but only for a moment; then I climb along the steep sides, careful to avoid the poison ivy. I scratch my palms and my fingernails collect dirt and I bounce down, unsteady, on the other side of the barrier. And I am walking fast along the creek, which crackles, not strong and overpowering like the Klamath but louder, bubbling, angry as it spatters against the rocks. The valley is lush with prehistoric ferns, bows of green turned black in the dark. The path meets a wide fire road running into the mountains. I glance toward the source as I step onto it, then gasp in surprise.

In the distance, at the mouth of the road, two headlights burn like round white globes. As I observe the lights, they shrink, sink back onto the road as the car reverses away from me. My heart is hammering in my chest. It was as if the car was parked there, waiting for me to arrive. I hear the sudden slash of an engine, as if someone's stepped on the gas. For a moment, it seems to surround me, and then it drops out in an instant, like the car met its vanishing point. I blink. The sound must have hidden itself around a bend in the road, but it felt like magic, like a knot to be untangled.

It could have been anyone, I remind myself. It could have been someone pausing on a long journey, or looking for privacy. *Not every road leads to you,* but I look up ahead, and I think, *This one does.*

I hurry, footsteps quick, tripping on the uneven ground. I stop when I see a hair tie yawning on the ground. I pause to pick it up. I imagine a world where I can get it tested, where I find your DNA, but the strands on it are long and blond, gleaming in the moonlight, so I know it doesn't belong to you.

I follow the creek, which must be the eponymous Fountain Creek, and the road bends and my heart slows and I see it, rising up in the dark so it's a shadowed, greenish color my eyes still recognize as yellow. It's your yellow house, just like I knew it would be.

I don't hesitate, like a kid in a fairy tale; I rush right up the porch steps to the door and I knock. I wait. The house is dark. The lights are out.

"Hello?" I say, afraid to say your name,

afraid someone is watching. "Hello?" I bang on the door. When no one answers, I try the handle. *We don't lock doors here* — your mother's voice comes back. *There's no point.* Your door is locked.

I stand under the eaves, looking plaintively up. I move to peer through the windows. My heart palpitates, and I realize I am expecting to see your body. I am looking for your bones: a cool, smooth shinbone, the eye of a hip. I am expecting to find your skull waiting, mouth ajar to tell me your story and the story is this: It's Murder, it's Missing, it's Conspiracy.

Then I hear her breath behind me. Her steps follow my steps. I turn abruptly and I see your mother glowering at me in the dark.

EPISODE 17:
SHE'S BEING WATCHED

It started with a feeling, like she was being followed. Then the notes appeared, little letters in her mailbox. They started off innocuous enough. "I think you're pretty" or "You looked good today." But over time, the content changed: "You stuck-up, dirty bitch. I'm going to saw your fat tits off."

We walk back up the trail in silence. I think about the passage in the burn book: *Either she's a fucking psychic or she's spying on EVERYONE.* When your mother sees me hesitate outside my cabin, she says, "There's something I'd better tell you," and I follow her across the ranch to the main house.

The inside is lavish — not modern or flashy, but clearly a rich person's house. There is a grand piano, an ivory statue of Christ flashing the holes in his hands, polished wood floors, a mudroom and a sitting room and a formal dining room. I follow your mother to the kitchen.

"Would you like a cup of tea? It's my own recipe." My chest contracts as I think of the bottles in the greenhouse, but I remind myself I have no evidence that she is a murderer. She may be tough, but she is probably not going to kill me. But she could. She could and I would be out here alone. How long would it take them to find me? What if they never did?

"I talked to my parents today," I say, just in case. "Told them all about this place. They're excited for me. My friend too." I never know what to call my ex-husband. "Ex-husband" feels too grandiose.

She puts the kettle on, fills two tea strainers with her own leaves. She takes her time with the tea and I watch her, reminding myself to breathe.

When she finishes, she brings the tea over — deep purple liquid in white cups on white saucers. She sets one in front of me. She takes the chair across from me.

"I did tell you." She taps her fingernails on her teacup. "Not to go down there."

She actually told me the trail didn't exist. "It was an accident. I got lost. It's easy to get turned around here, like you said."

I'm lying and she knows it; she must know it. I could lose everything now. I could lose everything for this mistake. You and my job and my place here and my tenuous grasp on your world. All because I wasn't careful. I feel thick with the guilt. I have let you down.

Your mother sits back. She exhales deeply. "I didn't want to tell you this." She leans forward. A light steam curls under her chin. "My daughter." My vision sharpens: the wooden chairs, the table and the paperwork piled on the desk in the corner, the lights over our heads break into a dozen hard shapes. "Was murdered."

"Murdered?" I can't believe it. Your mother said it, but I still can't believe it. "How? By who?"

"A gang." She nods slowly, soothing herself. "Down by the creek. That very creek."

"But what do you mean, 'a gang'?"

"They'd been harassing her for years." You never mentioned it.

"Who?"

"They had a big black truck. They dressed all in black. They wore balaclavas." I thought this was an unexpected word. "And white surgical gloves." It is like she is trying to block me from asking for evidence. She stops for so long, I think the story is over. Then, "My daughter was a great hostess.

She was great with the guests — the guests all loved her. She was the kindest person. She was my best worker." She wipes at her eyes but I don't see tears. She doesn't look sad, but her face radiates terror; it positively glows with it. "She didn't want to make a ruckus, even when they —" She gasps and moves her fist toward her mouth, overcome. "They threatened her. They stalked her and harassed her until she was terrified."

I am shocked. I can't believe this happened. I can't believe you never told me. All this time you were trying to save other people when you were the one suffering. How could you not tell me? How could you keep this to yourself?

"What did the police do?"

"The police?" Her eyelids squeeze out the light. "Nothing."

"Nothing?"

"She couldn't describe them, because their faces and their hands were covered." This is both convenient and incredible. "The police said there was nothing they could do."

"How could they do nothing?" Yes, we are familiar with police error, the mistakes and the cover-ups and the conspiracies, but to do *nothing*?

"They told her to get over it," your mother

spits. "That's what they're like out here. They don't care. They don't care about us." She adjusts her grip on her teacup. "This happened. But my daughter is strong. She wasn't going to let them run her off the land, her home, so she stayed. She refused to carry, even though Emmett and I begged her. She was so brave. But they came again and again. They attacked her by the creek. They followed her when she was driving. They ran her off the road. She tried to be strong, but it kept on happening."

"But who were they?" I interrupt, confused. It is as if your mother has taken your narrative, dragged it in a new direction, a direction I didn't anticipate. Maybe a direction I didn't want. A faceless gang? It's too far-out. It doesn't sound real. You told me, there is a tier: first the husband, then the family, then the lover. Those are the primary suspects. Not faceless gangs in the middle of nowhere. Not strangers with no motive. "I don't understand. She must have known them. Why would they target her?"

"I told you. They don't like us. The people in town don't want us here. Never have."

"But why? Why her? Who are these people?"

She shakes her head. "We don't know."

I squeeze my aching knuckles. "But this is

a small town. What about the truck? She must have recognized the truck?" I find it hard to believe that you wouldn't have noticed the details, that you would have been terrorized and not known by whom. You are a true-crime expert. You would have followed the clues.

"She didn't know," she hisses. My questions are irritating her. And I don't mean to victim blame. I just want answers. I just need to understand how all this could happen and you never said, you never told me anything.

"What happened next?" I grip my cup and the warmth turns to burning on my skin.

"They killed her." It gushes like cold water all through me, like I have been dipped into the Klamath.

"Was there a body?" My question is so clinical, it jars us both, but these are the questions, these are the questions we have to ask.

Your mother takes the hit and collects herself before she says, "I don't need to see a body to know my daughter is dead." A rush of relief. No body. No body means no crime, not yet. There's a chance you're still alive.

"Have you — have you looked for her body?"

"Where?" she says like there's nowhere beyond this house, beyond the perimeter in this place she doesn't trust. In here, we are alive. Beyond us, nothing is.

"Everywhere. Anywhere. You should be looking. Everyone should. If you truly believe she was murdered, the police should be involved."

"They don't believe me." She folds her arms, lifts her chin and shakes her head. "But a mother knows. A mother knows her child perfectly, the way God knows all of us." The way she says "God" gives me the creeps. "It's not safe out here." Her eyes dim and her chin drops. "That's why you should never go down to the creek alone. That's why you shouldn't shop in the stores or go into town. They could be anywhere." My instincts tell me "they" is a concept she constructed to control *me.* A way to keep me here inside the perimeter, the way she did with you, the way she made you feel like you could never leave. She knows that thoughts are contagious out here, and she wants me to catch her virus. "You're safe on the ranch, but you're not safe anywhere else. Do you understand me?"

I nod my head. "I'm so sorry. . . . I can't believe it." She sits back in her chair. And I slide closer. I put my arms around her, going through the motions. "You poor thing," I say. Her body stays rigid as I hold it against mine. "I'm so sorry this happened to you."

I don't believe you are dead. I can't believe it. I need to go beyond the perimeter. I need to talk to the people she doesn't want me to talk to. I need to find out what happened, and fast. I don't believe you are dead. But I do believe you are in danger.

I lie in bed and listen to Episode 37: *Your best friend should carry a list of names, a list of people to question, if something happens to you.* And I think, *Who is your best friend? Who carries this list?* There is no one here. I don't trust your mother, and I don't think you would choose her. There's your father, but I sense it is someone outside the family you would turn to. You never mentioned Jed. You never mentioned anyone outside of your immediate family, and I suppose I always thought you were like me: alone.

I need to find your best friend and your list. I need to go to Happy Camp, to talk to the police, to quiz the locals. And I need to get inside your yellow house. I don't believe what your mother said. You told me not to trust anyone. Stories are contagious out here, and I can't let myself be infected with

93

anything but the truth.

I fall asleep listening to you. In my dream I am running through the woods. They twist and re-form like a kaleidoscope in front of me, like a shifting maze. And then I see my own street up ahead, the street I grew up on, narrow, pedestrian, and I run faster. I run home. And when I am close — so close I start up the drive, so close my hand reaches out toward the doorknob — my body loses gravity. It lifts, a weightless thing untethered, and I float up into the sky. I hover there in a basin of stars.

Then I feel you behind me. Your fingers slide over the crook of my elbow. I hesitate, then slip my hand over yours. Your chin hovers over my shoulder as you lean forward and whisper in my ear, "Take this man or any man you can get your hands on."

It's like no dream I've ever had before. It feels so real. And I think we have crossed into another realm together, and I think, just as fast, that it's my own hand. I am touching my own hand and believing it's yours. And then you disappear.

I fight my way awake, through the various chasms of sleep, through paralysis, into one world where I wake up, sit up in bed only to realize I am still asleep, then dive back into a dream, then fight back, until finally I awaken and search for my phone to write down your words before I forget, only to find that I am still asleep.

I think of your words as soon as I wake up the next morning. And it's clear in the cold light of day that they are the same gibberish as any other dream directive. Dreams have a way of marrying intense emotion to absolute nonsense. Are you telling me your killer was a man? Are you telling me to get married? Sleep with any man I can find? Out here, that may be difficult.

I want to write the words down, even if they are nonsense, but I forgot to charge my phone. I think of the journal, and I slip my hand under the mattress. My chest hurts, like I've swallowed something whole.

I get out of bed. I lift up the mattress. My knees shake. My head feels light. The book is gone. I check the floor. I run my hand along the bottom of the mattress. I must have moved it, must have forgotten, must have taken it, half asleep, and hidden it somewhere else, but where? Why?

And then I think of your mother, of what all those people said, how she is always watching. Maybe she came to my cabin before she found me; maybe that's how she knew I was gone. Maybe she discovered the book. Of course she would want to get rid of it.

But it still bothers me. Why was she in my room? Why was she looking under my mattress in the first place? But then, it's not my room; it's not my mattress. Everything on this ranch is hers. I work for her. Even I belong to her, in a way.

My breath feels trapped in my throat, like I need permission to breathe. *I have never felt so WATCHED.*

What am I doing here? Your mother thinks you're dead. And there is no one around to contradict her. I should leave, try to put the pieces of my life back together. That is what the old me would do. Go back. Start over. End up in the same place.

But you wouldn't leave. You wouldn't give up. You would know this is only the beginning. The first clue. You wouldn't let one witness write the narrative. You would keep searching, putting all the pieces together, until you had a whole mosaic of truth.

My ears prick at the sound of an engine. There are trucks that pass on the highway, more often than I would expect, and because there are no other sounds, I can hear every one with startling clarity, but this one seems to roar right into my bedroom. I hop out of bed and walk outside. The horse fields are dewy in the half-light; the barn still holds deep shadows.

A black SUV has pulled up outside your mother's house. The dogs bark and circle as a man climbs out, with black hair and a curled body that hops as if walking over coals. He opens the back and starts to unload boxes from the car. Your mother appears at the door, rushes down to meet him. She doesn't greet him but moves straight to the boxes. Their voices bounce back and forth. This must be your father.

I don't meet him right away. Your mother wants me to take over feeding the horses, so I head over to the barn first.

The job is harder without her. I am supposed to slot two bales of alfalfa into the tractor loader, and I can't make them fit. I try to force them down. I try different angles, but no matter what I do, the flakes balance precariously, so if I move the tractor at all, they will fall off. I am wearing gloves, but the air is cold and biting and little stalks of alfalfa collect inside my jacket, down my shirt and in my shoes, poking me. The dust makes me sneeze.

Eventually I settle for the best I can do and climb into the driver's seat. I turn the engine twice, so the motor revs and crackles. I press the reverse pedal. The tractor doesn't move. I push harder. The engine crackles again, and I realize I have left the parking brake on. I release it and reverse. I come to a stop. The flakes sway but don't fall. I adjust the speed and press the forward pedal. Six flakes fall to the ground. I run them over.

I am near tears. I know it's silly, but I feel like an idiot. I am not the best employee; I tend to crack under pressure, lasting two weeks at one job, six at another. I have never felt so watched, even though your mother and father are inside the house. I am sure that I will be fired. That I will lose my place at the ranch and my connection to you. I will never find you. I will fail, like I always do. And you and I will disappear.

I give up on stacking the loader, and I carry a pile of alfalfa flakes by hand to the first pasture. I throw them too close together, and the horses fight, rearing up, snapping their teeth, tearing skin from withers and leaving bright patches of pink. Panicked that your mother will see, I crawl under the fence to separate the flakes. The alpha horse, a blood bay Arabian with nostrils flared, charges me. I wave my hands in the air to scare him, but he tosses his head and runs faster. I dive back under the fence. He skids to a stop behind it, then rears up again.

I lean against the tractor, heart pounding in my ears, adrenaline coursing through my veins. My head spins, like I can feel the highway twisting all around me.

These horses are not like the tame, stabled horses I grew up with. They are herd bound, with room to run and fight and ignite their instincts. And I can't do this, and I don't know why I thought I could. I have never worked at a barn, and I am afraid of horses, I suddenly remember. That was why I stopped riding. Because one day I woke up terrified of dying, and every time I got on a horse, horrific accidents would run through my mind, in *Anxiety Technicolor.* I would see myself flip over the horse's head and land on my shoulder — *crack* — and snap my collarbone. Or I would slip off the side with my foot still trapped in the stirrup and get dragged beneath the horse's pounding hooves. Or the horse would rear up and fall sideways on top of me, crushing all the bones in my legs to powder.

I force myself to stare straight ahead, to regulate my breathing. I startle at a shrill whinny, and then I see Belle Star. She is prancing with a limp. With every step her shoulder dives and snaps up abruptly. There is blood streaming from her nose.

Episode 21:
Something's Not Right

We all know when something is truly, deeply wrong. We know it in our bones. Sometimes we blame it on other things — our jobs, our lives, ourselves. But the truth is, there is evil around us all the time, infecting us. . . .

I stumble off the tractor and start toward the house, panicked. I run, like I ran in my dream, picking up speed so my lungs swell. I don't know if there is too much oxygen or not enough, but I can't breathe. I can't catch my breath, and the muscles above my heart contract like a fist. As I pass the lodge, I hear the plaintive cry of a phone ringing off the hook, but it only makes me go faster. I run all the way to your mother's house. I rap on the back door so electrified, I am shaking.

"Come in." Your mother's voice. I open the door to the mudroom. Beyond it, your mother and father sit at the breakfast table.

I try to catch my breath.

Your father blinks benignly. His eyes seem brown and blue at once, like he's wearing color contacts. He is unexpectedly small, effeminate. His hair is the same matte brown as your mother's, like they dye it from the same bottle. He pushes back from the table, sets his hands on his knees. "Nice to meet you, Sera. Addy's been telling me all about you."

"There's something — one of the horses is injured."

Your mother's brow creases. "Which horse?"

"One in the pasture by the barn." Something stops me from telling her it's Belle Star. I know she doesn't like her.

"Injured how?" Your father sticks a finger between his teeth and sucks.

"She's bleeding; her nose is bleeding. And she's limping."

"Which horse?" your mother repeats.

"Uh-oh," your father says in a goofy voice. "Looks like I better get the shotgun." He grins like I will find this funny.

I realize now that I shouldn't have come to them first. I should have taken Belle out of the pasture myself. I panicked, in the moment. This is their ranch; I thought I needed to get their permission. "We need to take her out of that pasture. I think the other horses are bullying her."

Your mother's eyes expand and contract. She knows it's Belle Star. "You can put her in the round pen."

"Should we call a vet?"

Their eyes meet over the table; then your father says, "I better have a look at her first."

And your mother says, "You're supposed to be feeding the horses."

I nod dumbly and walk out, shutting the door behind me. My limbs feel heavy as I walk back. I am nervous about going into the pasture, afraid the alpha horses will charge me again, but Belle Star stumbles right to the gate to meet me, as if she knows I am here to rescue her. I lead her slowly to the round pen, and she limps along beside me, blood gushing from her nose.

I think of your gang, and I run my hand down her face, trying to see if she's been hit, trying to find a fracture in the bone.

I find a flashlight in the tack room. I angle it so I can see into the long chasm of her nostril, but I can't figure out what's causing the bleeding. I think, *Stroke! Brain hemorrhage! Blunt-force trauma!* I can't even google it because I don't have Wi-Fi.

I think of your mother's expression, her

repeated questioning, as if she knew it was Belle Star or hoped it was. I think of the dead cat. The tumorous, wheezing dogs. I try to tell myself that this is normal on a farm. This is the "real wilderness." I am being too sensitive. But the part of my brain your podcast triggers thinks, *Serial killers kill animals too.* I bring alfalfa for Belle Star. There is no water in the round pen, so I drag in a water trough from behind the barn and fill it with the hose from a nearby guest cabin. Once she is quietly grazing, I leave to feed the other horses.

When I get back, your father is in the round pen with her, trying to look at her nose as she shies and throws her head.

He approaches her again. She balks and runs, tripping, to the other side of the pasture. He grins boyishly at me. "Might be time to send this one to the great big pasture in the sky." He points two fingers at her forehead, and she shies away.

"I don't think that's funny." My voice is steely.

"No," he says, chastised but still smiling. He slaps his hands together. "It's a flesh wound, m'lady! Merely a flesh wound!"

"Can we call a vet to make sure?"

"Where we gonna get that kind of money?" He plays the same game your

103

mother does. I think of the four hundred guns, the miniature train and the marble statue of Christ.

"I'll pay for it." I know I shouldn't put my foot down like this. I need to play along, to make them like me, but suddenly I'm wondering if working here is the right way to go about my investigation. They don't want me to go to the police. They don't want me to go to Happy Camp. They don't want me to go near your house. Maybe I am approaching this from the wrong angle.

But I remind myself that you were here. You lived here. You were here when you disappeared. And Jed will be back in a few days. Maybe he will be different from your parents. Maybe I will be able to trust him. I can't risk losing my foothold here. And anyway, I want to keep an eye on Belle Star. I need to stick this out. I need to play the game, and I need to keep your family close.

Your father frowns. "Okay! Okay! I'll ask someone to come by, but I think it's a waste of time." He takes off his hat and fans his leg. "They usually get better on their own. Or they don't. Anyway, we better get back to work!" He gives me a "stern" look, but every look is comical on his face, like he's a rodeo clown performing a normal life.

I get back to work, but I keep an eye on

Belle Star, as if someone might sneak in and attack her when I'm not looking.

The tack needs to be organized and cleaned. The other horses need to be checked out. One has a hoof cracked almost to the bone; your mother tells me to put oil on it. Half the horses have rain rot; their hair is matted and fungal from their being left to fend for themselves all winter. Your mother gives me a metal currycomb, and I scrape the infected hair out, leaving scaly patches of exposed skin. The horses are spicy. They've been off work all winter and they don't like to be separated from the herd and they kick and they bite on the ground and they buck and they balk under saddle. They are nothing like the pleasant ponies of my youth. They are hardy. They are furry. They are stooped and barn sour.

I am leading one down from the pasture, trying to avoid the clip of its teeth, when your father passes by on his ATV. He slows to smile radiantly at me and say, "We're so happy you're here."

It unbalances me for the rest of the day. *We're so happy you're here.* I can't put my finger on it, but those words are like a fissure in my spine, a tickle in my toes. I feel dizzy with the oxygen and heady with the view — the river below and the mountains above — and my body aches, my joints feel locked, and it haunts me: *We're so happy you're here.*

To my surprise, a vet appears that evening. He drives up in a big black truck. It sends a shiver down my spine and I watch him closely. His name is Moroni. He's thin and wiry with pale orange hair and a patch of crusted red skin on the back of his neck. Hank Williams Stage 2.

He greets your parents warmly, exclaiming over how well they look and how good the ranch looks and how does your mother get her plants to grow? Where did they find that particular shade of red to paint their shutters? How nice the air is out here!

"It's like you bought your own special atmosphere!" he trills dumbly as they show him all the new additions.

They take so long about it that I wonder if he is the vet at all, but eventually, they lead him to Belle Star. The blood has dried in a dark slash down her lips

Moroni hobbles into the pasture and confirms what your father said. "It's just a cut, inside her nose." Belle Star is lame from the shoulder. He says she probably strained a muscle in a fight with another horse.

"I don't think the other horses like her," I say. Your mother sniffs. "Maybe we should leave her here."

"That's an idea," Moroni says, noncommittal.

He shoots the shit with your parents for a while. Eventually I put together that he is friends with your brother, Homer, that they go to the same church, a church your parents used to go to, but they stopped because of the *goddamn liars and people in that town.*

I want to talk to Moroni alone, to ask him about you, but I need to be careful. Your parents are watching.

I decide to excuse myself early, even though I don't want to miss anything, so I can double back and wait for him outside his truck. It's parked on the other side of the lodge, out of view of your parents' house. I should be able to talk to him alone. Still, there is a chance one or both of your parents will walk with him, so instead of waiting out in the open, I duck into one of your mother's gardens.

I recognize the gate from the website, the careful swirl of the wrought iron. But in the pictures, there were roses and baby's breath and wisteria. Now there are blackberry bushes, tangled inside the fence, choking the gate, curling up the stand of a birdhouse and stuffed inside like a thorny nest.

This garden is a blackberry stronghold, so thick and high at the center, like it covers a blackberry planet. And along the edges, the vines bleed out, reaching farther and farther, so insidious, you don't see it at first, the way it curls along the edge of the barn, twists in a vine over the fence of a nearby pasture, stretches in a chain beneath every guest cabin.

It pricks my ankles, my arms as I duck down. The smells of mud and rot are warm around me. It is amazing how much life smells like death.

I wait. My left leg falls asleep. Then I hear footsteps approaching. I peer over the brush as nerves twinkle under my skin.

Moroni twists to look behind him, lips poised over a joint and a match. With a rush, I realize that I have seen him before. I recognize the mottled back of his neck. He's the guy from the coffee shop. The one that threw his arms around the woman who broke the teacup and said, *Where have you been?* He is alone. He lights the joint.

I stand, my leg encased in pins and needles. I untangle my feet from the branches that claw my ankles and step out of the garden. "Hi."

He lifts his chin. He doesn't ask why I was hiding behind a bush. He doesn't even look surprised. Instead he spews a massive cloud of herbal smoke, then shakes his head. "I can't stand that fucking bitch."

I am taken aback. Ever since he arrived, he has been praising your mother up, down and across: her gardening, her housekeeping, her taste. "Sorry?"

"That woman," he says, like we are on the same page. "I can't fucking stand her."

I step back. Something in his tone makes me physically afraid. He stalks to his truck. He grabs the handle and swings open the door. I need to ask him about you before it's too late. "Did you know her daughter?"

"Rachel?" He snorts. "That bitch was crazy."

My stomach burns, but I force myself to keep a cool exterior. "Crazy? How?"

This stumps him for a second. He holds his joint inches from his lips. "Well, first of all, she hated men." And just like that, I hate him.

"That's —" I bite my tongue. "Why do you say that?" My voice is saccharine, so I sound like a woman who likes, or at least tolerates, men.

He cocks his head. "Never had a boyfriend."

"I would imagine there weren't a lot of people to choose from."

"No. Not if you hate men."

"Did she have any female friends?"

"Nope." He rubs the lizard skin on his neck. "She just kept to herself. That's what I mean: psycho."

"How is keeping to yourself psycho?" He looks at me like *I'm* psycho, then climbs up onto his seat, happy to leave. How do men do it so fast? They make you feel like a "crazy woman" with one look. "What happened to her?"

"Ha!" he says like we both know what that means.

"What?"

"Well, look at her mother. You want to know what happened to her, look at her mother. It's obvious." I don't know if he means she hurt you or if she drove you insane. Or both.

"Do you think she did something to her?"

"Hey." He pinches his joint in an "okay" gesture. "I gotta say no more." He shuts the door behind him. "Probably? Rachel got outta here. Probably? She's on a beach somewhere sipping a margarita. Or else?" He points two fingers and the joint. "That psychopath peeled her face from her skull. But you didn't hear it from me!" He trills gleefully and the engine guns and he zooms past me, past the lodge and past your mother's house, out onto the highway.

I hear your voice, telling your story: *He told her exactly what happened, down to the grisly details. He warned her. But like so many witnesses before her, she didn't believe him. If only she had . . .*

EPISODE 25:
SECRETS WE KEEP

"It's always the husband." That's how the saying goes. And this time the rule held true — it was the husband. It just wasn't hers.

Before I go to bed, I make a plan. I set my alarm for one thirty a.m. I will go down, in the dark, alone, to your yellow house. I will try the front door again. I will bring a credit card in case it's a lock I can jimmy. I will try the back door. I will look for a way in. I don't know what I expect to find. But it's late enough that I will be able to search without being caught, and that alone makes me eager to go.

Your mother drawing the lines has made everything feel closer, like the perimeter is a purse string tightening. And even though I know I can leave — that she can't stop me, perhaps she wouldn't even try — I can feel the shape of the barrier in my mind, feel its hold on me, like a wedding ring, like a new job, like my parents' eyes.

Sometimes it seems easier to let other people control me. It's what I've done all my life. It feels safer, when I can't trust myself, to trust anybody else. Part of me wants to let Addy take control. And another part of me wants to break free, to break out, to be the psycho bitch Moroni said you were.

I push open the rickety screen door, ready to reset it when it swings off its hinges. Then I step down onto the dirt and follow the edge of the cabin to the trail.

I planned to use the light on my phone, but even that feels risky. Every tree shrouds your mother. Your father laughs under every rock. This land is theirs, so very theirs that I feel like I am trespassing even when I am inside my own cabin.

I take the far path, along the perimeter. Alongside it a cliff falls down to the highway below, and the edge is uncertain. The sheer drop unbalances me; I feel it always like a magnet, pulling me off center. I move from tree to tree, sometimes tripping on a root, feeling safer when I stay close to the woods.

The pathway brightens and the journey becomes easier, and it's only when Jed's house appears that I realize it's because his outside light is on. Was it on before? Has it been on all this time?

My nerves are like threads pulled taut. In my mind, Jed is cast as a villain. Was he really on vacation? Or was he hiding your body?

Jed returned to the ranch in the middle of the night. Sera Fleece left her cabin sometime after midnight. She left a trail. It ended outside his house.

I speed up. My feet crack the dead leaves. A figure rises from the dark. I open my mouth to scream, and he lifts his hand to stop me. I smack his hand away.

"Hey." He has an accent. "Hey, hey, hey now. Just take a breath. You scared the daylights outta me too . . . or the night-lights."

My breath is pounding. My fingers are numb. But I can't scream; I have no reason to scream, and I don't want to wake your parents but I want to scream. I feel like a scream has been waiting, like tears held back over years, like it's been waiting a long time to rise up and peel open the night. Jed's fingers brush my shoulders, directing me to the rock on the point of the cliff, the one that looks out onto the highway and the bend in the river. Only now it looks out into the black.

I perch, shuddering under his limp touch, so he releases me, steps back and observes me. I observe him too, in the glow that traces one side of his body. He is dressed like a cowboy, with jeans and boots and a flannel shirt. He has loose dark hair and dark eyes that seem to leak into the skin below. His lips are a ring. His hands are spread, like I might run, like he might have to catch me. "My God, you scared me," he says. "Who are you? What are you doing out here?"

"I'm Sera. I work here."

"Work here? Since when? Doing what?"

"Cleaning windows. Riding horses."

His expression sours. "She lets you ride the horses?"

"Yes."

He makes a derisive sound. "That woman. You know they hired me as a wrangler, their head wrangler. Been here six months. You know how many times I've ever ridden a horse?" He loops his fingers into a zero. He is still for a moment, staring at the ground; then he kicks the dirt. "God Almighty. That woman really is something!"

"I'm just glad there's someone else here."

This twists his lips up. "Name's Jedidiah Combs, by the way — Jed — although I don't doubt that woman told you all about me."

I want to ask him about you, but I know I should feel him out first. Everyone is a suspect, even the ones I would like to trust. I watch him closely, searching for signs.

He stuffs his hands in his pockets and moves up toward the cliff. "This is my spot. I have coffee here every morning. Sit on that rock." His eyes dart back in my direction. "What are you doing out here after dark?"

"Couldn't sleep." And then to mask it, "You were on vacation?"

"She told you I was on vacation?"

"That's what she told me."

"I was getting a divorce."

"You're married?" I say like I don't know.

He rubs his neck, gazes out at the black. "My wife and I came up here together 'bout six months ago. She lasted about a week. Then she went back to West Texas — Abilene, that's where we're from." He shakes his head. "I went back there. She won't take my calls. She won't see me. That's fine. I just want her to take my money." He stuffs his fingers in his pockets.

"I'm divorced," I offer. "Every time I say it, it seems like a lie, even though I know it's true."

He smiles back. "Yes, ma'am." He takes a

few steps toward the ridge. "Back less than an hour and already I can't breathe." He arches his back and pulls air into his lungs.

"It's so quiet out here, I can't sleep." I don't mention the voices, the way that sounds suddenly pop, and I can't tell if they're right outside or miles away. "I feel so alone," I say, and wish I hadn't. People are never supposed to confess to feeling alone, even in a place like this, where it's obvious.

"I wish I did. That woman is watching every goddamn thing I do and —" He stops short, as if he realizes how that sounds. "My apologies. I reckon I must be tired." He kicks the dirt.

"You don't seem happy to be back." Your name is on my lips, but I hold it back. Something tells me to wait. Someone who looks like *this* and talks like *this,* walking around without his wife. Someone in the middle of a divorce. I have listened to enough episodes to know: Jed is a prime suspect.

"Happy to be here? I'm not." He ruffles his hair so it curls in dark tendrils around his face. "Back home I worked on the rigs. Worked hard, long days. Never saw my wife. It's no kind of life. I thought this might be something . . . work outdoors, go fishing and hiking and hunting. But it's not what I was expectin'. And now I'm stuck out here."

"Why are you stuck?"

"Grace got Abilene in the divorce. I can't go back there." He checks my expression and explains. "I done cast my lot."

I try to keep my expression neutral but I am thinking: *He must have done something bad to make her leave.* I see the scribble of your face. His wife lasted a week. He's been here six months. He was here six months with you and your parents, alone. "You don't have to stay here," I say. "There are more than two options."

He cocks his head and smirks. "I always thought there was just the one option. I guess you learnt it different." He sighs. "They pay well, all cash, tax-free. A little corner of heaven, right? It should go down easy, but it don't. It should be a dream come true, but it ain't." He slides his hands into his pockets. "It is beautiful though. Even in the dark."

He stares ahead, hands tucked, like a romantic figure in a poem. I feel it like a pressure against my temples. My lungs hold tight. Is he really this dreamy character, or is he trying to appear that way?

I think of your life, all the pieces of it. The suspicious townspeople. Your radical mother. Your loopy father. And Jed, your backyard crying cowboy. It feels so contrived, like a game you designed for me to play. Or is that just because I have been trapped in my wheel for so long, stuck in stories of good and evil, that now everything feels fake? And then I get this scary feeling, like I have disappeared, like this ranch is my vanishing point, one last bend in the road and then I cut out like a candle.

And suddenly I want to tell Jed all of this, but I can't because he's a perfect stranger. Why is it that other people can sometimes make you feel the most alone? I have no one to talk to, no one close that I can trust. My mouth feels sewn shut. My heart is pulsing in my aching hands. I'm disappearing. And if I don't find you, I'll vanish without a trace.

"Heck, I better get some sleep." Jed swings his body around at once. "You want me to walk you back?"

I am torn. I want to go to your house, but I can't get past Jed. And I can't trust him. I can't trust anyone.

"No, I'll be fine. It's easy."

His voice drops conspiratorially. "It wasn't really a question. I can't let a woman walk home alone." I hate comments like that, but his accent softens my irritation. And as much as it embarrasses me to admit, I like the idea that somebody cares, even if it's just enough to walk me a few hundred feet down the path.

We walk back to my cabin, guided by the halo of his handheld flashlight. I want to trust him. I want to tell him everything — about the cat and Belle Star and the sick dogs and the way your parents seem sadistic, always laughing at something that isn't funny. But I think: *Suspect.* I think: *Wait.* Still, I don't know how long I can hack it out here alone. If you disappeared, someone must have taken you. If you are in danger, I am in danger too.

We stop under the eaves, by the front door. His nostrils flare at the smell, and I feel embarrassed, like this really is my home. "Sorry they stuck you here. You oughta just stay with me; there's three bedrooms. Lord knows I don't need 'em."

I feel the invitation catch in my throat, like we're on a first date and he's asked me to come back for coffee, forever. "It's fine. I don't mind it."

"Well, I'd invite you over for dinner but I can't cook worth a damn. If you ever need whiskey though, you can bet I've opened a bottle." He steps backward until he's five, ten feet away. He cocks his chin. "I hope you get along all right out here," he says, like we may never see each other again.

I fall asleep and wake up an hour later to the sound of a baby crying. Half in dreams, I think I'm another person, with a different life. I have to feed the baby. I have to hold the baby. I have to rock the baby. I am out of bed, cold lighting my bare knees when I realize I don't have a baby, and I shiver like it's something I should be afraid of.

I climb back onto the bed, ignoring the feeling of dirt and dust between the covers, and I look out at the swollen bellies of the blackberry bushes gathered in the garden outside my window.

The perfect place to hide bodies. I imagine the blackberries are so thick because they feed on human flesh, and I almost want to go out there and rip the bushes apart, cut them down so I can sleep without nightmares. *You could hide anything in there.*

Episode 29:
Open Season
at Fortuna Ranch

They found the bodies in a hunting freezer. They were stripped. They were cleaned. They were arranged to make the most of the space, so a bone was broken here. A neck was twisted there. They found seven bodies in one freezer.

The next morning, I am up on a ladder outside the lodge, cleaning the windows. I'd fed the horses. I'd checked in on Belle Star, who seems less agitated now that she's alone. Your mother roars up on her ATV. The dogs that follow her settle like sacks in the grass.

"Well." She cuts off the engine. "He decided to come back."

"Did you think he wouldn't?" I have not finished cleaning the inside panels, but I've moved outside, hoping to get another glimpse of Jed. There is something old-fashioned about this place. There's a new man in town, and I won't be able to sleep for days.

She gazes out at the ranch, where Jed is, invisible to us. "I didn't know, the way he took off. Here for six months and he wants to go on vacation? What does that sound like to you?"

It sounds perfectly understandable. This place is isolated, even more so by the rules about not going into town, about not traveling past the perimeter. I can understand that after six months he might have felt like he was due a vacation.

"He was supposed to bring back his wife. Did you see her?"

It's not my place to tell her about his divorce, and anyway I'm not supposed to have met him yet, so I say, "No, I haven't."

"Well." She leans forward on her ATV. "We'll just see how things go now you're here." She starts her engine and speeds away before I can ask her what she means.

I work for three days, falling into the routine even as the pressure inside me builds. I clean windows. I ride horses. I clean more windows. I ride more horses. But on the inside, I am frying, burning up. I tell myself I am building your family's trust, burying myself deeper in your world, but every day

123

the case gets colder.

I pass by Jed a few times a day. He works on the roof of cabin seven, making repairs, shirtless, sweating. And I am no closer to you, no closer to him, no closer to anyone. I work and I read *Dear Mad'm* and I plan for the weekend, when I will search your house, search the ranch, search Happy Camp.

I hope your parents will go to Ashland to resupply, but I know Jed might be here, and I don't know how I will get around him. How can I look for you when there is always someone watching?

There is a scream sewn backward inside my lips. My hands are aching, desperate to do something. The air is hot. My neck glistens with it, but you are cold and getting colder. And I need to do something. Yesterday, today, *now*.

At night I listen to your podcast, every episode a clue, a hint, leading me toward *Murder, Missing, Conspiracy.* Every morning my head feels thick; my chest feels tight. Every day I am angry with myself for not getting closer, for not working hard enough, for not finding you.

On Wednesday, your mother comes into the tack room and tells me they won't be going to Ashland this weekend — they have enough supplies from the last trip. Isn't that lucky? And I need to do something. I need to start asking questions, so I do.

"Why doesn't Jed ride? Isn't he the head wrangler?" I am cleaning the silver rings of a saddle with a toothbrush. I keep my head down, working diligently.

"He doesn't know what he's doing on a horse," your mother snips. According to Jed, she's never even seen him ride one.

"It would be nice to have another person." I pause, careful. "The horses are better when they're together."

"They'll go out together enough in the summer."

"But isn't that what we're practicing for now?"

The thought has begun to climb on me, that this feels like the beginning of an abusive relationship. You have told me many times about how they progress, the relationships that end in *Murder, Missing, Conspiracy*. They often start the same way. They often start with this: *He isolated her.* Your mother tells me not to go to town. She makes me work alone. She buys me food so I won't have to shop. Food and clothes and toilet paper so I won't have to leave. I remember what you said about growing up here: *It was the middle of nowhere, and I*

125

couldn't escape.

I need to break out. I need to find you. I can't always please your mother. I can't always please everyone. So I push.

"I don't know the guest trails. And you told me it wasn't safe to go past the perimeter. I need someone to show me." Jed told me he had spent months clearing the trails, even though he wasn't allowed to ride them. "I need someone to come with me so I won't be alone."

Your mother cocks her chin. I know she doesn't want to go with me herself. She doesn't like to leave the ranch. But she knows I am right. If I am going to lead the trails, I need to know where they are.

"Fine. I'll talk to Emmett, see if he can let Jed go for one or two mornings. To show you the trail." She bounces on her heels. "Heck, it's not like Jed is any use to him either."

You never said a word about Jed, which surprises me because he's the kind of man women gush about: toned and tailored, with a habit of licking his lips, glaring moodily at shadows. He is attractive, and he is angry at the world, which makes him even more attractive, in my book. The next morning, as we tack up Angel Two and Jewel, Jed

126

watches the morning mist like it stole something from him.

I ask him easy questions first. This is what you taught me.

"How long have you been riding?"

"Forever. Since I was a baby." He grew up in a small town. He worked on a ranch from the age of seven. I can tell he knows his way around a horse. I wonder aloud why Addy suggested otherwise.

"She's punishing me."

"Punishing you?"

"It's what she does." He gently tightens the cinch and tucks the leather.

It's a crazy notion, but haven't I noticed a sadistic streak? The way she laughed when she drove too fast on that first day? The glint in her eye when she asked me to climb up a fifteen-foot ladder unsupported to clean the lodge windows?

I walk my horse to the mounting block; Jed swings on from the ground.

"I'm supposed to take you down to the beach today; it's across the highway." He reins his horse around. I follow him down the main thoroughfare, past the lodge. The phone is ringing again.

"That phone is always ringing," I say.

"That's the reservation line," Jed says. "Far as I can tell, they're pretty lacksydaisical about taking bookings. I wouldn't be surprised if the summer comes and we're still the only ones here." I smile because I've never heard anyone use the word "lackadaisical" in real life, even if he did pronounce it wrong.

We are both quiet as we pass your parents' house. Jed's shoulders stiffen and he watches it uneasily. Then we head down the drive, toward the highway. A wide semitruck blasts around the bend in the road, and Jed pulls Jewel up.

"They always show up right when you're about to cross," he mutters. Jewel prances as we wait for the truck to pass, and then we cross the road together.

On the other side, we head down a steep trail. I glimpse the river through the trees: heavy, brown, propulsive.

"This is the trail," he says. "Apparently it's a 'showstopper.' "

It is beautiful, but so is everything out here, and I don't care. We are off the property. It's like I've been holding it in. I can't contain it anymore. I can't hold on to you. "Did you know Rachel?"

"Rachel?" His horse slips. It slides down the trail, and he leaps into action to rebalance it, twisting his back and angling his seat until the horse comes right underneath him. He peers back at me, up the steep hill. "How do y'know who Rachel is?"

"Addy told me."

"What did she tell you?" His eyes bore into me, searching for you.

"She told me what happened to her."

He pauses, works the words through his mouth like a crank. "What did she say happened to her?"

"About the gang. Addy thinks she was murdered."

He goes quiet then, stiff through his spine like he's been run through with a rod. His body sways with the horse as we reach the bottom of the incline. Before us the land crawls out, awash with sand. It's a deserted beach, like the island in *The Black Stallion,* wide and pale with scribbles of brush.

"Wow," I say appreciatively. And then, "Is that what happened?"

He flips the long strands of his reins to the other side. "I don't know what happened to Rachel." I can't tell if he's choosing his words carefully or if it just sounds like he is because he talks slowly.

"When was the last time you saw her?"

"I guess around Easter, maybe."

"What day specifically? And what time? How did she seem?" I wish I had a tape recorder, a calendar, some way to quantify exactly when and how you disappeared.

His voice shallows. "You seem pretty invested in a stranger's story."

I debate telling him the true reason I am here. He is just as likely as anyone to be involved in your disappearance. But in spite of this, I want to trust him — maybe only because I have no one else to trust. And the truth is, I'm not getting anywhere on my own. I need someone on the inside, someone who was here when you disappeared. I need someone.

"I listened to her podcast." His hips slide forward on the horse, but I can't see his face. I look for clues in the line of his broad shoulders. "Before she disappeared. That's why I came out here. To find out where she went."

"You're shitting me," he says, but not to me. He speaks out into space, as if speaking to you. Then he ducks his head and lowers his voice. "Let's just keep on with the trail."

He quickens his horse, directs it toward a copse of trees. My lower back stiffens. Where is he taking me? Is this really the trail? Or have I trusted the wrong person? Is he taking me into the woods to cut me up? (*Forty-six stab wounds in the face, so we know it was personal. The bullet entered her head at her temple, no exit wound. Signs of struggle. The first place to look for DNA is under the victim's fingernails.*) Did his wife really go back to Texas? Has anybody verified it? Or did he murder her and bury her in the woods? Did you find out? Did he kill you too?

He leads me away from the beach, along a lilac-strewn path. In spite of your mother's warning, I am not carrying a gun, but I consider all the weapons at my disposal:

I could gallop away on my horse. (He could gallop faster.)

I could wrap the reins around his neck and choke him to death. (He could cut them with the knife sticking out of his pocket.)

I could charge him on horseback. (He could clothesline me, tackle me to the ground.)

I could use his knife to slit his throat. (He could turn it on me, thrust it in my neck so my blood would spit warmly on his fingers. What would it feel like to die that way? Would the pain sharpen or would it feel like a gradual loosening, like all the knots in my nerves were untied?)

And I think: *Trust. I have to trust someone.*

We reach the woods. He doesn't say a word. And after a while it becomes clear that he's not going to kill me or tell me your

131

secrets. He's not going to do anything at all.

"I need to find out what happened to her." I squeeze the reins between my fingers.

"Why?" he says, genuinely confused.

"She did for all those people, on her podcast. She cared enough. To look. To find out. To try to save them. I have to do the same for her."

"She didn't save anyone." He reins his horse up. "She lost herself." Satisfied with his conclusion, he continues up the trail.

I let my horse jog to catch up. "What do you mean?"

"What do I mean? I mean, she saw murder everywhere, ill intentions. She got lost in her own stories. Thought everyone was out to get her."

"Like her mother does?"

"Rachel is nothing like Addy; don't you say that." Anger flashes through him. I can see what he would look like in the killer role. Because he *is* angry. Beneath his cool, slow words, his anger is aimed, always at your mother. So why does he stay? Is tax-free money really enough to burn alone in isolation? Or is there something else that keeps him here?

He sees that he has let himself out too much, and I watch him enforce a new relaxation, rock with his horse, flick his reins and lean back. "You don't understand what it's like out here. What it gets like. Even leaving for a couple days, like I done, you start to see things clearly you just weren't seeing before. It was just the four of us out here for a long time. And Addy's a psychopath, and Emmett's a nut, and Rachel, she was chasing crazy, or maybe she was running from it, but either way, she was so close, things started to overlap." He cranes back in his saddle. "You know how they say, 'You can't see the woods for the trees'?"

"Yes."

"Stay here long enough, you'll know what they mean."

"But where is she? Where is Rachel?"

"She left. Lucky girl."

"Her mother thinks she's dead."

"Her mother —" His accent sours on the words, and he corrects it. "Her mother thinks whatever happens to work best for her at the time."

"But Rachel loved it here." He seems surprised I know so much about you. "On her podcast, she used to talk about keeping an MMC Pack."

"MMC?"

"Murder, Missing, Conspiracy. It sounds stupid when you say it," I add off his look. "But it's information a person keeps with

133

someone they trust. Information that might help locate them in the event of their disappearance. Medical files, names of close friends, jobs, education, anything that might —"

"I don't know anything about all that."

"Did she have a close friend? Was there anyone she trusted?"

He seems irritated by my questions, and I can't help thinking that's a clue. Why doesn't he want to find you? Why doesn't he seem to care? He has the bitterness of someone who once cared too much.

"Rachel? Ha. It was a point of pride, to her, not to trust nobody."

"But she must have left clues."

He looks at me like I'm a child — no, he looks at me like I'm an adult *acting* like a child. "She didn't leave clues because nothing happened. Simple as that."

"So you just think she's gone. Just up and left with no explanation?"

"You didn't know Rachel."

"I did too know her." I want to say I knew you better. I knew your heart. I knew the real you, the secrets you confessed in the middle of the night in my bedroom. The words you whispered in my ear.

"You're making more of this than there is. Her parents are crazy. They drove her crazy.

134

She left. She doesn't want to be found."

"What about the police? What do they think?"

"The police?" he asks like it's a dirty word.

"You never told the police? That she just disappeared?"

"She didn't vanish into thin air; she walked out. Goddamn, I admired it. I wish I had the gumption."

"We need to talk to the police."

"We?"

"Don't you want to help? Don't you want to find her?" He says nothing, and it bubbles up inside me. His apathy, everyone's apathy. The world goes around and people are murdered and attacked and kidnapped and tortured and everyone just looks the other way. You disappeared and everyone just goes on living like you were never here. "This is exactly what the problem is, this is exactly what she always talked about. Terrible things happen and people just go on with their lives. They don't want to get involved. They don't want to help people. This is the reason evil exists!"

He has gone flat with me, statuelike, but his eyes burn. "If I thought Rachel really was in trouble, I would do something."

"But you can't always see it! You can't always see it when someone's in trouble."

"You're in trouble; I can see that pretty clear." He looks into my eyes for one, two seconds, and then he moves on down the trail.

Later that night I am outside Jed's garage. I feel guilty, like we are already aligned, like I am mean for not trusting him. But I can't trust anyone. And I think Jed knows more than he said. He was here with you for a long time.

The garage is fifty feet from his house. The door is open. If I am quiet, I won't get caught. I step inside. I find a truck, a motorcycle, an ATV, everything big, black and shiny except for a lone pink helmet on the wall: his wife's? I take it off its nail, examine it like evidence but don't find anything. I set the helmet back on the nail.

At the back of the garage, a silver hunting freezer hums. The sound rises as I move toward it — piercing, off-key. My imagination bleeds a vision of your body, curled inside the silver box like a child playing hide-and-seek.

I know I won't find anything pleasant in there, but I have to look. *Seven bodies in one freezer.* What if you suspected? What if you found out? What if you were talking about Jed?

136

I square up to the silver box, try not to think how it's shaped like a coffin. I press my fingers under the handles on either side and I force the door up. The cold wheezes out. It oozes over the bare skin on my face and neck.

It's not human, but it's so unexpected, so serene, that I leap back in surprise. I wait for a smell, and when it doesn't come, my nerves bubble and burst along my back.

There is a dog alone in the silver box, like a picture of a frozen life. It's a pit bull, and it's looking up at me, like it's waiting for its master to let it out.

My heartbeat throbs in my throat. It takes my head a while to come up with a convincing narrative. The dog must belong to Jed, but why is it here? Why has he kept it? And, more important, how did it die?

EPISODE 33:
THE PREACHER WAS A MADMAN

Their bones were buried in the garden outside the chapel, beneath the flowering rhododendrons. Some were never identified. Some weren't even human.

The rest of the week, I am never alone with Jed, but I see him everywhere. Up on a roof, flying by on his ATV, walking up to the shooting range with his rifle at his side. There is something haunted and fragile about him, and I know I can't rely on him for anything. I can't rely on anyone but you.

I make it my goal to get to Happy Camp; I need to see the ranch from the outside, to get perspective. I need to *think,* without other people thinking for me. I tell your mother I need Benadryl, tampons, a copy of *The Handmaid's Tale.* She tells me allergies are a myth but gives me a box of maxi pads, then says she has something better for me to read and hands me *Dear Mad'm.* Your parents are so proud of their self-sufficiency that your mother is insulted every time I try to concoct something she can't provide.

I spend my evenings with Belle Star, petting her, brushing the burrs and knots from her golden mane and tail, teaching her to accept the saddle and the bridle without throwing a fit.

On Friday, I tell your father I want to visit the book exchange in Happy Camp, hoping he might agree and influence your mother. I have read *Dear Mad'm* three times. Jed overhears and says, "I have a copy of the Bible, if you want to borrow it," peering sideways at your father like he stole it.

And it gives me an idea, the perfect alibi, the one thing your mother can't give me.

There is one church in Happy Camp. It's a place I never would have found on my own, on an unmarked road in a brick building with no signage. The congregation is fourteen people from two families. There are three Moronis (one I recognize), all with fair hair and red necks wrinkled like chicken skin. One sits next to the woman from the coffee shop. The other family is yours: your brother, Homer; his wife, Clementine; and their daughters, Aya and Asha.

The service is two hours. I will stay for

ten minutes so I have ammunition if your mother asks questions. Then I will walk down the mountain to the police station.

I was so excited to get off the ranch this morning that I forgot to take a Dramamine. My head is swimming when I arrive. My vision pulses as I slip into an empty chair near the door in the white box room. Along the back wall there are two windows with the shades drawn. There is a clock on one wall, its cardboard face lightly punctured, and a plain wooden pulpit at the front.

At nine o'clock, your brother takes the stand and welcomes us all to the meeting. He is dimpled and strong jawed. He is exactly the kind of man my mother wanted me to marry, someone who could pull off a sweater for the Christmas card, someone whose face would look great in miniature, boy and girl.

My parents strongly objected to my divorce; it was the first and only time I ever outright disobeyed their wishes, but as soon as the papers were finalized, as soon as there was no going back, my mother started setting me up. We were sucked back into the past, like we could solve a problem (me) with the same old solution.

As your brother talks, his eyes fasten on me. I didn't consider how conspicuous I would be. I didn't consider that he might report back to your parents if I leave early. Sweat pops down my back. My hands ache as he announces the first song.

I take a hymnbook from the floor as two older woman shuffle in: gray hair, crinkled skin, stocking straps visible beneath the uneven hems of their skirts. There are dozens of open seats, but they stand beside me, waiting for me to move down. I slide down three seats, a Moroni on my other side. I am locked in the row. They dart curious glances in my direction as they pat their hair, creating clouds of dust or powder.

The congregation starts to sing. There are so few people that I can hear every voice, hear my own voice; I try to pick the parts where it won't be heard but it always becomes somehow exposed, flat and plaintive. They bless and pass the sacramental bread and water. I don't know whether I'm supposed to take it or not — I think not but I do anyway; being in such close surroundings makes me nervous to separate myself from the group.

Then your brother announces that this is a testimony meeting, which is where the members take turns standing in front of the congregation and saying, evidently, whatever comes to mind. The first Moroni tells us that this week he was sprayed seven times by the same skunk. This leads naturally to a lecture about the state of politics *in this country,* which your brother swiftly derails.

"Remember what we talked about, Moroni." He taps his nose and activates his dimples.

Moroni drums his fingers on the pulpit, says, "Hmm," out loud so we all know he's thinking about it, then ominously concludes, "I think the skunk was a Liberal."

After the first Moroni and the second Moroni, a few of the children are pushed to the front. Soon everyone has spoken except me. The entire congregation sits in silence. The clock grows heavy with the weight of our eyes.

"No one has to get up," your brother says encouragingly, bouncing on his heels.

I want to leave, but if I stand, they will think I'm volunteering to talk. I don't have any idea what to say. Apart from not knowing what these people actually believe, I don't have a lot to say about God. I don't think you did either, although you never talked about it specifically, never wanted to get "political" or be "too earnest." But I think we know better than to believe in some divinity overseeing everything. If there was a God, there wouldn't be *Murder, She*

Spoke. There wouldn't be Laci Peterson's fetus washing up the day before her own headless, badly decomposed body appeared on a shore in San Francisco. There wouldn't be three Oklahoma Girl Scouts raped and murdered on an overnight camping trip. Even just sitting here, in a too warm, too clean room, pretending there is a God we are all praising, makes me kind of angry, if you want to know the truth. It makes me think about how the patriarchy was preserved for thousands of years because organized religion gave men magical powers and made women their servants, and now here we are in a world where women disappear and men run congregations.

But everyone is watching me. And I am supposed to blend in, to make alliances. I am supposed to be brave, and most of all, I am supposed to do *something,* so I stand, and when my knees sway but don't buckle, I let them take me to the front.

I cling to the edges of the pulpit, suddenly seasick, like I can feel the road that took me here still swaying between either temple.

"Um, obviously I'm new." A polite titter. "I just wanted to say thank you to everyone for welcoming me to your church. I've never been to such a small church before. It's neat." Apparently, I am auditioning for their friendship in the fifties. "I look forward to getting to know all of you better." I hope that's enough, and I move toward my seat. I have left out the part about my faith in God, but I didn't accuse a skunk of Liberalism, so I feel like I'm ahead of the curve.

"Tell us where you're from!" shouts a Moroni.

"Visalia."

This unbalances them enough to get me back to my seat, but then the Moroni presses on. "What brings you here?"

You, I think. *I am looking for a woman just like me who disappeared. Her parents think she's dead, but don't care to confirm it. Her brother has electric dimples. Her coworker knew her well, but not well enough to wonder where she went.*

Thankfully your brother stands. "Let's save questions for after the service," he cautions, although there is still half an hour and no one left to speak.

He unbuttons the top button of his coat. He brings out his Bible and he sets it on the pulpit. He turns on his dimples and then he shares the story of the prodigal son. He speaks engagingly, as if he had planned to speak all along, like he knew I would be here, like he chose this story specifically to tell me it's not too late for me.

144

" 'My son, the father said, you are always with me, and everything I have is yours. But we had to celebrate and be glad, because this brother of yours was dead and is alive again; he was lost and is found.' "

He takes us to the bottom of the hour; then we sing again and pray, and then the first session ends. I have one hour to quiz the police, one hour before I need to head back to the ranch.

I stand at my seat as the others turn to face me. I want to get out as quickly as possible, but the two women form a wall.

Your brother, the ambassador, is moving toward me. "Welcome. Welcome. What brings you out here?" The entire congregation, all fourteen of them, press in and I'm surrounded. The clock ticks weakly on the wall.

I debate lying, but the community is too close; it will cross wires. "I'm working at a ranch."

Your brother's shoulders lift. "Which ranch?"

"Fountain Creek."

The congregation freezes, holds its pause for five, four, three . . . then shivers and splits apart, like your home is a way to break up a crowd.

Your brother wipes a finger over his brow.

"Aha!" he says like he's discovered something. His wife steps in beside him.

"I'm Clementine." She offers a hand with thin, collapsible bones. "I hope you're okay out there." She speaks casually but her words are odd.

"I just started."

She nods like that adds up. "We have our women's group now, next door. I teach the young women, but you're welcome to come with me if you want." I only see two "young women," and they are her daughters, your nieces. They step in beside her so your brother's family all stand in a perfect row. Your nieces share your brother's DNA. They are so beautiful, I feel sad that they are living where no one can see them, but then I remind myself their beauty is theirs, that a woman's beauty doesn't have to be shared.

Everyone is very eager for me to stay, which I didn't anticipate. I imagined myself going unnoticed, like I do everywhere else. Instead Clementine's eyes glow with a soft thrill, as if she can will me into friendship. Instead your nieces smile and shyly curl their necks to giggle over their hands at me. There are so few people out here, it creates a hunger for human contact like I have never seen, but all I want right now is to be alone, under my own control.

"Actually — I'm sorry — I have to run a few errands. Just while I'm in town. I have to do a few things." I stop, realizing the more I explain, the less likely it sounds. Why can't I run my errands an hour from now? And the funny thing is, I know I *can.* Your mother has warned me about town, but she hasn't forbidden me from going there; she hasn't threatened me, but still I feel like I must follow her advice. She is not a woman to be crossed. I need to stay on her good side.

Finally, the two women shuffle out of the aisle, and I seize my opening, rushing to the door. "I'll be right back!" I shout stupidly.

A random Moroni steps in front of me. "You been here long?"

I spin to slip past. And I think: *They will tell your mother.* And I think: *She will know. She will ask why I left, what I needed. Can't she give me everything I need?* But I banish the thought and escape to the hall and out the door.

Down in Happy Camp, the emptiness enfolds me, the sense of abandonment that drifts through the cracked streets. I would have thought that out here I would crave people more, that I would miss them, but that doesn't seem to be the case. Even the fourteen members of the church felt like a crowd, their wants so heavily imposed on me. With so few people around, it's like we are volunteering to live inside each other; sometimes we seem to share a head. That is why your mother's wishes have such a strong effect on me. You felt this way too; you described it to me: *I'm easily influenced. I need to be alone to think straight, but even out in the middle of nowhere, I am never alone enough.*

I walk past the Forest Service, up toward the high school, toward the police station. You told me it was open only four hours a day, but as I reach the station — a narrow building crowded into the corner of an empty parking lot — I see an officer inside studying his phone. He has peels of dark hair around a crown of pink that glows under the fluorescent light. His gut hangs in the hammock of his belt.

I pause outside the door. This is a big moment, I know. In all of your cases, the police statements define the narrative. They are the frame the rest of the story hangs on. Today, I will spur the police to action. They will start their investigation. They will quiz your parents, your brother, Jed. They might even interview me. Your story will be on record, and I will be that much closer to finding you.

I feel unequal to the task. I know so little of what happened. I wish Jed were here. He could provide details of the day you left, your state of mind. But he left the ranch at five o'clock Friday, roaring past the house like he wanted your mother to know about it. I may not know as much as he does — but I care more. I won't let you disappear.

A bell clangs over my head as I walk in. The officer doesn't look up. The station is quiet. It doesn't look like a station. It looks like the intake office at an airport car rental company.

"Hello?"

The officer pulls away from his phone one body part at a time: eyes, shoulders, chest, chin. And then he looks hard at me, like I am the next in line on a prank that has lasted eons.

"I need to report a missing person."

His jaw moves once, twitching over imaginary tobacco. His name tag reads *Officer Hardy.*

"Rachel Bard."

He doesn't move. Doesn't grab a pen to take notes. Doesn't even blink.

"Don't you want to know how long she's been missing for? When she was last seen?"

I am ready with these details.

"It's not a crime to be missing." He rolls his jaw. "Especially not if you're a Bard."

"But — what if she's been kidnapped? Or murdered?" My voice rises on the word. I sound silly, hysterical. And for a second, I'm the busybody, the crazy old woman. (She has to be old, because to a man, there are only two things a woman can be: young or crazy.) I can see that person in his eyes when he looks at me, and I curl in on myself and I want to go, I want to hide and I want to disappear but I won't, I can't, and I insist, "Her mother thinks she's dead."

He pinches his pink face, stands back. "Who are you? I know you're not from around here," he says like that's the bigger crime.

"I'm her cousin." It may not be a good idea to lie to a police officer, but it's the only way I can express my closeness to you, the authenticity of our connection.

"The Bards don't have cousins." He says this gently, to my surprise.

"I'm her best friend." My neck burns. *Am I?* I know we haven't met but I'm the only one, the only one looking for you, the only one who cares. I have even considered that you might have left your MMC Pack with *me* and searched my own belongings.

He leans on his elbows. "I want you to listen. I don't know how you know Rachel or if you even know her, but this girl has gone and disappeared about forty-five times. The first time, she was maybe fourteen. We were worried then. But then she kept on going missing. It became something of a local joke. It got so people didn't even care. Some people just want to be missing. It's better than being wherever the hell they are."

I put my hand on the counter. He jumps like I threw my fist. "She didn't want to be missing. She was terrified of it." I know you were; we both were. This is why we are obsessed by it, by *Murder, Missing, Conspiracy.* Because we always knew it could be us. This man is wrong about you. This man can't understand what only we knew. "You need to open a file. You need to be investigating. I'm telling you, something bad has happened to her. I know."

Suddenly I'm angry. Because isn't this just typical police? Isn't this just the police *we* know? Again and again. They miss the clues. They come in too late. They wait until the case goes cold, the evidence is compromised and corrupted, then flap around ineffectually, pin the crime on whoever is weak enough not to put up a fight, while we, the

151

people who care, we *burn.*

He steps back. "You're new around here, so I'm just gonna let you know, we used to get a lot of noise from that Bard woman." He flaps his hand. "She used to bother us all day. Thought this whole town was out to get her. Everyone had something against her. Then she went quiet. So we're just not gonna mess with that." He puts two hands up.

My thoughts click. "When did she go quiet?"

He wipes the sweat from his pink brow. "I dunno, few weeks ago."

"But that's when Rachel went missing! Don't you see? There might be a connection." Do I think Addy is involved? I have promised myself not to jump to any conclusions, but Addy is in prime position.

"We don't investigate connections; we investigate crimes."

"But what if something did happen?"

"Then it happened. I'm a cop, not a time traveler."

I shake my head, filled with disgust, your disgust, our disgust. "So you just sit here on your phone while people go missing, get murdered? And you call yourself a cop?"

He covers his ears. "My God, it's like that woman all over again." That shuts me up.

Once it is clear that I have shut up, he takes his hands off his ears and puts them back on his phone. Finally, he says, "If you can provide me with something concrete, a reason to believe a crime has occurred, something beyond whatever all nefarious ideas you got twitching up in your little brain . . ."

"I'll find your evidence, and when I do, you'll be sorry you never listened to me."

He looks up, and our eyes connect, and his voice softens as he says, "Hey. You want some advice?" He cracks his neck. "Get as far away from the Bard family as possible." His chin drops and he mutters to himself, "Now, I consider that going above and beyond the call of duty."

I don't want to go back to the church, can't stand the close feeling of it. If your mother finds out I left early (how could she?), if she questions me about it (why would she?), I will tell her I felt sick. It isn't a lie. My head is still dizzy from the drive and my guts are twisted from the visit to the police station, so I walk past the church and into a wide park that opens onto the river basin.

I walk down a wet trail to the bank, then perch on a rock above the water and watch ducks slide in and out on the opposite side.

I work my hands, testing my aching joints. I almost wish for windows to clean, for something to do, just to stop feeling so useless, helpless, nowhere near you.

Maybe I am imagining things. Maybe you haven't disappeared. Maybe you did run away. Maybe you are far away and happy now, free in your new life, but for some reason, I can't believe it.

I check my phone but I have no service. I want to call my ex but maybe it's better that I can't. He will just tell me I am getting carried away. He won't believe I'm doing well, won't care how hard I'm working at my job, how I'm keeping everything together, even all the way out here, where I could fall apart and nobody would know, nobody real would know.

I burn a little more fire, thinking about the police and how they don't care, and then I burn a little more, thinking about Jed and how he doesn't care.

Then I start up the lawn. I see Clementine and her daughters on a picnic bench. I think how strange it is that Clementine is my age and her daughters are teenagers. They sit across from her with the same rapt expression: her lips, her lashes, staring back at her. And I wonder if seeing herself reflected in the faces of her children tricks her into believing she has a higher purpose, like it wasn't a purpose she herself selected, like she couldn't walk away at any time.

I swing wide to avoid being seen by them, cut through the brush on a trail that thins until I'm bushwhacking through reeds.

I finally make it to the parking lot. As I approach my car, Clementine appears, walking up the wide path from the park. Her daughters don't flank her. Your brother is nowhere to be seen. It's just me and her, alone.

She plucks white fuzz from her purple top. "You're out at the ranch," she says like she needs double confirmation. "Do you need a ride back?"

"No. I have a car." I gesture. "Where do you live?"

"We have a place in Happy Camp."

"Addy said Jed's house . . ."

"They wanted us to move in but" — her mouth chews unspoken words — "it wasn't a good fit."

"I'm not stupid," I blurt. I am frustrated with the police, and I am taking it out on her. But I want her to know that I know everyone hates your mother and father. I know that. I am not naive, and I am not a fool, like the police and everyone else seem to think.

She is startled, confused. "I'm not saying you are — I'm sorry. I think maybe there's been a miscommunication."

"Sorry," I allow, although I hate to apologize to anyone. One day, I realized that I apologized too much and so I decided to stop — but sometimes it's hard to know when an apology is earned. "I just — I know it's not a great job," I say like I'm embarrassed to be blue-collar. "I'm here for a story, actually."

She smiles. "Oh, you're a writer! I teach at the high school. We'd love to have you come in," she says like I am Stephen King. I haven't even been published. I don't have any intention of being published. I'm not even a writer, except that I tend to get creative with my own reality.

"Maybe," I say, because it's the nicest way to say no. "I better get back."

She nods like she knows exactly what I mean. And I think: *Clementine is nice.* And I think: *I want to be her friend.* And I think: *Were you?*

And I know it's not smart, but I have to ask her, "Did you know Addy's daughter?"

"Rachel?" Her smile smears. I nod. "Well, of course I knew her."

"Were you close?"

Her nose wrinkles. "When we were

156

younger, but everyone was friends when they were young."

"Did she have many close friends? I thought it might be nice to meet some people around my age," I add when I realize how strange this must sound.

"I'm your age," she says, but she doesn't seem like it. She must have had her daughters when she was a teenager. She has that completed look of a woman with children, like someone switched the lights off on their way out. "But Rachel, Rachel wasn't really close to anyone. Except Bumby. Her cat. He was probably her best friend." I think: *What an offensive cliché of a single woman.* And I think: *You're being too sensitive.*

I fake a laugh and I get into my car.

"See you next week!" she calls.

I wave out the window, and I catch Homer's face in the glass door behind her. He has dimples even when he frowns. He shoves the door open. The gesture looks odd with his wholesome figure; the scowl doesn't fit on his happy-go-lucky face.

"I thought I told you . . ." But his words dim as he gets closer. And I can't reverse, so I pull away, back down the twisted trail toward the ranch.

The wheels turn and my head swells, and I think about what she said. I think about the pictures of Bumby you posted on Instagram and Twitter. Yes, there are about three dozen cats on the ranch with the same coloring as the dead cat I found on that first day. I try to remember if it had a collar, but I'm not sure. I assumed it was Bumby immediately. I didn't look closely. I was afraid to get my hands dirty. And I scold myself: *Details, details — you always told me to remember the details. What gun did they carry? What gloves were they wearing? Where were they at two o'clock on Thursday afternoon?*

Your mother said she would bury the cat in the pet cemetery. She also said the trash collector comes once a week.

The trash bin is on the other side of the lodge, out of view of your parents' house. It's boxed behind a latticed fence, to hide it from the guests. I slip inside the fence and shut the gate behind me so no one will see. The stench of garbage fills my nostrils, but underneath it something else lurks, something every living thing recognizes instinctively.

Bang! A shot fires. I jump back against the fence, heart pounding. I scratch my cheek on the splintered wood. I remind myself it came from the shooting range, but it felt as if a shot was fired right behind me, the way the sound surrounded me.

When I drove in I saw Jed marching up the hillside, carrying a rifle, with an oddly fixed expression, like it was something mental he was about to take aim at. Your parents' house was quiet as I drove past. Your mother didn't come out to scold me about being late like I thought she would, and I wonder how much of her character is a product of my own imagination. Am I being paranoid? Does she care what I do, or is she really just trying to protect me?

Another shot cracks, pops the air open so everything looks sharp and bright. Then the ranch goes quiet. I am wearing the rubber gloves I use to clean the windows. I grab the edge of the trash bin, and I bounce, one, two, and spring up, but I am not as athletic as I imagined and I lose my balance, put out my arms to catch myself. The bin rattles and warm trash cushions my fall.

I wade through evidence of everyone. There are a surprising number of empty beer and whiskey bottles I assume are from Jed. Empty cleaning product containers. Receipts for flashy cowboy gear. And my own minimal waste. I sift through, dig deeper as the smell swells. My stomach lurches, but I order myself to be cool, to stay calm, to do something. Find something, finally. My fingers press into a scrim of skin.

I find the cat inside a trash bag, a tangle of fur and folded bones. His face is looking up at me, mouth twisted down by death, milky eyes still slightly open. I run my fingers down his stiff head, and I feel the hard ridge of his leather collar. Vindication gushes through me, and I slide my fingers around it, lovingly, until I reach the metal buckle and move to unfasten it. The stench has dropped in volume, as if we are getting to know each other now. The buckle releases, and I pull off your cat's collar.

I enter it into evidence.

One leather cat collar
Fountain Creek Ranch dumpster
Found by Sera Fleece

My heart flutters when I see the name, in loopy script, the same stamping system you used on the horse's tack: *BUMBY.* And around it is a small metal tube, where you're meant to keep emergency details — *address, phone number* — in case your pet goes missing. I slip out the tiny roll of paper. I pinch the end and roll it out carefully.

There is no address, no phone number.

Instead there is a list of names. You did
leave clues.

Instead there is a list of names. You did leave clues.

EPISODE 37:
THE IDEAL ROOMMATE

Thirty-year-old Gina Love was last seen on Monday morning, May 22, 2017, at seven fifteen a.m., by her female roommate. She was on her way to work. Her coworkers never flagged her disappearance, never contacted the police when she didn't show for the next three months. She had no close friends. Her roommate didn't feel comfortable searching her bedroom.

"I didn't know her that well," she said. "She was so random. She liked to be alone."

So it was only after three months, when her roommate was clearing the room for a new tenant, that she discovered that Gina had left behind her purse, her wallet, her house keys, her ID.

"I feel like a lot of people blamed me," her

roommate said. "But I was just respecting her privacy."

BANG! Another shot ricochets through the valley. My knees wobble. I am heading up the perimeter trail to the shooting range. I am going to find Jed.

Part of me thinks I should continue my search alone, but another part of me accepts that I can't. I have been alone for the past year, trapped on my bed in my room, listening to you. I have accomplished nothing, apart from memorizing your every word. And now you are gone and no one is looking.

I know I shouldn't trust Jed. I shouldn't trust anyone. But the truth is, I don't believe in myself. I don't believe I can do this alone. And given the choice between your mother and your father and Jed, he is the only choice.

I find him alone on the range, rifle balanced on his shoulder. His back is rigid and he swings around, eyes wild. It takes him a second to lower his gun. "Lord! Don't you know not to sneak up on someone holding a gun?"

"What are you afraid of?"

He grimaces, wipes his brow. I think of the bottles in the trash bin, and I notice the evidence on his face: the looseness in his lips, the shadows under his eyes, the soft sheen on his forehead. "What are you doing up here?" He sets his gun nearby and leans against a tree.

"Where have you been all weekend?"

He shrugs. "I had to get out," he says like he hasn't only been back for a few days. "I just bummed around, went to the Bigfoot Museum in Willow Creek." With his accent he says it *Willa. Willa Creek.* "I wouldn't recommend it." I imagine him walking alone around a deserted Bigfoot exhibit. It's so sad that it's kind of endearing.

"I found something."

"What'd you mean, you found something?"

"First I need to ask you a question: Why is there a dog in your freezer?"

He pulls down his hat, to hide the red spots on his cheeks. "The fuck were you doin' in my freezer?"

I made a mistake. I was so excited by this new evidence that I forgot myself. Of course I shouldn't have been in his garage. Of course I shouldn't be snooping. Wasn't I mad at your mother for doing the same thing to me?

I take a risk. "Before you came. The freezer in my cabin wasn't working. Addy

164

said I could use yours." It's a total lie and it burns coming up, but I have no choice and I hold still. I have a feeling he will accept anything I blame on your mother.

He exhales, carefully, like he has to swerve around the prickly parts. "That's my dog. Had her for seventeen years. She didn't last a week here."

"I'm sorry," I say, and I mean it. I've never had a pet, specifically because I'd be afraid to lose it. "That's terrible" — I try to be delicate — "but why is she in the freezer?'

"Huh," he laughs, and sets his hat back. He uses it like curtains: open for business and closed when he shuts down. "I wasn't about to bury my dog on her land." It's surprisingly pagan but sort of sweet, the way he wants to protect his pet.

"Then why didn't you take her with you to Abilene?"

This unbalances him, like it never even occurred to him. "It wasn't that kind of trip." He wipes his cheek. "Now, what is it you wanted to tell me about?"

I can see he wants to change the subject, which means it's the perfect time to get him talking about something he otherwise might not reveal. "Were you and Rachel involved?"

"Involved?"

"Romantically. I need to know."

"You might remember, I was married."

"I haven't forgotten."

He tips his hat down again, and I can see his southern side, see that he is probably younger than I think. "Rachel . . . she didn't think much of me, and that held a certain attraction. I like it when people share my opinions, 'specially on the things that matter."

I nod, satisfied that he is being honest. I hand him the piece of paper. "It's a list."

His lips furrow. "Where did you find this?"

"Don't worry about that."

He reads aloud, " 'Rachel Bard. Tasia LeCruce. Florence Wipler. Clementine Atwater.' " He looks deflated; I wonder if he wishes his name were on your list.

"I know Rachel," I say. "And Clementine. And Florence — she was the subject of Rachel's first podcast."

Episode 1: On the Murder Line. One blue-skied summer day, four teenage girls in tank tops and cutoff jeans hopped on the eleven thirty bus from Happy Camp, headed north. One was never seen again.

That is an addition I don't know what to do with. If this was a list of people to contact if you disappeared, why would you write down the name of a girl who had disappeared? Why would you write down your own name? In the episode, you named Florence, but you never named the other three girls that took that ride on the Murder Line, the wilderness bus route for criminals and drifters, for people who wanted to disappear. You never said that you were one of them. Maybe it's a clue, or maybe I just want it to be one. "I don't know who Tasia is. I was hoping you might?"

He crinkles his brow. "I wonder if that's Happy Camp Tas."

"Who?"

"Girl who works at the coffee shop."

"I've met her," I say, slightly thrilled, like I have been putting things together all along. "Were she and Rachel friends?"

"Not that I knew." His lips curl in that verboten smile. "Like I told you, Rachel didn't really have friends."

"Well, we need to talk to her."

His eyes drift down me in a way that makes my bones feel loose. I think it's the inclusion of "we." A horse screams far off in the fields below, but it bounces back so it sounds like the horse is just behind us, ready to charge. I don't want to do this alone.

"Well, I'll be working all week, same as you."

"Then we need to go today."

"They close at five on Sundays."

"Then we need to go now."

His lips purse. His eyes move back and forth, fast. "What are you thinking, you and I just drive off together, right in front of Addy?" It's strange how we both think she wouldn't approve. It's strange how we both fear her disapproval. We work for her. We live in her houses, on her land. In isolation, it's strange how quickly the rest of the world fades away.

"What about the fire trail? By the creek?"

He considers. "We could walk down through the creek, but it's another few miles from there."

"Don't you have an ATV?" I say, but I know that's stupid. We can't drive an ATV on the highway.

He bites his lip. "I have a bike. A motorcycle. We could roll it down the hill."

I nod; this could work. "We better hurry."

He scoops up his gun, and I follow him along the upper perimeter trail. We are quiet all the way to his house, knowing how sound can catch and throw and distort. I wait in silence as he takes his bike, rolls it down the trail toward the creek.

Ever since your mother warned me not to go to the creek, it feels imbued with evil, thick with the closed smell of your empty house. Even the bright greenness feels false, like it's hiding something, the persistence of the shadows, how they wind with the wind and the vines. I watch Jed's hips rock as he walks down the trail, and I shiver. I think about you on this path, coming and going, your own little place away from the ranch.

"Did you ever come visit Rachel down here?"

"Why would I come down here to see Rachel?"

"I just assumed you hung out together."

He stops. "No, I mean, Rachel didn't live here."

"What? But this is her house."

He looks down the trail. "No one lives there. They can't. There's no electricity. And no water hookup. And getting one all the way down here would be an endeavor."

"Why would they build a house without water and electricity?"

Jed makes a face. "I don't know if you noticed, but these people don't exactly think things through. They like the appearance of things, but if you look closely, just about everything here is falling apart or being swallowed up by blackberries."

He's not wrong. "They really are every-where."

"Addy has it in her head that she can make a poison to kill them. She carts it around in her ATV. She's been working on it since last year. Rachel used to joke that she'd kill us all. She thinks she can solve everything, that woman, like she created life and death itself."

"Is that what the bottles are, in the green-house?"

"There are bottles for that and just about everything else you can imagine. She calls them her 'cures.' If the cure for one problem is a bigger problem, I reckon she might be onto something. Grace used to hate that stuff. Said it was witchcraft." His face softens when he mentions his ex-wife's name, like it carries its own kind of magic. "I would stay away from that place and anything she tries to give you. The most dangerous people in the world are the ones who think they know something." I like Jed. I can't help it. There is a smoky poetry to everything he says.

"If Rachel didn't live in the creek house, where did she live?"

"With her parents."

"But — I thought . . ." You took pictures, wrote captions about your house, your perfect house. You lied to me. But I won't believe it. Jed must be mistaken. Or maybe he's lying. "I thought it was Rachel's house, like your house is Homer's. Didn't they build it for her?"

"Probably they just built it to torture her with, like they do. Probably they built it so *no one* could have it." He sets his teeth, seeming happy with that answer, with any answer that paints your mother as a villain.

"Did Rachel work on the ranch?"

"She did some things, here and there. Took the horses out. She used to love Belle Star."

"Addy said no one's allowed to ride her."

"I wouldn't believe just every word coming out of that woman's mouth."

"What's going on between you and Addy?"

His spine straightens. "She don't like me."

"Why?"

"Don't think I'm good enough."

"Good enough for what?"

He cocks his head at the slipping sun. The mountains claim it early here. "Whenever they interviewed me, on Skype, way back in Texas, I remember she asked me if I would mind bein' treated like a 'dirty farmhand.' I thought she meant by the guests."

"What did you say?"

"This was my dream job, Sera. My dream. But these people? They don't want employees; they want to own you."

"Like they're buying their children back."

He flinches in surprise. " 'Sactly. It's essactly like that."

Jed winds his bike around the blockade at the edge of the highway, then comes to a stop. He passes me the pink helmet.

I put it on and climb up behind him. It's strange to be this close to someone else. I can feel the life puffing in and out of his stomach, which feels softer than I expected, more real. He stomps the kick-starter and the bike comes alive, shaking with teeth-chattering power.

He says something I don't catch and then we're off. I clasp my arms tight around him. A semitruck races around the corner just as we reach the road. They always appear right when you're about to cross, just like he said. Jed jerks to a stop, waits for the truck to roar past, rattling us in its wake. Then he accelerates and steams in behind.

The bends in the road are worse on a motorcycle. The bike lists sideways and I hold on tighter but he doesn't laugh, like your mother did. And I'm overcome with a warmth that stings around my crown, melts into my shoulder, like it's special when people aren't cruel.

The valley opens up as we cross over the river on a long suspension bridge. Light flashes on the water, and for a second, I am someone else and the weight of you and everything softly rises. The bike travels faster, and I can feel Jed's stomach muscles tighten as he crouches forward and I think: *I am in a beautiful place, with a beautiful person.* And then I keep moving, and the world is flashing past: mountains and trees and breathtaking vistas, all a blaze and a dart past my eye.

When we reach Happy Camp, I am unsteady, overwhelmed. Jed pulls easily into the parking lot outside the coffee shop, and I want to ask him, *Why did you stop?* I want to tell him to keep going, all the way through the winding canyon until we come out on the other side. But instead I wobble off the motorcycle. He reaches out to steady me.

"You okay?"

"Sometimes this place makes me sick." I work my aching knuckles. The sun has dropped now, dipped below the mountain. The earth is painted black and blue.

He sighs and guides me away from the bike. "I know what you mean."

We walk toward the store as the lights go out.

"No!" I race forward, shove the door, which swings helplessly open, and step into the dim shop.

"I'm in here alone all day and you come *now*?" A soft light emanates from the back office, throwing her into shadow.

"All right, Tas?" Jed says in a loose, familiar drawl, and I wonder how well they know each other.

She puts her hands on her hips, makes her eyes long. "Jedidiah. Been a while."

He walks over to the counter and rests his elbows on it. "How you been?"

"All right. How are you keeping out there?"

"Well, you know what it's like. . . ."

"That I do. . . ."

I take a step in closer and Jed remembers me.

"This is the latest recruit." He raps his knuckles on the table. "Sera." They both look back at me, wide-eyed.

"We've met, actually." I try to remember some defining feature our conversation, something that will clear the clouds from her eyes, but I can't. "You dropped a tea-cup."

She blinks blankly, like I could be anyone; then she looks back at Jed.

"She wanted to ask you some questions.

About Rachel."

I frown. I can speak for myself, and I wasn't sure if I wanted to go right into it. It would be better to work my way there slowly, like the best investigators, like you always told me. You start by shooting the shit, getting your target comfortable. Then when they're lulled into a false sense of security, you snap on the lie detector and cut to the bone.

But it's too late for that now. The shop is dark and your mother is expecting me at the ranch and Tasia is looking at me like I have exactly two minutes. So I make them count. "Before she disappeared, Rachel wrote a list of people to contact if something happened to her. Your name is on that list."

"She didn't." Tasia freezes; her hair frames her face in long, lazy dreads. "Why the hell would she go and do a thing like that?"

I glance at Jed. "We're trying to figure out where she is." Tasia is silent. "The cops don't care. Her parents think she's been murdered." Her eyes flicker. "We were hoping you might be able to help us."

She says nothing, and her expression stays constant, so it's impossible to guess what she is feeling: angry, elated, caught?

"Were you friends?"

This breaks the spell. "No. I mean, I guess

we were friends once, when we were kids, but . . . that was a long, *long* time ago." She huffs, like she is really put out by all this.

"How long?"

"I don't know, high school?"

"Why aren't you friends anymore?"

"I guess we grew up. And Rachel didn't."

"What do you mean, 'grew up'?"

"Clem got married. I got married." I want to tell her that being married doesn't make you a different class of person, while at the same time wanting to assure her that I was married too.

I settle for "I don't think being married has anything to do with it."

"That's not what I meant. I meant, we moved on."

"Moved on from what?"

"Look." Her eyes go flat. "Rachel was crazy." I hate this word. Even more when it's said about a woman. (Which it always is.) Even more when it's a woman saying it about another woman.

"Define 'crazy.' " I wish somebody would.

"She was sick. She was obsessed with sick stuff." I shrivel a little. I wonder what Tasia would think about me. "And she liked to cause trouble." She gives Jed a look, like he will understand. "Look, I'm not saying I'm happy she's gone or anything. All I'm saying is, I don't really understand how my name ended up on some list when I've barely said a word to her in about fifteen years."

I am speechless. I stare at the floor, feeling dizzy, like your story is the winding road I came in on, bile rising in my throat. I am trying to process this. You are not sick. I know this. You care about people. You care too much; that is why *Murder, She Spoke* exists, because you wanted to talk about the people everyone else had forgotten. If you were obsessed, it was with answers. I know you.

But then I think about your house. How you lied to me, told me the yellow house was yours, posted pictures, provided captions. *This is where I go to find peace. I'm so lucky to have this little corner of heaven!*

You said the house was yours, but Jed said you lived with your parents. My head is spinning again. How can I tell fact from fiction? I need evidence. I need to focus on the facts, but everything feels slippery out here, like everyone's thoughts are jaws opening, to swallow mine.

Jed and Tasia look furtively at each other. They think they look over my head but I see them; I know what those looks mean.

"I'm sorry. I don't really know what you

177

want from me," Tasia finally says.

"Sera just wants to make sure Rachel's all right. . . ." Jed tries to help.

"I have no idea how Rachel is. Real talk? I don't care. I don't know why my name is on that list." She spreads her fingers. "All I can think is, she didn't have many friends. Maybe our relationship meant more to her than it did to me."

"What about Florence Wipler?" I try to keep my voice even, but the name sounds like ammunition. "Her name is on the list too. Do you know where she lives?" I ask like I don't know.

Tasia's eyes go veiled. "Florence was a girl who went missing, in our class. It was a big deal." It is what inspired you, what made you feel chosen. It is what led to *Murder, She Spoke.*

"Why would Rachel write her name down?"

"I don't know." And when she realizes that won't work, she adds, "Rachel was obsessed. She rewrote history. Suddenly she and this girl were best friends. Suddenly she knew everything about her and none of us cared. And when that wasn't enough, *Rachel* went missing. She would disappear for days, come back with these wild stories, say she had been kept in a basement or grabbed off

178

the street or dressed up like a doll." She shudders. "Really disturbing stuff. That's when she got kicked out of school. No, that's not right. She was 'asked to leave.' "

I take a stab in the dark. "You were on the bus that day, with Florence."

"I —" She cranes back; her eyes narrow and contract, like she is getting a new read on me. "Yes."

I play it light. "What happened?"

"I told you; I don't know. We were arguing and Florence ran off."

"What were you arguing about?"

"She — Wait, hey." She checks in with Jed. "This is so none of your business." She folds her arms and steps back. "I'm done *talking* now, by the way. Nice of you to check in. Nice to finally meet you." She seethes like I am scum, and I am scum. I don't care about her. All I care about is getting to you and I want to apologize, but then I feel like I shouldn't. I am just asking. I'm just trying to help. A woman is missing; this isn't a tea party.

"Thank you," I say. Jed shrugs like he's apologizing for me. I start toward the door. The overhead bell dings.

"Hey! By the way?" I turn but she is half in shadow. "It really sucks. When your friend dies right after you've had a big, dumb argu-

179

ment. In case you were wondering. It really fucks you the hell up."

My stomach sinks as Jed and I walk into the parking lot. The air has chilled in our absence, and I shiver with surprise, raise my hands to rub my bare arms.

"Well, that was pleasant." Jed hands me the helmet.

"I don't believe her," I say, too quick. He inhales sharply. He is frustrated with me, and I don't want to care but I do. I want him to like me. I want everyone to like me and I also want to find you, and it is becoming clear that I can't have it both ways. "Is that the Rachel you knew?"

"I guess I didn't know her that well." He waits.

"Did you see Tasia's reaction? When we first told her about the list? Did you see how shocked she looked? That didn't look like the face of someone thinking about something that happened fifteen years ago. I think she's lying. I think there's more to the story. It was almost like she expected us. Like she was afraid. Like there was a real and present threat." I can feel my heart lift, the beginnings of getting carried away.

"I don't know." Jed climbs onto his bike and waits for me.

"Well, I do. I know Rachel." And I do. I know you better than anybody else. And I'm not going to give up on you. "We need to keep digging. We need to talk to Clementine. Doesn't she live in Happy Camp?"

"I've never been to her place. Have you?"

"You could ask Tasia," I say, but the lights are out. The door is locked. The town is deserted, in the way of small towns on a Sunday night.

Jed is limp, like he is worn-out already, like he doesn't want to find you. Like he doesn't care. "Maybe we should just call it a night."

"Fine, but we're not finished yet. We're just getting started." I force the helmet over my head, ignoring the swirling sensation in my gut. You wouldn't give up. You never gave up, no matter how cold the case seemed to be.

As we move out onto the highway, the space between my hip bones swirls. I hate this road, especially on a motorcycle, especially in the dark, where I can't see the curves in the road until they take us, slanting sideways. The air is cold and it slips under my shirt, under my skin.

We are sliding through a turn when a black truck appears behind us, its lights fully bright. The driver lands on his horn, as if we don't know he's there, and the sound ricochets from ridge to ridge, so it seems to amplify, open up my eardrums.

I move closer to Jed, to ask him what the hell this guy is thinking, but of course he doesn't hear me. I lean forward and the wind whips my cheeks and the truck presses behind us so close, I swear I can feel the heat of its metal grille, the smoke of its exhaust. And it rides even closer, the driver jamming the horn down again, swallowing us in the sound.

Jed goes rigid as the bike starts to skid. He turns to look behind us and I turn with him, but all I can see are two bright white lights, a tall black chamber; then the grille is so close that I swear it's underneath us. The bike twists and we bounce off the road, toward the edge of a cliff.

"Get the fuck out of this town!"

EPISODE 41:
MURDER OF A JANE DOE 1

Graphic Content Warning

She had been stabbed eighty-six times. The skin of her cheeks had been clawed from her face, down to the bone in places. The murderer bleached her fingernails, then gave her a manicure. They used a curling iron to style her hair, and left a postmortem burn on her forehead.

The women who found her said, "At first, I thought she was a doll, as silly as that sounds. My mind just couldn't comprehend. I thought she was an enormous doll."

The bike spins, flattening through the dirt. Jed drops his boot, drags his leg to pinwheel us to a stop.

I force myself away, wanting to get as far from the hot, clicking metal as I can. My knees shake, in delayed reaction, and I trip, falling awkwardly against a rock. Jed lifts his helmet and pitches it at the two little red lights glaring backward at us from the highway. They slip and disappear behind a curve, and the sound of the engine cuts out quickly. Everything is quiet.

"Fucking asshole!" Jed yells. "The goddamn, fucking assholes in this fucking place!" He rolls up his jeans, and I can see his leg is torn up, road rash where he slid to stop the bike. He sits down hard on a rock. "What the fuck is wrong with people?" He presses his finger to the wound and hisses. "Shit."

My heart starts to race, swelling in my chest. "Do you think that was them?"

"Who?" he says, hissing again.

"The gang!" I blurt. My voice takes a slightly hysterical edge, and I try to quell it, but we were just run off the road. "The people Rachel talked about! The ones who ran her off the road."

He raises a skeptical brow at me. I can tell he is not impressed by my apparent gleefulness. "I think it was an asshole — that's what I think."

"Maybe they know we were talking to Tasia, and the police — maybe they don't like it!" I try to keep the victory from my voice, but I can't help being a little proud. Maybe this is a sign that we're on the right track. Maybe this is a warning that we're getting closer to you.

He sets his leg down. "What do you mean, the police?"

"I talked to them this morning." He shakes his head like I did something bad. "They weren't helpful, if that makes you feel better. Officer Hardy. He told me to get as far away from the Bards as I could."

"Ha." Jed snorts. "That sounds pretty helpful to me." His knee jerks as he starts to stand, so he rocks back down. "Hey, will you give me a hand here?"

"Are you okay?"

"I'm fine; I just can't stand up." I take his hand and guide him to his feet. He hovers beside me for a moment, hand on my shoulder, testing his leg.

"Are you all right?"

"I told you I was fine," he says, and then he squeezes my shoulder once so I feel it melt down through me and he steps back, away. "That bike" — he points — "is not fine."

"What do you mean?"

"I mean" — he puts his hands on his hips — "I hope you're wearing comfortable shoes." My heart rate jumps again. "You can leave the helmet here. I'll come pick this thing up once we get back." Jed starts up the highway, testy on his bad leg.

"What about Addy?" I'm not quite sure what I mean. She is not here and she has nothing to do with this situation, but still I can't help but consider her first, like she holds a primary spot in my brain.

"We don't have a whole lotta options. We can't call anyone without a signal. We could go back to Happy Camp and knock on doors, try to borrow a phone, but I don't reckon you want to call up Addy for a ride neither."

"How far is it?"

"I reckon it'll take us about an hour, if we're quick."

"What if that truck comes back?"

He glares at me. "Sera, it was just a truck. People out here are like that. They come out here because they don't like other people, and sometimes it shows."

I follow behind him, wading in the light from his phone. "Is that why you came out here?"

"I told you why I came out here: I wanted a better life."

"Then why did you stay when your wife left?" He bristles. I have gone too far. What was I thinking, saying that to him? But it's

186

like I can't stop pushing; I can't stop looking for answers. His wife only lasted a week.
It was six months before he even tried to
see her. You vanished and no one is looking
for you. If this place had another name, it
would be Apathy. Apathy County, locked on
the Murder Line, in the dead center of
Nowhere, USA. "I just mean, I would think
you would have gone after her," I say before
I realize I'm not making things better. I have
this insatiable need to know people's dirty
secrets. I need to understand everything,
while everyone else can live with things
never being resolved or explained.

"Well, this is nice." Jed slaps his good leg.
"I ride you all the way out here even though
I think this whole idea that something happened to Rachel is downright crazy. We get
into a goddamn accident, fuck up my bike
and my leg and now what? You gonna tell
me I'm a bad husband? I let my wife and
my life slip away. You think I don't know
that?"

"I don't mean . . . I let my life slip away
too."

"All right." He throws his hands up.
"Don't go looking for your answers in me.
Come to that, don't you go looking for your
answers in Rachel neither. You know that's
what all this is about, right? I don't even

know if I reckon you care whether something happened to her — you'd rather just get caught up in someone else's disappearance instead of dealing with your own."

I am quiet. I don't think he's wrong, but I hate to admit it. Maybe I did want to get lost in you. Maybe I wanted to disappear in your story.

We walk along the highway and for once my mind is quiet. There is no podcast playing on my phone, no crazy thoughts, no useless anxiety, just the cold and the mountains and the trees and the rivers and the knowledge that I messed up.

If I had to define the exact moment, the day I started to disappear, I think I could. It was the day the divorce became official, the day there was no going back, when I decided to be a woman, alone. But that's not true. Because my ex would argue that for most of our marriage, I was already gone. So maybe it was the day I lost the baby. But that's not true either. I think of the wedding, how it just went on and on. And everyone was so happy, and I was just there. And the happier they were, the more *there* I was. I go further back, to the day we met. I knew we would get married right away. I knew it like it had been chosen for

188

me. I said to myself, *Here is a man I can stand. Here is someone I can definitely put up with.* So maybe it was before that. And I think of being young, how women are taught, piece by piece, how they fit into the world. But that's not where it started either. I was born a woman. I was born to disappear.

I want to tell Jed he's wrong, that he doesn't understand how deep this thing goes. But I also want to demand that he marry me, that he save me from this. *Take this man or any man you can get your hands on.* Maybe that is your wish for me. Maybe that's the solution, the only way I can stop myself from disappearing.

The next week rocks me back into your world without you: riding horses, cleaning windows, riding horses, cleaning windows. Every day at five o'clock, I go back to my cabin, force down a peanut butter sandwich and fall asleep. My body aches but it's oddly pleasant, and I think, *Maybe I should give up. Maybe I should let go. Maybe I need to accept that you can't find someone who was born to be gone.* But every night, I still switch on your podcast. I still fall asleep to the sound of your voice.

Episode 64: They told her she was crazy to think anything nefarious had occurred.

Episode 18: They looked the other way.

Episode 37: The case went cold.

All the missing women, and the story ends the same way. The story ends when people stop looking, when they stop searching, when no more evidence is found. I won't let your story end that way. I won't let my story end that way. I won't give up. I won't stop looking. If Jed is right, if I'm looking for you because I'm lost too, then finding you will save you and me both.

I still have my list of names. I still have Clementine. I think of what she said about you, that you were friends when you were young, when everyone was friends. Tasia said that same thing, and I think how alike we are in our aloneness. I think that no one would look for me if I disappeared. But then I think you might.

I make a plan. I will offer to speak to Clementine's class. And I will make her tell me everything about you to return the favor. I rub the windows like I can force everything to be clear.

A couple times a day, your mother checks in on me. She admires my work ethic, my dedication, the fire in my belly.

"You're a hard worker," she says. "I like that."

She tells me stories of the latest disasters — the PC culture is destroying this country; all those shootings are a government conspiracy to get her to give up her guns; the people that own the land across the way are growing cannabis and they want to get her out — and all the potions she has conjured to solve them: thoughts and prayers, lavender to sleep, calendula around the perimeter to overpower the stench of cannabis. Then she sighs and says, "We're so happy you're here." Over and over.

One night she invites me to dinner at the main house. "We're going to have everyone over. All the staff." I assume she means me and Jed. "We'll eat out on the patio."

"Do you want me to bring anything?" I ask although the concept is ridiculous. What could I bring? I'm not supposed to leave.

"Just yourself." She flashes a smile that flushes hot youth through her face, and then she leaves me to my windows, to the meticulous, solitary, bone-crushing work of making glass disappear.

I think about you almost all the time, often in an exhausted, abstract way, but other times I examine Tasia's words for clues. She seemed so angry at you — why?

Because you let yourself be affected by a girl's disappearance? She seemed angry and afraid, and she didn't like you? What was she afraid of? And what did you argue about the day Florence disappeared?

After work, I lie down for a moment and fall asleep. Heated dreams swirl through my head, and I hear your voice, hear your angry voice like it's right outside.

I get out of bed, still off-balance. I put on one of the shirts your mother gave me, a bright orange flannel with daisies embroidered in a chain around my neck. I walk across the ranch as the sun lowers, throwing dapples through the trees.

As I pass by the garden, I notice a brown patch where the blackberry bushes have died. Was that there before? I step closer, timidity infecting my limbs. The thorny bushes have gone a pale beige color, shriveled and receded, revealing what lies beneath. I step forward. I tip the thorny bush with the toe of my shoe, and that's when I see it, the shape of a tiny pale hand, fingers outstretched.

My heart throbs in my chest. My neck breaks a sweat, like I've been found guilty. I swivel my eyes around the ranch, feeling watched.

"There's something here," I say out loud,

even if no one is listening.

It's a baby. There is a baby in the bushes.

I crouch down on my knees. I feel sick and then I think — *Don't leave your DNA!* I cover my hand with my shirt and peel back the blackberry bushes so I can see the body, laid out in the shadows.

It's a doll. It's a doll, and somewhere I knew that. But I remember so many episodes where real dead bodies were described: *I thought it was a mannequin. I thought the blood was spilled red wine.*

I know that I should leave it, but I use my sleeve-covered hand to drag it out. The displacement in the bushes releases a rich, rotting smell that pushes me back. The doll falls on my lap. There are puncture wounds in her chest and scratch marks on her cheek. I am reminded of *Murder of a Jane Doe 1,* like I have found the body you told me about. And for a moment it is as if that story is not just real, but here with me. Like everything you told me was not only true, but also tied to this ranch, to you, to me.

We had a nursery; that was the worst thing. We had a nursery with yellow walls like the walls of your yellow house. I tried to move the furniture so many times. I tried to redecorate, make it an office that no one worked in or a guest room that no one slept in. But really it was just an empty room, yellow and empty, like your house.

And I'm sitting alone in the dirt, holding a doll. Who is the crazy woman? Who is the one losing her mind?

I hear the sound of a party before I arrive, and I think I must be imagining it. Your mother hates everyone. Who would she invite? I left the doll propped up at the side of the greenhouse. I felt bad leaving it, but I also didn't particularly want to take it home with me.

When I arrive at the house, I see another big black truck parked outside. Does everyone in this town drive a truck? I find a group of people weaving in and out the back door under your mother's command. I don't see Jed. Instead I see the two women from church, parked in patio chairs with their bare legs crossed, jawing to each other as gnats swirl overhead. Your two nieces, dressed in long skirts, carry plates and cups in prairie patterns. They look up fast when they see me, then look away. Your brother is here.

I walk into the house to see if I can help. Plates of organic food steam on the counter — the food is brighter than the plates and smells like earth and nettles. Beside it, your mother is seething already.

"Can I help with anything?"

She flaps a dish towel. "Is Jed here yet?"

"I haven't seen him."

Your brother is helping your father use the computer in the corner.

"You don't need to type in your password," he says. "It's already saved."

"I don't want it to be saved." Your father makes a grab for the mouse.

"They're all saved because you keep forgetting them."

"No! How do you unsave them?"

"Dad, come on. I can't keep resetting them for you. Trust me, no one wants to log into your Prime account."

"That's how they get you!" He taps the side of the computer. "Next thing you know, it's tickets to Aruba on your dollar!"

"Please stop talking, Dad."

Your mother told me they didn't have Wi-Fi. Obviously, she doesn't want me to use it. I wonder if you used it. I can't imagine you broadcasting from here, in the middle of your parents' living room, but I still want to search their computer.

"You have Internet," I say to your mother.

"It's for business use only," she snaps. "We don't like you kids going on there and mess-ing things up."

"But if I —"

"Emmett, Homer!" Your mother flaps the towel again, shooing away the heat. "We need to start dinner. Where's Jed?"

I want to push, but what's the point? I can't search for you with a crowd gathered. I need to come back when everyone is gone.

"Hi again." Clementine appears at my elbow. I shift away in surprise, but then I remember she is on your list.

"Where's Jed?" Your mother asks again. It's unclear who she's asking.

"I think I saw him heading down." Clementine's smile stretches between her ears. "He was looking at the ducks."

"Looking at ducks? Has he lost his mind?" An image comes to mind, of me unearthing a doll from the blackberry patch; maybe he's not the only one. "I said five thirty. Didn't I say five thirty?" Again, it's unclear who she is talking to. Clem and I both scan the room for her target audience.

"Why don't we start setting the food out? I'm sure he'll be here just in time for the prayer," Clem says brightly.

Your mom's face sours, but she hisses, "Whatever." Then she stalks to your father. "Get off the computer and help!"

I take up a tray of smashed potatoes.

Clementine smiles gratefully. "You know, I'd still love you to come to my class."

"I'd be happy to."

She is taken aback by my sudden change of heart. "Oh, okay, great," she says, and I wonder if she is one of those people who make offers to sound nice. "What about Friday?" I guess not.

"I'd have to check with Addy." My stomach does a little flip. Your mother will never agree to this; she doesn't want me to leave. But I don't need her permission. I don't need anyone's permission, and I wish I didn't have to remind myself of that every time I do something someone else doesn't like.

"I can check with her," Clementine offers, and I want to hug her. She knows I am afraid, and she is helping me. Her daughters join us. "Asha and Aya hoped you would be here," she says like they are one thing. "We've been talking about you all week." I don't know how that can be. They barely know me. Surely, they can't know enough to fill a single conversation, let alone a week's worth. But I also realize that out here, the littlest things can be magnified, become an obsession.

"Where'd you get that shirt?" Aya asks me.

"Your grandmother."

"Told you," Asha snaps, and sticks out her tongue.

"Help," Clementine orders, mom-style, and they pick up the hot plates with square pads.

I carry the potatoes out through the living room. Asha and Aya step in on either side of me. "We want to watch you talk to her class," Asha says quickly. "Tell our mom." And then they both go out ahead of me, their long skirts swirling in sync.

As I pass the stairwell, my eyes drift upward. I want to go up there — maybe I can ask to see the house? I wonder what your room looks like now that you're gone. Have your parents preserved it? Would knowing that tell me what they really think happened to you? If your bedroom has been preserved, would that mean they expect you back, or could it mean they have left it as a shrine?

Clementine comes back in and finds me. "It's a beautiful house, isn't it? Addy hand carved the sconces."

"Yeah, it's amazing. Do you think maybe I could go upstairs?"

Clementine blinks in alarm. "Why?"

"I just thought it might be fun to see, you know, what they've done with it."

"Addy's kind of a private person. But

198

you're welcome to come see our house anytime!" Clementine is nice. Maybe I can trust her. Maybe she is a better choice than Jed, who appears right then with one leg soaked with mud past his ankle, looking like he really has lost his mind.

We haven't talked since Sunday night, when it took us well over two hours to walk back to the ranch. Over two hours not speaking, as the forest rattled with night-time sounds, angry calls that chilled me to the bone. Not a single car passed, and I wasn't sure whether that was a blessing or a curse. Would someone have offered us a ride, or would they have played chicken, tried to run us off the road? When we were finally about to cross the highway to the ranch, a semitruck appeared. Jed laughed in spite of himself, caught my eye and shook his head. But once we crossed the road, the spell was broken, and he walked me to my door and left without saying good night.

Your mother is incensed by his late arrival. "Where have you been? We've all been waiting."

"I thought I'd go swimming," he says. Asha and Aya giggle frantically and each slaps a hand on the chair between them.

"Jed, sit here!" They say in unison.

"I got a tattoo." Asha slides up her sleeve

to reveal her wrist.

"It's fake," Aya butts in. "When are we gonna go shooting?"

Even the women from the church seem to perk up in his presence. Only your mother bristles.

We pray and then we eat. The food is rich and it goes down heavy. Your brother and Clementine are quiet, keeping their heads bowed over their plates, breaking their silence only to exclaim over your mother's food, your mother's garden, your mother's ranch. Elodie and Geraldine, who work at the ranch every summer, sing even heavier praises to your mother, marveling at what a strong woman, what a good cook, what an inspiration she is, like she is royalty, like they are lucky to be hosted on her land, in her kingdom.

But every time she leaves the table, every time her back is turned, their faces droop, their shoulders sag and they look like loan sharks tallying up debts. I think of Moroni, the way he praised your mother to the sky, then called her a witch behind her back. I think of what the man on the street told me, that first day in Happy Camp: *We take bets. On how long you all will last.*

I can understand why they don't like her; she is a tough woman to like. But they also rely on her. There are not a lot of opportunities in Happy Camp. The surroundings are so beautiful that sometimes the poverty catches you off guard. Elodie and Geraldine wear the same dresses they wore to church. Sitting across from them, I can see that what I thought were patterns are actually the kind of sweat stains that never go away. The darkness of their hairlines comes from the dirt caked underneath. And even though Addy's food tastes like fertilizer and is probably loaded with herbal remedies not approved by the FDA, they still eat all of it.

In a place like this, Addy is glamorous, a queen. And I wonder if that's why she stays, even if she claims to hate it. The truth is, I can't imagine her anyplace else.

All through dinner I prickle with the need to mention you. I try to think of ways to bring you into the conversation without drawing attention.

Your daughters are beautiful, Clementine. Addy, what about your daughter?

Homer, what was it like growing up here? What was it like growing up with your sister?

But instead I eat you mother's food and feel light-headed in the fresh air. Whenever I'm asked a question, I say, *Yes, yes, I love it here. Yes, I'm so lucky to be here. Yes, yes, yes* until all I want is to run, run to the perimeter and cross it, cross it so I can breathe and see the forest *and* the trees.

The girls buzz around Jed, so enthusiastic that it exhausts me, makes me wonder if I ever had that much energy, and why I never used it for anything good. For his part, Jed is polite but distracted. Every time our eyes meet over the table, it feels like an accident.

"I better get back." He pushes out his chair, and everyone at the table moves at once, like he has broken the spell.

"I made dessert," Addy says. Everyone looks from Addy to Jed.

"It is getting late," I say, which your mother doesn't like.

Jed gets unsteadily to his feet, like it is physically difficult to leave her table. "Thank you for dinner."

"You'll stay for dessert, or you'll be rude." The table is quiet. I think oddly of the gun at her hip, as if she will shoot him for leaving; that is how thickly her will is imposed on everything. It's like she has brought a glass dome to the table and we are all trapped inside it and I think of what you said — *It was the middle of nowhere, and I couldn't escape* — and I wonder if you meant from her, how you said, *The Murder of Dee Dee Blanchard: I get that. I get that so much.*

Jed and your mother lock eyes. I think she wants him to fight her. You said she liked strong people. I think she misses you. You were strong and now you've vanished and all that's left, the only people for her to play with, are broken and lost.

Jed takes a deep breath and sinks back into his chair.

Your mother brings out brownies, which are her own special recipe. "The secret," she informs us, "is the hot sauce." She pours it over each brownie as she serves it, so hot that the brownies collapse, leaving gaping holes. And the chorus begins.

There is nothing like overpraising food for turning it to mud in your mouth.

Dinner finishes and Jed escapes, stalking along the main path to the other side of the ranch. Everyone watches him go. Your mother shakes her head. "That man is up to no good." Elodie and Geraldine hurry in to placate her.

"Your dinner was amazing."

"The dessert was top-notch."

Clementine is taking the dishes back to the kitchen. I follow her, through the house with the glowing white Christ statue, the slick black piano. It's quiet in the kitchen, a hollow where the echoes can collect. I want to ask her about you right then and there, but someone could come in at any moment, so I say, "Friday?"

She gasps at my voice, surprised that she is not alone. "Yes." She smiles her useful smile. "Don't worry about Addy. I'll work it out with her."

I glance toward the living room. My words gather in my throat, then all run out almost at once. "I wanted to tell you something; it's about Rachel."

She catches my eyes. "Not here," she says, and I don't know why. Her eyes are wide, and then she passes into the shadow of the hallway so I can't read her face.

Homer appears suddenly, coming from outside, and moves in beside her. "There you are." He is so casually handsome, like the lead in a Hallmark movie, and he slides his arms around her waist, kisses the tendon on her neck.

"Sorry," she says to him. "Just trying to help your mother." She takes his hand and presses it, like she's ensuring their connection, and then she moves on to the kitchen, leaving him with me.

"Well, hello," he says like we haven't been sitting across from each other for the past hour. He leans easily on the counter, crosses his arms. "We really enjoyed you at church."

Church people say the weirdest things.

"Um, yeah, it was really interesting."

"We don't have a lot of people in our congregation. We used to have more." Like that might convince me to come back.

"It was really fun." The more I say it, the less we both believe it.

"I hope you'll come again."

"Of course." I have no intention of ever going again. I glance quickly, into the dark living room, then say, "Did Rachel go to church?"

"Rachel?" Like he's trying to place her. "No."

"That's too bad."

"Yes." He scratches his neck, like his mask itches. "Rachel and I were very different. I believe in forgiveness." What wouldn't you forgive? "I believe people can change."

"That's nice," I say.

"I think so."

We finish cleaning up, and your mother loads me down with leftovers, dry, papery food so dense, it feels like dumbbells in my hands. I pass through the group, saying goodbye. I feel the uncomfortable burr of loneliness, thinking about going back to the staff cabin, the stink and the stuffiness, when your mother's house is so clean and cheerful.

I say goodbye to your mother, your father, your brother, your nieces, Elodie and Geraldine. Clementine is waiting by the door. She moves in to hug me, then tilts her head so she can speak into my ear. A thrill runs up my spine; I think she will finally tell me something important.

"Do you feel safe here?" she says instead.

"Yes."

She pulls away. "Okay." Then she follows her family out to the car. I watch them leave from the shadows and wonder why she thinks I wouldn't feel safe.

EPISODE 45:
THE QUEEN OF THE FLIES

The compound was stationed close to the PCT, on the border of California and Oregon. At the height of the summer, the cult members would drive out to the trailhead and wait for hikers to pass by, exhausted and half crazed with hunger. They wouldn't take just anyone. They targeted women, women who traveled alone. They drove them to the compound, where they offered them a feast. They let them eat their fill and then they feasted on their flesh.

As I walk back to my cabin, my stomach roils with your mother's food, which is like nothing I have ever tasted before, like she invented a new cuisine. I tell myself there is no reason to believe it's going to make me sick, that I'm not the only one who ate it, but then I think of the bottles lined up in the greenhouse: the reeds like hair, the white slices of fish bones. Surely your mother would know better than to put something like that in her food?

I wander through the ranch with the lights out, so the guest cabins cower, the horses move like phantoms in the shadows. I feel like I am running out of time, like I am an hourglass with a hole at the bottom, emptying, with no chance of turning it all around. It's not a feeling that is specific to you, although this time you are at the heart of it.

It's the first night I have noticed the stars, and I gaze up as I walk slowly toward my cabin. There is a blanket of them, wildly flecked, like paint splatters across the sky, and I regret that I didn't see them before.

I wonder how I got here. How I'm over thirty and, instead of living, I'm disappearing. The idea of life has always been, I thought, that as you got older, your life multiplied, that you became bigger and bigger, more and more, not less. But I think about you (*Missing? Murdered? Conspiracy?*) and I realize the place I thought I was going, the place I thought we were all going, has scattered like the stars away from us.

I walk along the duck pond; I can see the rough battle of Jed's feet, diving in and out of the water. I observe the thin layer of surface, and I fantasize about finding your skull, wish so hard I can almost see it glimmer, see your crystal bones. Like the bones of Lynn Messer found in an open field two years after she went missing. Lying out in a cow pasture, and nobody saw her, search parties and police dogs, even her own family — *for years.* And her husband remarried and her kids' heads spun and her body was out there with the cows, drying in the sun, rotting in the dark, and no one noticed. I won't let that happen to you. I won't leave your bones waiting.

My stomach lurches. You are out here somewhere. Are you drowning in the water or are you baking in the sun and why does nobody care? Why is nobody looking? Why has everyone accepted your vanishing? Why don't you matter? Why don't *we* matter? Because the truth is, Rachel, growing up out here in a population of four, you are just as missed as I would be, solved like a problem that could never be fixed any other way: She disappeared.

She was crazy, she was a bitch, she was alone. You never fit, and so you make more sense as a mystery, a disappearance. And maybe that's why I was drawn to you in the first place. Maybe we always knew that we would disappear and no one would care;

maybe that was why we cared so much about the people who disappeared before us.

I reach into my pocket and take out your list. What is the secret? What is the tie between the names? Four girls, four girls who used to be friends. Four girls who haven't been friends for a long time.

I follow the perimeter of the lake, still looking for your bones. I pass by the promised pet cemetery, tucked under a tree. Names are scrawled on homemade tombstones: *Lulu, Gigi, Grace.* And in front of Grace's, a bundle of discordant wildflowers. I shiver in surprise. Isn't that Jed's wife's name? Maybe the family pet shared the name. Maybe Grace, in the week that she was here, made a grave for herself, for fun?

The ground drops out from under me. Bile rises in my throat. I think of Jed's muddy boot. He was up here, leaving flowers. Maybe he made a headstone for his own wife, but why? And then it strikes me: What if she never left? What if Jed was lying? But it doesn't make sense, that he would murder her, then bury her out in the open, where anyone could see — but then, who would see? Who would ever know but your mother and your father? What if they are all in on it, everyone at that dinner party? And my stomach lurches, and I hear Addy tell me, *We're so happy you're here* and Homer say, *Rachel and I were very different* — "were," past tense, like he knows you are never coming back. What if they are all planning to kill me? I think how easy it would be, to pluck people off, out here, in the middle of nowhere, in Apathy County, where no one cares.

I move away from the river, following Jed's weird footpath until it disappears on the packed dirt road. I almost trip over another dead cat, stretched long across the path, like it was flying, like it fell from the sky. I hear a strangled call and look up. I search for the vultures — do vultures sleep, or do they just circle? Do they feed off the sleep of the dead?

Up ahead, I see the greenhouse glitter in the dark, a mirror for the moon. I feel the witchy food turn in my stomach, and I brace myself against a tree, cough once, then watch it pour out of me.

It looks the same on the ground as it did on the plate, and then I hear heavy panting, the trot of footsteps, see the glint of yellow nighttime eyes, and your mother's dogs appear, surround me like a pack of wolves. They approach slowly. I call to them but they ignore me. They gather at my feet, and then they lap up my vomit from the ground.

The next morning, I finish feeding the horses and arrive back at the tack room to find Jed saddling two horses.

"Addy said I could take you up to Eagle Rock today," he says, lifting a saddle onto Jewel's back. "It's the all-day trail for advanced riders. Probably take all morning, if you want to bring a sandwich or something." He doesn't look me in the eye. I think of the grave in the pet cemetery.

I hesitate, realizing we will be up there alone. I can say no. I can refuse to go. But then I think of you. You weren't afraid to put yourself at risk. You weren't afraid of being "crazy." You weren't afraid of pushing, when everyone else let go.

I can drop out. I can quit, like I quit everything. Or I can be fearless. I can be the person you assumed I was, in every episode, whispered in my ear. Told me grim secrets because you knew I could handle it, that I wasn't like other people. You believed in me. You knew I would save you, if you ever needed to be saved.

"I'll be okay." I step in to finish tacking up my horse. It's quiet for a few minutes, except for the flap of tack and the huff of our breath, the occasional nicker of our horses. And then we mount and ride out past your mother's house, along switchbacks up the steep mountain, deep and deeper into the woods.

Too soon, we are so far up that the ranch appears like a cluster in the palm of the mountains. I take a breath. Jed glances back and gives me a knowing look.

"I sometimes don't realize how close we all are down there," I say.

"I do," he says, flicking his reins to stop his horse trying to grab at the plants along the trail.

"So, how's Grace?" The question activates a rod in his spine. I can't see his face to gauge his expression, but his body tells me he is not happy with the question.

"I'm sure she's all right," he says stiffly, like I should know better than to ask.

"In Texas?"

"I reckon." His voice is light but then he pulls up his horse. He looks down at the ranch below us, and I can see there are tears forming in his eyes.

My first impulse is to say, "Sorry."

"S'okay." He wipes an eye. "Need to stop having whiskey for breakfast."

"You didn't see her at all when you went back?"

"No. I told you she wouldn't see me." He

wipes an eye again, although the tears have gone.

"But why wouldn't she, if you came all the way down there?"

"Sera, this might shock you, but I have a little bit of a drinking problem."

"I thought you were just a cowboy."

"That too." He sighs. "If I thought I deserved to see her, I would." He flicks the reins and urges his horse forward.

"So you don't even try?"

He stops again. I can see him swallow. "Now, I don't go telling this to everyone, but I reckon you might understand. I haven't exactly been honest about what brought me here. I . . . I guess I've been hard on you because I can relate a little too much." He sighs again, all through his body, but instead of making him look defeated, it makes him look stronger. "Back in Abilene, I got into a real hole. I stopped working, just fell to drinking. I hid it from my wife, did all kinds of things, just trying to hide from her, all lyin' and cheatin' and stealin'. I got a real sick kick for any bad thing." He shakes his head. "God love that woman. I don't know how I ever thought I could live the life we're supposed to live, with a wife and kids and a job. I guess I knew I couldn't, but my mistake was, I done it anyway. It just acted like a vise on me. I couldn't do it. I just can't." He pleads like he knows I will understand, and I do. That's why I'm here.

"Coming out here," he continues, "it was kind of like a last-chance saloon, you know? One last chance to start over, make it all work right. I promised Grace I'd cut out the bad stuff, swore up and down and on my life. But I didn't. I didn't stop at all, and when I came home drunk, just one week after we come, away from her family, away from everything she ever knew, she was done. She got far away from me, just like she shoulda done. So if I don't follow her, if I don't look for her, it's because I don't want her looking for me. I want better than that for her."

I nod, but my voice twitches when I say, "Okay."

He tilts his head, like he knows me too well. "What?"

"It's nothing."

"I can see you got something crazy in your head; you might as well just say it."

I think of the Buck Knife in my pocket, the gun at his hip, consider how everything could change suddenly, if he is the killer. But somehow, I know he's not. "It's embarrassing." He groans, encouraging me. "Last night, I was walking out by the lake where

215

the pet cemetery is. I saw these headstones and I thought — I thought one had your wife's name on it."

"Jesus."

"I'm sorry." I squeeze the reins. This is not how I saw this playing out.

"You think I murdered my wife?"

"I didn't —"

"You think I'm a murderer, and you rode all the way up out here, to the middle of nowhere, alone with me, and I'm armed, and you ain't." He brushes his gun. "So you could ask me about it?" His hand is shaking slightly, and I wonder if that's from the alcohol or something else.

He's right. I can't seem to stop myself from telling him everything, when I should be treading carefully. And I wonder if it's really because I trust him or if it's because I need him to like me, even if he is a murderer.

"I didn't say that I thought *you* did it," I say, although he was my primary suspect. You always taught me, family first.

"Lord Almighty, you have a death wish!" I am quiet. He doesn't kill me. He doesn't try to. Does that mean I was right to trust him? He still hasn't offered an explanation and at length he continues. "You seen the cats?"

I think of the cat I found by the lake last night, and Bumby, and the sea of cats in the chicken coop. "Yes."

He sniffs. "When Grace was here, she used to try and look after all them cats. Addy told her not to, but that was just Grace's way. She loved animals. Would just stand for an hour petting a horse or something. Anyway, she found some kittens in there — of course she did; there's about a dozen at any given time — and one of 'em was sick." He tugs nervously on the reins. "So Grace took it. Drove out to the vet in Yreka and they offered to rescue it, to take care of it, for free and all. But Addy found out somehow. And she tracked Grace down and accused her of stealing her property. She demanded she bring the kitten back. And Grace did, though it broke her heart.

"The kitten died the next day. And Addy made this big production, about how they'd bury it up there in Grace's honor."

"That's terrible."

"I know. I was working that day. It was just Grace on her own. I didn't know anything about it until Rachel told me. She really lit into me, all how I'd dragged Grace out here and abandoned her. I'm not saying she was wrong, but I do have to think Addy was a little to blame." He shakes his head and clucks his tongue, remembering. He tightens his grip on the reins. "Grace had a real bad feeling about this place. She was real religious — I met her at church and all. She was the good girl from the bad family; I was the boy she shoulda stayed away from. You know the story. I never saw her pray more than she did that week she was up here."

"You left the kitten flowers." It's sweet.

"She woulda wanted me to." He flips his reins. "I'm not all bad, you know. I do have the occasional decent impulse."

I nod, gazing down into the pit of the valley.

He catches my eye. "You satisfied?" And then I have a glimpse, like a whistle all through me, that this is a lie, that this is a conspiracy and they are all part of it. I see Addy and Jed, last night's entire dinner party, out in the woods after nightfall with a fire lit, blood painted on their faces and a ritual killing on the menu. Episode 45 of your podcast, *The Queen of the Flies,* about the cult that lived off the grid in the woods, and every year at the height of summer, they feasted on the flesh of an outsider. *Missing, Murder, Conspiracy.*

I know it's crazy, but I also know it's true. It happened. So how do I know it's not happening now?

"I won't be satisfied until I find Rachel."

He blows air out of his cheeks. "Darlin', it must be hard being you." He reins his horse around and continues up the steep trail. And I have a choice: I can keep trusting him or I can let myself go off the deep end. But the truth is, there isn't a place isolated enough to escape the fact that you have to trust someone, sometimes. There's no way around it and I urge my horse. I follow him up the hill.

The horses pick their way through, over fallen branches and poison ivy.

"I talked to Clementine last night," I say. "Tried."

"What'd she say?"

"She said, 'Not here.' And then Homer appeared. It's like she didn't want to say anything in front of him."

"Homer's a good guy."

"What makes you say that?"

"He just is," he says, voice rising in annoyance.

"Everyone's a suspect."

"You don't have a crime."

"Why did he leave? Why did Homer leave the ranch? He's this great family man. They built a house for him — why isn't he here?"

"I reckon I can guess."

"Why?"

" 'Cause no one can take Addy for too long. She's too controlling, gets under your skin. That's why they take bets out in town on how long people will last. You and I are defying the odds. Why do you think Addy is 'so happy you're here'? 'Cause she can't believe you're crazy enough to stay." He shakes his head. "He probably couldn't take it, so he left. You can imagine, it's not easy to find a job out here. This is about the only place that pays in money. Eventually he found Jesus; that's how bad things got. And then he got a job at the lumberyards with the Moronis."

"I'm surprised they come for dinner."

"You and me both."

The trees drop away on the right. We are high up in the mountains and we can see the sweep, the rise and fall of the peaks with the trees stacked up and the sky so wide, and I think it is more beautiful than anything I have ever seen. And I think how much you loved it. And the view is so expansive that it stretches in my mind, lifts away all the restrictions, and I think that I could stay here forever, that I could love it here, love everything about it, that I could have this place forever and make it mine. But it's too big, and it's too wild, and it doesn't belong to me.

"Rachel loved it up here." Jed reads my mind as the trail joins the fire road and becomes wide, flat, hemmed with bright green grass. "We can let them run, if you want? Rachel and I used to do it all the time. . . . Addy doesn't like it."

"Yes." I tear my eyes away from the view, gather myself and my horse. "Let's go."

Jed smiles and then he hoots at his horse, Texas cowboy–style. First the horse dodges sideways but then it splits. Mine comes in fast behind it and we are galloping, racing along the fire road through the woods with no one around for miles on top of miles, and we are free, we are absolutely free out here. Disappearing makes us free.

Finally, we pull our horses up, prancing, at the top of Eagle Rock.

"We better brush 'em out really good so Addy doesn't see the sweat," Jed says. An eagle calls in the distance, and below us the land falls away in peaks and valleys, lassoed by the winding river.

That afternoon I am cleaning the windows in cabin eight when I hear your mother pull up on her ATV, potions clattering in the basket, her daily check-in to deliver bad news: The world is going to hell, and also there is a conspiracy to make us believe the world is going to hell. The old dogs groan and swirl around her, then spread out on the lawn as she comes up the steps.

The screen door flaps shut behind her.

"You were gone a long time this morning." She steps close to inspect the curtains I have left on the table. I say nothing. "I told Jed to take you up there, but I didn't tell him to take so long about it. Rachel, are you listening?"

I look up but she doesn't catch it, and I don't correct her. The truth is, it thrills me. This is how I will find you. This is how I will know you. I will become you; I will step into the mystery the way you always tried to with *Murder, She Spoke.* The way you memorized every detail. You knew Elizabeth Lowe's stepfather got a call from California days after she went missing. You knew Emma Bernhardt's mother went swimming after midnight on the night Emma disappeared. You sank into their real lives, into the minutiae, so you saw how every piece worked, how everything came together, but still you didn't know everything, still the mysteries stayed unsolved, still you could never really know because you couldn't go back, you couldn't *become* your victims, but I can and I will. I will step into your story and I will examine every piece; I will become you because that is what I need to do to know what happened to you. I will risk myself to save you.

"We went straight up the mountain, and straight back," I tell your mother, my mother. I don't mention the hour we spent at the top, letting the horses graze, just talking, our hands in the dirt, our heads tilted up at the sky.

"A ranch," Jed said. "I grew up next to a big 'ol Texas ranch — everything's horses in Abilene — and all I ever wanted was to have a ranch of my own one day. A big-ass, fuck-you ranch. 'Course I just ended up on the rigs. You can make a lot of money that way, but you pay with your life."

"And now you're here."

He sighed into his belly, crushed a daffodil. "For however long that lasts. They're angling to get rid of me. Have been all along. And now they have you."

"I'm not pushing anyone out."

"No, you're just another pawn in their game."

Your mother shakes her head. "I don't like him around my horses. He makes them crazy."

"I like Jed," I say, but her words shake something loose in my mind. Didn't Jed tell me your mother never let him ride the

223

horses? But this morning he told me that both of you used to gallop on them all the time. How much time did he spend with you? How well did he know you?

"Ha! He's useless." She crosses her arms. "I wouldn't spend too much time around him," she says like Jed wrote her lines.

"Why not?"

"He's not good enough for you." Good enough for me or good enough for you?

EPISODE 49:
ALL THE GIRLS

That morning when the students arrived at school, they found that all the girls' lockers had been marked with a slash of blood, which was identified as animal. The principal was appalled but refused to confirm that the girls had been targeted specifically.

"It was just completely random," he said. "It was a silly high school prank."

Clementine comes through for Friday so easily, it makes me wonder if I am imagining that your mother is controlling. On Thursday evening your mother says, "You can take the morning off to visit Clementine's school."

Jed offers to drive me. I think he just wants an excuse to miss work but I accept it, like I accept everything from him, because it's easier to see myself as sane if I have a man beside me.

On Friday morning he is waiting outside the staff cabin in his big black truck, looking just-woke-up pale and fiddling with his keys.

I pass the dry patch in the garden. It looks bigger, but I don't have time to investigate it. The vultures are still circling. The sunlight is starting to bake the grass, bringing up the smell of mulch and dead wood. All I want is to get out of here, as quickly as I can.

I climb into his truck and pop a Dramamine. We pull past your parents' house, dip down the drive and wind along the road to Happy Camp.

"What is it that you're doing for Clementine?" he says once the ranch is no longer in the rearview mirror.

"I'm talking to her class." I was so focused on the other part, on trying to get her to tell me about you, that I completely forgot I will have to talk first. I feel the slip of motion sickness, like the world is coming untethered. I should have taken the Dramamine earlier.

"About what?"

"About writing."

"You're a writer?"

I loosen my seat belt. "I am if it means I get to talk to Clementine." He keeps quiet,

226

and finally I allow, "I probably should have prepared something."

He glances over at me with a ringer's smile on his face, and I wonder what would happen if we just kept driving. I almost say it out loud. I look ahead at the bends in the road and imagine a place where it straightens out, widens into a highway, eight lanes across, where you can get more than static on the radio stations, where the real people live. I feel like Jed would be a different person off the ranch, and I wonder why he doesn't leave, and then I let myself imagine he is staying for me. I wonder if you ever felt that way.

"How well did you know Rachel?"

"We've been over this."

"Yesterday you said you rode together all the time. But you told me Addy never let you ride the horses." As I speak, I wonder why I am always letting him off the hook, confronting him about everything, giving him a chance to defend himself. It's like I want him to be innocent so badly that I am not giving him another option.

"Addy didn't know about it."

"But then you must have known Rachel better than you said."

He takes a moment to craft his answer. "You came out here because of her podcast.

Think how compelling she mighta been in person. Yeah, we spent some time together. Yeah, we shot the shit. But I told you, I don't even think she liked me."

"Then why did she hang out with you?"

"Because, Sera, out here there ain't a lot of options."

I set my jaw. I feel awkward, but I need to ask the question. "Did you sleep together?"

"I mean, o' course we did." His answer catches me off guard, and I don't know what to say, what to think. You slept with Jed.

His truck slows as the road opens to reveal Happy Camp. "You want me to come in with you?"

"You don't need to."

"I don't mind."

"You don't have to." His eyes are pulsing. "Do you want to?"

"I can."

We park in the lot next to the police station and approach the school. *Home of the Indians, Heart of the Klamath.* There is no security. The school is smaller than the ranch. I remember what Tasia told me, how you were asked to leave. There is a crooked patch of dead grass outside the window, marked up to look like a football field, and I can't blame you if you did make up stories, just for something to do.

I follow Clementine's directions to her classroom. When we get there, I peer through a small square window cut into the door. Clementine stands at the front next to a stained whiteboard. She has written the words "ontological" and "epistemological" on either side with a weak dry-erase pen.

She points to the board. "What is an example of an ontological truth? Anyone? Anyone?" She scans the classroom, hopeful even though there are only six students, then glimpses me through the glass. "Oh, just a minute. Hold on. Our special guest is here!" She comes to the door. She is surprised to find Jed there with me. "Oh," she says. "Jed. You're here."

"I was headed out this way anyway." He lies unnecessarily.

She brings us to the front. All six students are girls; two are your nieces. Their eyes follow Jed and their lips stretch in easy, pleasing smiles.

I have nothing prepared but maybe that is for the best. I have nothing to say to these girls anyway. Looking at their bright, clean faces just makes me sad. I think of Alissa Turney. I think of Laci Peterson. I think of Florence Wipler, who disappeared in these very woods. I think of myself. And all I want to say is *Be glad. Just be glad you're here. You don't need anyone to tell you anything. You're still here.*

"Everybody, this is Sera Fleece." Clementine beams hopefully. "She's a writer and she's going to talk to you about writing."

I got here on a lie and I have nothing to say. The sooner this is over with, the better, and I can join Clementine for lunch and ask her about you. But first I have to get through this.

"Thank you." I smile unevenly. Jed folds his body into a too small desk.

The students are younger than the high school students I remember. Their expressions are unset, their faces still emerging, flecked with pimples. Once you get past a certain age, people love to ask: *What would you tell your younger self? If you could go back and talk to your younger self, what would you say?*

I would say, *You're in for it.* I would say, *I'm so sorry.* I would say, *Run.*

But I can't say those things to these girls. So I pretend to be someone else, like everybody does, like I used to do proficiently, once upon a time. I ramble, ironically, about being prepared and then about discipline. "The thing about writing is, no one is going to make you do it. . . ." I drift.

230

"That's probably true about most things, as an adult. That's probably the main problem with being an adult. It would be a lot easier if someone would just come in and tell you what to do.

"The thing is, with writing, you never have any security. That's another thing that's true as an adult, actually: marriage, jobs, children." I laugh inexplicably. "For some reason we teach kids that you make a choice and it lasts forever. I guess to keep the college system going? But the truth is, you're going to lose everything, probably earlier than you think. And you're going to have to start over. And over and over and over."

And then I feel this is too depressing, so I throw in a little true crime. "But it's important to remember how lucky you are. There are people your age who have been murdered, kidnapped. All the time. Every day. There are people who just disappear and are completely forgotten. . . . So you should be grateful."

A light pall has settled over the room. Clementine's jaw has loosened. Even Jed looks taken aback. Finally, Clementine says, "Does anyone have any questions?" and then cringes like she shouldn't have asked.

Six hands rise at once, and my chest loosens a little. Maybe I did make an impact. Maybe it was refreshing to hear an adult be honest for once.

Clementine calls on a girl with a YouTube tutorial's worth of makeup slicked on her face.

"Are you from Texas?" she asks. I am confused until I realize she is talking to Jed.

He stretches back in his seat and says, "West Texas," like anyone knows the difference.

"Wow," one girl says.

"Like a real cowboy," says another one.

"Does anyone have questions for our guest speaker?" Clementine interjects. "About how to make a living as a writer, maybe?" I don't think anyone knows the answer to that question.

One diligent girl raises her hand. "What are you working on now?"

"A murder mystery."

This makes the class stew and Clementine looks concerned.

"Is it a true story?" Asha asks.

"I'm not sure yet."

"How can you not be sure yet?"

"Because I'm in the middle of the story."

Jed clears his throat. "What time d'y'all have lunch around here?"

The audience is sidetracked.

" 'Y'all'!"

"Oh my God, his accent!"

Clementine steps in. "All right, well, we still have ten minutes, so why don't we all thank our guest and then have silent-study time?" Her eyes flit over me and I feel my cheeks burn, feel my chest hollow. I was terrible. And I couldn't even talk for fifteen minutes. The class thanks us and Clementine leads us the few steps back to the door. "You can wait for me in the teachers' lounge. Left outside, then third door on the left."

Jed and I follow her directions down the halls, which smell conflictingly of age and teenage pheromones. I try not to think about what I said, to replay the moments in my mind, but I can't resist any opportunity to hate on myself. I am disappointed, and I am angry I am disappointed, round and round in a vicious cycle.

I have to remind myself that I came here for you, to talk to Clementine about *you*. So what if I sounded psychotic? So what if Jed is walking carefully around me, like he expects me to crack at any minute? I did what I needed to do.

I sit on a plastic chair next to a stained wooden table in the teachers' lounge: a closet with a coffee machine. Jed makes a coffee, then sits down beside me, too close to me in the tiny room. Then he grins.

"Well, that was entertaining."

"Don't laugh at me."

His smile leaks out his eyes. "I'm not. I'm not laughing at you." He puts his hand over mine and exhales. "You have to admit, we make a pretty depressing pair, Sera Fleece."

My eyes meet his and I feel something turn over inside me and that annoys me. It annoys me that I'm in this picked-apart lounge in the middle of nowhere with an alcoholic West Texan divorcé and I feel just as lusty as I did as a teenage girl, hanging pictures of River Phoenix on my wall. It was supposed to be better; it was supposed to be more. Jed looks at my lips.

I take my hand away as the bell rings — even in a tiny school in the middle of nowhere, they use the same screaming wail.

A few teachers trickle in to use the coffee machine, but they all back straight out. When Clementine appears, it's just Jed and me.

"Thank you so much for coming," she says, although I'm sure she regrets her invitation. "It means so much to them to see . . ." She drifts off, in the process of pulling out her chair, perhaps realizing that what they saw was a woman twice their age who was just as lost and confused as they are, if not more. "I appreciate the effort."

Jed tries to hold in a laugh and ends up snorting.

"You're very welcome," I say as she takes a seat. "And now —"

"How's your week?" Jed jumps in, shooting me a look like I was born without manners. Manners are the last thing on my mind right now; this is an investigation.

"Fine." Clementine sighs and I can see she might be tired, although it is hard to tell with mothers. "There's been a mite infestation at the lumberyard, so everyone's a little on edge." It is clear that by "everyone," she means Homer. I think of how he appeared in the kitchen, how he caught her outside the church. *I thought I told you . . .* What? Was it something about me?

I look pointedly at Jed, making sure he's not about to interrupt me again. Then I begin, "I wanted to show you something." I start to take the list from my pocket. Jed watches closely as I lay it out on the table in front of her. "This is a list of names Rachel Bard wrote."

Clementine jerks like she's about to leave the table but stays seated. "Rachel Bard. Tasia LeCruce. Florence Wipler," she reads from the top.

I point. "Clementine Atwater."

"Where did you find it?"

I clear my throat, try to keep my voice even, determined. I am an investigator. I am not a joke. You are missing and I am going to find you. "Do you have any idea what it might be?"

She sits back, ruminating. "It would help if you told me where you found it."

My stomach twists. My shame keeps finding new depths. What can I tell her? That I went digging through the trash to find your dead cat because I thought he was your best friend? That sounds insane and they both look at me — they both look at me like they pity me.

"Never mind the list," I say with all the efficiency I can muster. "I'm here because of Rachel."

Clementine rocks back in her chair. "Because of Rachel? What do you mean?"

"Her podcast. I used to listen to her podcast."

Clementine's eyes flit from Jed to me, confused. "You moved all the way out here and got a job at Addy's ranch because of a podcast?"

"I need to find out what happened to her." It seems almost silly under her smile. "Addy said that people were harassing her, chasing her in a big black truck."

"Everyone out here has a big black truck. Did Addy tell you who it was?"

"No." This just keeps getting worse.

She drums her fingers on the table, once. "How would she not know? This is a small town."

"Why would Addy make it up?" I can't believe Addy is my key witness.

She sits back to think, gazes at the coffee machine like it's a window onto someplace else. "I wonder if that was what Rachel told her." She catches my disbelief and scoots closer in her seat. "Maybe Rachel wanted to leave, but she didn't know how, so she created this wild story — she was always good at telling stories. Maybe she thought it was the only way her mother would let her go. If she thought she *had* to leave, for her own safety. If she was in danger."

"Then why did Addy tell me she was dead?"

"Addy and Rachel were very close. I think it's hard for her . . ." She drifts, but catches herself. "I think it's hard for her to admit that Rachel would leave her. Or maybe she just doesn't like you asking questions."

This has a ring of truth, but everyone tells a different story. I try to tell myself that's a good thing. If it was a conspiracy, they would all tell the same story. But the question is, who can I believe? I thought Clementine was a "good person," but it feels like she has never even considered any of this, like she is making it up on the spot. Is she really so content with her life that her sister-in-law can disappear and she never even questions it?

"Have you heard from her?" I clench my fists.

"I — *no* — but that's not unexpected. We aren't really close."

"So you think she's still alive?"

"Of course she's alive." She gives me an earnest look. "I wouldn't worry about Rachel. She always took care of herself."

I bite my lip. I can't believe it. Can it really be that simple? Did you just leave? I drop my chin and spy the paper on the table. "What about Florence? Florence Wipler?"

Her eyes dance back and forth. "What about her?"

"Didn't she disappear too?"

"That was a long time ago."

"It meant a lot to Rachel, didn't it, her disappearance?"

"It meant a lot to everyone. When you're a kid, that kind of thing stays with you." She pauses, but when I don't respond, she resumes talking. "Florence became a kind of local celebrity, had her picture posted everywhere. I think Rachel — We *all* were affected by it. Rachel, maybe, more than others, but she was always very . . . just *more* than everyone else."

I am very careful with what I say next. I feel it tight in my nerves as I breathe. "Tasia told me about the argument."

Clementine shakes her head and sits back. "None of us knew what was going to happen. If we had known . . ." She power-sighs. "It all seemed like such a big deal then. . . . Moroni felt terrible about it." A bolt traces my spine. *"Terrible."*

I feel my heart beating in my chest. Does she mean what I think she means? Even Jed is quiet.

"He was young," I say weakly, trying to seem like I am on her side, even if I don't know, don't have any idea, what she's talking about.

She exhales, relieved. "Exactly, exactly. They were both so young." She breathes unevenly, like this is her mistake, her burden. "And I know Tasia feels bad about it, but it was *her* boyfriend, and she was — what? Fifteen? Fourteen? We just couldn't understand why Florence would do that. I mean, what was her intention? But then, young girls do dumb things. I try to remember that, with my girls."

239

I put the pieces together in my head. Florence and Moroni hooked up. The other girls found out, got angry, and Florence ran off and was never seen again.

"And Tasia still married Moroni."

"Yes, well." Her laugh has a slightly hysterical edge. "If we didn't forgive them, we'd all be single."

She scoots forward in her chair, taps the list. "Can I ask you something?" She runs her hand down the list. "Did you find this in Bumby's collar?" My heart drops, like I am the one who has been caught. Humiliation heats my jaw. I remind myself she doesn't know Bumby's dead, that I crawled into a dumpster to find this "evidence." "I remember when she made it." Her voice is reassuring. "When he was a kitten. She put all of our names down because she was so paranoid that he would get lost; she wanted to make sure someone was contacted." She sits back, warmed by the memory. "It was sort of sweet."

I think: *Idiot.* I feel myself sinking and I know Clementine thinks she's disappointed me and she has. I should be happy for you. I should be glad to think you've escaped, that you're out there somewhere, alive and well. Instead I feel crazy, unmoored, like losing you is tantamount to losing my mind.

240

How can I be so wrong about everything? It's like my senses have rearranged themselves, like I am just off track. Somewhere, in the past few years, I lost whatever it was that made me like everyone else, and now I am lost, so lost that I am seeing crimes that aren't really there. *Murder, Missing, Conspiracy.* What if there is no bad guy? What if I'm the bad guy? What if I am the victim and the villain of my own life?

Episode 53:
Murder of a Jane Doe 2

Her body washed up on the coast. What was left of her wore a beat-up pair of jeans, a T-shirt tied at the waist and a friendship bracelet, the kind they make at summer camp.

My footsteps are heavy as we walk back to Jed's car. I wish I hadn't let him drive me. I can see that he is pushed back, away from me. I know he thinks I'm crazy. It makes me think of my ex, in the days after I lost the baby, the look on his face like what I had been telling him all along was finally confirmed: that we were different. That I was different.

Clementine thinks you left of your own accord. Jed does too. Why is it so hard for me to believe it? Maybe I just resent it. Maybe I am just disappointed you left without saying goodbye. Like your mother, I need to believe something happened to you, because the alternative is that you never really cared at all, about the podcast, about your listeners, about me.

"Do you believe her?" I ask.

"I don't know. . . ." He is hesitant to disagree with me. "I guess I do. I guess I think Rachel just wanted out."

"No," I insist, but am I just being stubborn now? It's almost like I want something bad to have happened. Have I been listening to too many podcasts? Jed said you lost yourself, that you thought everyone was out to get you. Is that what has happened to me? "I don't believe it." Is that just what I want to believe?

"Sera, you didn't really know Rachel." He puts his hand on my arm but I shake it off.

"Yes, I do. I know her. I know her better than any of you. Her whole podcast, the reason she did it, was to find answers. She wouldn't do this. She wouldn't leave behind any questions."

"Maybe you're wrong."

"What do you mean?"

"I mean, maybe you ain't right about her intentions." His accent is thicker when he's impassioned. It tangles his words, contorts his lips. "Maybe she wasn't looking for answers for them. Maybe she was looking for answers for her. Maybe she wanted to

243

disappear and she was tryin' to figure out how."

"Then why broadcast it? Why publicize it?"

"Rachel was a lonely soul," he says with a strange finality. "She didn't connect to people like you or I do."

"I don't."

"Fine, maybe you don't." He throws his hands up. Two hectic spots blossom on his cheeks. "Maybe you do understand her better than anyone. Didn't you do essacty the same thing she did? Didn't you just up and disappear? You're looking for her — who's looking for you?" He goes stiff, like he's shot himself but he can't figure out why or how. "Rachel, I'm so sorry."

He doesn't catch the mistake, and I don't correct him. "You never really wanted to find her anyway. Why would you? You don't care about anything, except where your next drink is coming from." I snap around and walk away, through the parking lot, out toward the deserted Main Street.

When I am too far away, he calls out, "Hey!" He snaps his fingers. "Hey, hey, Sera!" But it's too late. "Don't you need a ride back?"

I keep walking.

"Don't be like that."

I put my hands up. "We're done, right? Case closed. I don't need your help anymore."

He shakes his head and walks in the other direction.

There is no bar in Happy Camp, the man behind the counter at the convenience store tells me. The Snake Pit, which was once the apex of all local crime, was shut down five years ago, so the criminals could scatter, I guess. To make them harder to find. I buy a forty and I take it down to the river, where I sit in a break in the brush and drink with determination.

Did I want to disappear? Or was I secretly hoping someone would come looking for me? Did I wish something bad happened to you just to save me from the bad thing happening to me? And what do I do now?

I think of the last person, the only person, who ever really cared about me. I think of the baby, and when I take my phone out of my pocket, I am surprised to see a signal. So surprised that I call him before I can stop myself.

"Sera?" He still has my number saved.

"I didn't want to have a baby," I say so fast, I wonder if it's really me saying it.

I can feel the pressure as his breath

escapes his lungs. "Yeah, I figured."

"Everything was happening so fast and I . . . I thought we were supposed to do it. I thought we were supposed to get married. I thought we were supposed to have kids."

"We were supposed to."

"But who said it? Who says?"

He sighs. "Sera, as much as I love spitballing with you, the great thing about not being married is I'm not contractually obligated to."

"I wished it."

"Wished what?"

"I wished I wasn't pregnant. What if God granted my wish?"

"I wouldn't put it past Him."

"Everything is so fucked up," I say, and then I can feel the enforced silence, feel that he didn't and doesn't want to reveal anything.

I gaze across the fast, muddy river. "I don't know where I belong."

"No, Sera, you just don't want to belong. This is all your choice."

"Is it? Because it feels a lot bigger than that."

"Do you know what I think your problem is? You never had any friends."

"Thanks."

"No, I mean, like, girlfriends."

I think about all of the time I have spent chasing you, and I think he might have a point. I kick a rock. "Sometimes I forget how great you were."

He groans and then he sighs. "God, why the fuck are you doing this to me?"

"I wanted to apologize."

"Thanks, Sera. Gee, thanks. I feel a fuckton better now." We are quiet and I listen to the river running. I thought this call would cure something, but I don't want to go forward and I don't want to go back. "Are you still in the woods?"

"Yes."

"What are you doing out there?"

"I'm working at this ranch. I told you, remember?"

"Sure."

"What are you doing?"

"The same shit. The same shit we used to do. God. You know, sometimes I do miss you."

"Sometimes I miss me too."

There is nothing left after that, so I say goodbye before the signal drops and I look out across the river and I wonder how I can make the right choice by leaving him and regret it forever at the same time. And I wonder what the fuck I am going to do now.

■ ■ ■ ■

My eyes snap open. I drifted off, but now I wonder. I could stay. Your mother and your father like me. Every day they tell me, "We're so happy you're here." And Jed likes me, and I like Jed, and maybe together, we would both be happier. We're both lost, but what if we found each other? I think about your list of names, your best friends, the ones you lost. Maybe I have been looking at this the wrong way. Maybe you didn't disappear so I could save you. Maybe you disappeared so you could save me.

I get up off the dirt, feeling embarrassed, even if there is nobody around, is never anybody around. My signal has vanished, so I throw away the rest of my beer and walk back up toward the coffee shop.

I startle when I see Jed's truck pull out of the lot, but he is too far away to stop and I watch him slip behind a bend in the road. Maybe he was waiting for me, but I've missed him.

I hurry into the coffee shop. The bell dings over my head but the shop is empty.

"Hello?" I call but there is no response. I wonder if Tasia forgot to lock the door. I walk to the counter. There is a small kitchen in the back with a phone on the wall.

"Hello? Tasia? I'm going to use your phone." I pick it up quickly, before anyone stops me. I call the ranch.

I am caught off guard when your father picks up, am irritated by his goofy voice as he jokes, "Happy Camp? All the way in Happy Camp?"

He agrees to pick me up and I set the phone on the cradle. The coffee shop is still empty. It feels a little eerie with no one here. I wonder if Jed was in here alone.

I scan the windows, then duck behind the counter. I don't know what I'm looking for but I can't help looking. I find an empty flask, a pack of American Spirits and a handgun. I am so used to guns out here that it barely registers.

"What are you doing?"

I jump so fast, I feel impact. Tasia walks in from the back of the store, fixing her hair.

"Sorry. I had to use the phone."

"Ask next time." I don't point out that there was no one here. "I'm about to go on break."

I want to ask for her friendship but I can tell this is not a good time, so I say, "Thank you," and walk out. I hover in the street, checking out a billboard of events that have already happened.

Your father is there faster than I expected. His SUV gleams black and my mind darts to that night with Jed, the car that ran us off the road. It was black and the headlights had a similar feline quality. But it wasn't your father; of course it wasn't. Jed is right. I need to stop seeing ill intentions everywhere.

"I'm really sorry." I climb into the front seat and buckle my belt. My stomach is already soupy in anticipation of the drive. "To make you come all the way down here."

"No problem. Beep, beep." I'm not sure what that means. Your father is the type to make a joke in tone only, so you know where the laugh is expected but you rarely know why.

My head swirls as he accelerates into the first curve. I read once that motion sickness is caused by conflicting signals from your eyes and your ears. If you focus on something inside the car, the dashboard or a book, your eyes think you are not moving, but your ears know that you are. And the brain's reaction is to believe it's being poisoned, and the nausea is caused by the brain's desire to vomit out the poison.

This is how I feel about your disappearance. My brain is telling me that I was wrong, that you left, found a way out, but

250

something else — my heart, maybe? — is telling me that's not true, and the conflict is poisoning me, making me sick. I grip the side of the car.

"You feeling all right, pard'na?" Your father is so annoying.

"Yeah, fine. Just a little carsick." Your father drives like a maniac, rushing into the corners and then braking quickly, like he didn't know they were coming, like he hasn't driven this road a million times before.

"Stare at a point in the middle distance," he says with the singsong gravitas of a quotation, but it is not immediately apparent who he is quoting. He smiles and a twinkle twitches his eye. Then he dives headlong into another turn and rushes to slow through the curve. "You know, Addy's really happy you're here. We both are. We're so happy you're here."

"That's great," I say. "I love it out here." It's not a lie. This place may be isolated but it never feels empty. The spaces that would be populated with people are instead filled with mountains and trees and flowers and streams. There is something sustaining about it, something that makes me feel healthier than I have in years, in spite of everything.

"We hope you'll stay with us a long time."

My stomach flips. I grip the bar of the door. "Can I ask you something?" We are closing in on the ranch.

"Well, Sera, you just did." I hate your father.

"It's about your daughter. I . . . I was wondering what happened to her." Your father is the only person I haven't asked.

His face stiffens, like we have finally landed on something that isn't a joke. And without a joke his face is hard and strange.

"Addy said she thought she had . . . passed?" I don't mention that others have said you are still alive. If it was all a hoax, your parents are the ones you pulled it on.

He accelerates and aims the car off the road. I cling to the door handle as we careen off the highway, toward the edge of the mountain. He drives to a stop at the end of a turnout. My heart is pounding. My body senses physical danger. He snaps off the engine.

He says nothing for a while. It is impossible to fathom what he is thinking. Although I know he is a father — I know he is *your* father — he is such a stagy character, it's hard to empathize with him; it's hard to see him as a father who's lost his only daughter. Finally, he exhales, and as ex-

252

pected, it's an exaggerated sound.

"It was Easter Sunday," he says. "We were all gathered round the table: Homer and Clementine and Tasia and Moroni and Jed." My heart skips, overwhelmed. He is the first person to go straight to the details. He is making a meal of it. "I could tell something was amiss, right from the get-go." There he stops, like that is the end of the story.

A long time passes before I say, "What happened?"

"It was before dessert. Rachel disappeared."

"What do you mean, disappeared? She just walked out?"

He frowned. "I don't know whether she walked. You wouldn't get far on foot out here," he says in a silly voice, and I don't know if all of this is a joke. I know your mother is unbalanced but I've always thought your father is just goofy. Now it strikes me that he is possibly batshit crazy. "Addy made brownies."

"And you all just did nothing? You didn't look for her? You didn't call the police?"

"She did it all the time." He strokes the steering wheel. "Ever since she was a little girl. She would just disappear. It was kind of a game for her."

"But she always came back."

"Always came back," he repeats.

"Was she ever gone this long?"

"That" — he flicks his key chain — "is a very good question."

"Was she?" I repeat, undaunted.

He shakes his head, looks out over the river to the opposite side, where deer have gathered on a natural salt lick. It's majestic, picturesque. It's beautiful, like everything here is, except us. We don't fit.

"This is a funny place. People just snap." He snaps his fingers. "One day they're peachy keen. The next, they're acting a little . . . shall we say, erratic?" He gives me a withering look, at odds with his words, at odds with the moment. Your father is a matching game where nothing goes together. "And then *swish*!" He wriggles his fingers. "They're gone."

"Was there anything she was upset about? Was there anything unusual that might explain why she would leave?"

"Nothing above the usual unusual," he jokes, and then he starts the car abruptly. Whatever moment I had of lucidity, of seriousness, is gone. "Hey, don't you worry about Rachel. We're just so happy you're here. Addy and I are so happy you're here."

He steers back toward the highway as another car appears around the bend.

Instead of waiting, he sails in front of it, then brakes to cut the car off more effectively and the horn blares and your father ignores it. And I think: *You're dead.* And I think: *They killed you.* And I think: *That's crazy.*

I am at the end of the line. I am at the last of your clues. I have talked to every available person on your list. I have met your family. I have talked to the police. I have ridden your horses. I have lived on your ranch. I have taken apart and cleaned every window. The only thing I haven't done is get inside your yellow house.

I think of the house. I think of the windows. I realize how easily I can take them apart.

As we pull up the drive, I feel bile clawing up my throat. I hear the phone ringing in the lobby. I think, *Are they ever going to get that?* But I feel too sick to say it. Your father drops me off in front of the staff cabin.

"Thank you." I stagger out of the car. "Thank you for driving me."

"You need to watch yourself, getting lost all the time," he says in his silly voice. "All the way in Happy Camp!" He hits the steering wheel for emphasis, sweeps his eyes over an imaginary audience, then peels away fast.

My heartbeat is drumming in my ears. I wait until his SUV disappears behind the lodge. Then I take the trail to your house. I am careful to stay in the woods. I pass Jed's house. I drop down the path to the creek, swing smoothly down the switchbacks. I follow the fire road around the bend and your house appears; a patch of sunlight turns the apex of the roof a deep red. I remember all the pictures you took, of Bumby, of the house, but I'm not sure if I ever saw the interior. I wonder why you said it was yours if you lived with your parents. Most of all, I wonder what is inside.

I step onto the porch. I try the door first, but it's still locked, so I move to the windows. I have been taking apart the same windows all week, in the lodge, in every cabin. They are all the same make. These screens are missing pull tabs but I take the Buck Knife out of my pocket and use it as a counterweight until I pop one out. I set the screen down on the porch, then move to the window. I place my fingers exactly as I have a dozen times this week, and I press hard, deep with my shoulders, and I try to open your window. It doesn't budge. I try again, press hard with my shoulder. And again. But it doesn't move. It looks the same as every other window, but there is something different. I step back and peer up at it. It's almost like it's sealed. I try another one, and another. I try every window on the first floor. Not one will budge.

I step back from the house, breathing heavily. I gaze up at the eaves and I am so frustrated, so tired of getting nowhere, of always being wrong, of dead ends, out here and out there. Why can't I just break through?

I look around me, the meter rising in my veins, clogging them, packing them with adrenaline. What if I broke the glass? They do it all the time in movies. What if I hit it as hard as I can? What if I kicked it?

I punch it once, as hard as I can, without even stopping to think. My knuckles soften but I don't even make a dent. What am I thinking? I'm lucky the glass didn't break; I could have severed an artery. And if I had managed to break through and not injure myself, what would I have done then? Crawled through the hole my fist made? I need to get ahold of myself. I need to think.

Pop! An enormous rock zings past my head, hits the yellow wall so hard that it leaves a mark, then topples to the floor at my feet.

I gasp, wheel around, so the yellow house is behind me, pressed beneath my fingers. I scan the scene, but there is no one there. *There is,* I remind myself. *They are just invisible to me.*

"Hello?" I say. Was that rock intended for me? Were they trying to hit me? Will they try again?

Oddly, in the face of actual danger, I feel calm, brave even. I step forward on the porch. "Is anyone out there?" I say as if there's a chance the rock grew wings.

I can't hear anything over the babble of the river. But I think, *There must be, there must be someone out there watching me.*

"You can talk to me," I start. "You can tell me —"

I jump as three birds dart into the air. I hurry forward in their direction. I hear an engine — out on the highway or up the fire road — hear it roar and then cut out, like it has disappeared around a bend.

I wait. My heart pumps in my shoulders. Then I look down at the rock, my evidence. It's hefty enough that it's hard to lift. Whoever threw it must be strong. Or they must have been close. I flip it over in my hands and see one word written in thick black marker. My heart rate rises. My blood rushes with the river. The message thrills me.

RUN.

EPISODE 57:
LAST CALL

Before she disappeared, Leah made one odd phone call, to her best friend, in the middle of the night. It was after three in the morning but Leah didn't apologize. She spoke like it was any normal time. She complained that she had been feeling sick all week. At four oh one a.m., she said she needed to lie down.

I go to Jed's house. I knock on the front door, call softly, not wanting anyone outside to hear. I have hidden the rock sealed in a plastic bag in my backpack, just like you taught me. I will preserve the evidence.

Jed doesn't come to the door. There is no sound inside. I step back, try to see the whole house at once. And I question myself.

If I am thinking like you taught me, Jed should be the prime suspect, the one who threw the rock. He lives the closest to the yellow house. He could have seen me pass.

And he has been encouraging me, all along, to leave. Maybe he finally wanted to up the ante. I glance at his open garage and start — his truck is there, parked beside his broken motorcycle. Was it there before? And if he is here, why isn't he answering the door? I knock again. "Jed?" And then, "I can see your truck." And, "I know you're in there." A funny feeling creeps into my veins, like I am being watched.

I hang around for a while, walk around the back and look deep inside the garage, hoping he'll return, but he doesn't. And I can't imagine him at your mother's, I can't hear him at the shooting range and I can't imagine him anywhere else. Where is he?

I slip the rock out of my backpack. I wonder if I could get a handwriting sample, to compare. Before I can stop to question my ethics, I try the front door. It's unlocked.

"Jed?" I say again, and then I push the door open. The house is open-plan, so I step into the kitchen and the living room and the dining room all at once. It looks like he has just moved in, bare but for the odd pile: an expensive-looking rodeo saddle on a rack, a seven-foot safe where I assume he keeps his guns. The kitchen is unfinished; there are no doors on the cupboards, and they are filled with prairie-patterned dinnerware and the liquor cabinet is crammed. There is an enormous cross on the wall. A fan swings lazily up above, clicking with every rotation. I don't know where I will find a handwriting sample — do people use pens anymore? Instead I find myself drifting through the rooms.

Grace must have left in a hurry, because her clothes are still here. Everything is clean but oddly frozen, and I wonder, *Did Grace have a car? Why didn't she take her shoes, or her toothbrush, or the dresses in their closet?*

But it doesn't make sense. If something happened to her, if Jed knew, if Jed did it, wouldn't he have gotten rid of her stuff? Or was this a strategy, a way to make him look innocent? Why would he keep everything?

I need to confirm that Grace went back to Texas, but I am not sure how to do that. Jed told me she did. Your parents said she left. I could check social media but the only Internet access is inside your parents' house and your mother doesn't want me to use it.

In the bedroom, I find my handwriting sample. There is a letter on the nightstand, tucked into Grace's Bible, and I read,

I'm so sorry about the other night. That's not me. That's not who I am. It's like there's the real me and then there's this thing, this monster I can't control. Whatever happens, I hope you can still have it in your heart to pray for me. I understand you wanting to leave. Sometimes I wish you would. Just save yourself the trouble and know that I love you more than anything in this world. I love you. But the truth is, I guess I hate myself more.

My fingers feel numb, strange, like he has confessed my own secret. I set the note on the bed and force myself to take a picture on my phone, even though the words on the rock are written in block letters and I don't see an immediate similarity.

I catch my breath and I scan the room around me, wondering if I should be looking for more evidence, but evidence of what? It's not a crime to hate yourself.

When I open the door to the staff cabin, I am hit with a chemical smell. The windows are open, so the space is cold, but the floors are clean, the sheets have been washed, the furnace is polished. At first, I suspect your mother. Instead I find Jed standing over the kitchen sink, ringing out rags.

I startle, feel surprise pulse through me. "What are you doing here?" I think how I just came from searching his house for evidence, while he was here cleaning mine.

He cocks his head. "I'm sorry."

I think of the note, and I feel it like shame and stimulation through me, like I am Grace. Like I am the one he is in love with.

He sets the rag down. "You okay?"

". . . I'm embarrassed," I answer honestly. "I was going to clean it. I —"

"It's okay." He reaches up and presses his thumb into my chin. Did he kill his wife? Did he kill you? "I just wanted you to know I . . . I think it's good, what you came here to do. I — I think you're a good person." He thought Grace was a good person too. "Maybe I just want to believe that Rachel got away, that nothing bad happened. But I do believe it."

I cross my arms over my goose bumps. "Maybe I didn't just come here for Rachel. Maybe you're right. Maybe I came for me too."

He steps closer to me, invading my space. I don't step back.

His words are written on the back of my skull, gleaming and bright: *It's like there's the real me and then there's this thing, this monster I can't control.* What if he killed her? What if he . . .

"Can I?" He lifts his hand, and I feel this

tremendous pressure, dead fear, on either side of my skull, and when he touches me, when his fingers brush my cheek, it tightens. Only it tightens so fast that it's like a high. And he curls his fingers behind my neck.

What if this is the end? What if this is the vanishing point and I embrace it, fearlessly? What if I dared the world to swallow me, not slowly, over time, but all at once?

He kisses me, careful at first, like we are trying to find a spark and then it catches and he deepens the kiss.

"I need something," he gushes, and I let him push me against the counter.

When I was younger, I used to dream that I would wake up one morning to find that all the people in the world had disappeared, except for me and the one boy that I wanted, like I couldn't imagine any other way to get him. And once we realized we were alone in the world, only then could we fall truly and deeply in love, because we needed someone and we had only each other. One gorgeous boy and me, alone in the world. This is exactly what I dreamed about, almost.

The sun goes down and the pitch black is the perfect setting. The fear serves just to heighten everything. We have to be quiet.

We have to be fast. Every moment is stolen. Every thrill is ours only.

We do it in the kitchen first, up against the counter. Then we do it on the living room floor. Then we do it in the shower. My body rises to a crescendo, that stuck-on-the-ceiling, taffy-pulling feeling, and I am afraid I won't come down, afraid he will leave me trapped. So I beg him to get me where I'm going, to release me, and he does, and I come again and again.

I haven't had sex in a long time. I think I was afraid to. Afraid of this feeling, of being at someone else's mercy, of being exposed and vulnerable and trapped. My body is like frayed wires strung too tight. And if you play them there is always a chance that they will break, and that threat radiates through the whole instrument, brings the night to life. Damaged people have the best sex.

When it gets too late to keep pretending that the sun will never come up, he kisses me and speaks into my neck. "I don't wanna leave."

I kiss his collarbone. "You better."

He kisses me again. And I watch him through the windows, watch him fade into the night. And I'm all mixed up. I don't know who I am or where I'm going. And I wish I could follow him into the dark.

■ ■ ■ ■

The next morning, I pass your mother in the garden on the way to the barn. She is knee-deep in blackberry bushes, with a determined grimace, spraying them liberally from a red glass bottle with no mask or gloves to keep the chemicals off her skin. There is no denying that the blackberry bushes are dying, but she will kill everything. The whole garden will have to die to save us from blackberries.

The doll is sitting outside the greenhouse, where I left it, but its face is splattered with holes. I wave at your mother as I hold my breath.

After I feed the horses, I look in on Belle Star. She nickers when she sees me now, and I rub her poll and massage her crest.

Your mother drives up on her ATV, bottles clanging, followed by her herd of crooked dogs. They collapse onto the grass as she climbs off the vehicle. I move away from Belle Star, remembering I am supposed to be working, but your mother doesn't seem to care.

As your mother approaches, Belle Star backs up, tosses her head and trots out into the pen. "She looks better," your mother says.

". . . Yes."

"She should go back in the pasture." She rests her foot on the red fence.

"But this proves it was the other horses attacking her."

"If they attacked her, it's because she's weak. She needs to learn to be strong."

"She's not ready yet."

Your mother tosses her head, pauses like she's considering it. I think she wants me to know that it's her decision. I think she wants me to feel that I am at her mercy. I think of what Jed said about her: *She's punishing me.* Suddenly she beams. "Emmett and I were talking this morning. We're both so happy you're here. We'd like you to come stay at the house."

I startle, so caught off guard that it takes me a second to figure out what she means. "Stay at the house? Like, live there?"

"Yes."

It strikes me as a weird coincidence that now that the staff cabin is clean, now that it is actually livable, she offers me a place in her house. Almost like she knows Jed cleaned it. Almost like she knows Jed was there, with me. Almost like she knows everything. I feel myself flushing. Does she know I was down by the yellow house? Did

267

she throw the rock? Does she want to keep me close, to keep an eye on me? Does she know I slept with Jed? I know it's none of her business, but I still feel like I've betrayed her somehow. Does she want me to feel that way?

"I don't think it's safe," she says, "for you to stay in the staff cabin." She tosses her head again, an oddly girlish gesture. "I don't want to scare you, but I think there may be rats."

There have been rats all along, from day one. Even after being cleaned, the place still stinks of rat shit. They scuttle around the attic, day and night. Sometimes I see them darting between the floorboards, dropping from holes in the ceiling

She leans against the rail, speculative. "You could stay in Rachel's room."

My heartbeat quickens. Your room might provide the break in the case I am looking for. And I can sneak down to use the Internet to check Grace's Facebook account, make sure she really is back in Texas. She has me. I can't say no, but I can still negotiate. I stretch back from the rail. "I think we should leave Belle here."

Your mother sniffs, like she knows exactly what I'm doing. She looks at me, her eyebrow arched. "That's a wonderful idea."

■ ■ ■ ■

As soon as I finish work, I pack up my things. I put them in my car and drive across the ranch to your mother's house. She greets me at the back door, outside the mudroom, where I remove my shoes. Dinner is on in the kitchen. Your father is sitting at the corner desk, humming to himself. After the staff cabin, it's jarringly cozy. The house is warm, impeccably clean and suburban.

"Why don't you set your bag down and wash your hands and come help me finish making dinner?" your mother says, smiling as she leads me into the kitchen. I drop my bag in the corner, next to the stairs.

"Good evening. *Que será, será.*" Your father turns from the computer to wave. It looks like he is shopping for another boat for the lake.

Your mother is cooking and she asks me to chop avocados and tomatoes and peppers, and herbs from her garden. We bring the bowls to the table, where we pray and then we eat. I look around me and I wonder if this was your life. Dinner at the table with the family, a statue of Christ in the living room and, underneath it all, a sense of pageantry, like we have all agreed to play at perfect.

"Isn't this nice?" Your mother smiles warmly at me, at your father. "I told you this would work out. We're so happy you're here."

After dinner we play a board game with patterned tiles. Last night catches up with me and I am so tired. I can't remember the name of the game and the rules elude me. I lose every round, and your mother gets frustrated.

"Rachel was good at this," she says as if I'm not living up to you. But she likes to win, and she and your father smile at the end when the points have been tallied and I have been beaten again.

Then your mother shows me up the staircase. Your father carries my one small bag. I stop in your doorway. The first thing I notice is the telescope, gold and pointed out the window. I remember seeing it before, not realizing it was in your room. Next, I notice the floors, which are littered with papers, all kinds of papers in files and folders and boxes jammed against the wall. Your case notes. They were here all this time, and I allow myself a moment of pride for being patient, for playing my cards right.

This is what I need. This will lead me to you.

"This is all Rachel's mess," your mother says, as if you are still here, still in high school. "But I washed the sheets." She moves to the door and looks wistfully back at me, crossing her arms. "We're so happy you're here."

She leaves the door open and goes down the hall. I shut the door immediately. Panic rises up in me, out of nowhere. Nerves bumble along my shoulders. Suddenly, I feel afraid. Suddenly, I want to run.

What am I doing here, living in the bedroom of a woman who has disappeared? What am I trying to do?

I pace, feeling claustrophobic in this space, your space. I stop and peer into one of your boxes. I hope to find case files but I am surprised to find school assignments, going back years, every test, every paper, every note. I am always surprised by people who save these things. Do they ever really look back? Do they ever really need to see them again? And the way they are arranged, in piles in the middle of the floor, makes it seem as if someone dumped them here, although your mother claims they're your mess.

I start to sift through, but my chest feels

271

tight and my throat feels narrow. I breathe deeply. I sit at your chair, at your desk. I remind myself there is nothing to be afraid of, but then I think, *This is instinct. My body knows something my heart doesn't. Run! Get out now, before it's too late!*

The gold telescope is in front of me, trained not up at the sky but out at the ranch. I stand up, curious. I shake my hands out, rub my knuckles and walk to the telescope. I bend down, peering through. A face flashes in front of me. I jump back with a start, knocking my ankle on the sharp corner of a box.

I catch my breath. My heart hammers in my chest. I remind myself that the face is on the other side of the telescope, not in here with me. I force myself to look again. It's Jed, standing under a tree on the far side of the ranch.

It takes me a second to piece together that this is not a coincidence. That he is waiting for me, that he knew to wait for me there because he used to wait for you. I wonder how I can get out of your room without your parents noticing. I stick my head out the window, but I am on the second floor, and there is no ladder, no trellis, no pipe.

It takes me actual minutes to remember that I am not a prisoner, that I can leave for any reason, at any time. I open the door. I walk down the hall. Your mother's bedroom door is open. I can hear the sound of water running, see the oversized dresser against the far wall. I pass by the open door and walk down the stairs. Your father is still at the computer, still scrolling through dozens of thumbnails of boats.

"Everything okay, Sera, Sera?" He has picked up this habit and he is not going to put it down.

"Is everything all right down there?" your mother calls.

My face heats up. My back hollows. *Run.* "I left something in the cabin. I'm just going to grab it."

Your father scratches behind his ear. "Why not wait until tomorrow?"

"Emmett, is everything okay down there?"

"I'm just going to get something!" My voice rises so I almost shout. I almost sound hysterical. "I'll be right back!"

My hands ache and I press my nails into my palm, wanting to break the skin. And my head spins and my throat narrows and my heart beats in overdrive and I rush to the door before they can chase me, before they can stop me. And I am fifty feet away in the bracing cold before I realize they won't. Why would they? They have no reason to. I can walk outside alone. I can do whatever I want. I am my own person. I don't belong to them.

Still I hurry, past the lodge, out into the ranch, where I find Jed standing under the tree, lit by the moon, like a lost cowboy in search of a love song. In spite of everything, all the evidence surrounding him, I just can't see him as a killer. He is too busy killing himself to kill anyone else.

"This is all my fault," he says.

"What is?" I say, disoriented.

"Don't stay with them." He steps forward, grips my wrist but presses too hard. I automatically pull away.

"I have to. I'm in Rachel's room. There are files. I think they might have clues."

"Sera!" He sounds angry. "When are you gonna let it go?" His eyes widen in alarm. He was too loud. He knows it. The valley threw his voice from here to there. The dogs bark in the distance. Out on the highway, another truck roars past.

He steps back away from me, kicks the dirt. "Shit. Lawd."

"What is it?" I step forward softly. "What happened?"

"Someone was in my house."

My bones chill. "How do you know that?"

He wipes a hand through his hair. His jaw

is loose. I wonder how much he has had to drink. "They moved some stuff." He finds his breath. "They moved some stuff around."

I think of the letter. Did I put it back? Or did I leave it out on the bed after I took the photo? I was so distracted, distracted by the words and what he wrote, and I can't remember. "Maybe you're imagining it." I feel the pull of guilt and I know I should confess but I can't. He's already mad at me, for not dropping this thing, for taking it too far. And it's not just that. He's fragile. I can see that now, like whatever guise of strength he had has been ripped off by our intimacy and now I can see him clearly. I thought he was strong but maybe he is weaker than me. Maybe he is more lost than I am.

He shakes his head, and that's when I realize he is shaking, shivering without his jacket in the cold where he has been waiting for me for who knows how long. And I want to hold on to him but I can't because I'm afraid and he says: "She knows."

"How could she?"

"She knows everything." He shakes his head miserably. "You don't understand. You don't understand what she's like. She's jealous."

"Of what?"

"Of everything. Of anything she can't control." He is trembling everywhere. He has always been on the edge, but now he is losing it, right before my eyes, and I don't know what to do. I don't know how to help him.

"Jed, calm down. I don't know why you're so afraid of her."

"Man alive, neither do I. I'm losing my shit. This place gets to you. It just gets to you. The other day, when I was in Willa Creek, I saw vultures circling, miles out up the road, and I knew they were here. I knew they were circling the ranch. And they were. If you look up. All day, every day, there's vultures circling here."

"Jed, breathe. You need to breathe."

"I think she's bugged the phone at the lodge. I think she's listening when I call my mom, when I call my brother."

"Jed." I feel sorry but I also feel slightly fearful, like it might be catching. I remember what your mother said, how thoughts are as contagious as colds out here, and I don't want to catch whatever he's got, but I don't want to leave him sick either. I put my hand on his shoulder. "Hey, you need to pull it together. Everything's okay. Everything's fine — Hey!" I say again, and then I pull him into me.

He shivers, ten seconds, and then he melts into me, and then he sobs, "I did something bad."

I step back quickly. He moves away too, allowing it. "What do you mean? What did you do?" My mind goes straight to you. Did he do something to you?

"It's like I got a death wish." His thoughts are jumbled and I don't understand what he's trying to say.

"Did you do something to Rachel?"

He shakes his head. "No, listen to me. Rachel is not —"

"Sera!" We both jump a mile. Jed dashes his shoulder into the tree, eyes wild.

Your mother stands behind me in her nightgown. The glow of a distant bug light makes a crown around her head. "I thought you were going back to your cabin," she says to me, her voice so calm, it cuts through us. "You know I don't like you all standing around in the dark. It's not safe." Jed has stopped shaking. His whole body is rigid. "Jed, remind me where you live."

"Yes. Yes'm." He ducks his head and walks off, swaying slightly.

"I'd keep my distance from him if I were you. Crazy is contagious," she says like she read my mind. "Now, what were you wanting from your cabin?"

My possessions are so meager that I can't think of anything and I finally say, "I just realized I forgot to wash some rags and I didn't want to leave them there."

Your mother stretches her lips, close to a smile but not quite. "How thoughtful of you," she says. "To clean up. Why don't we do it tomorrow?"

I swallow and I nod and then I follow her back to the house.

EPISODE 61:
WHY THEY STAYED

They did whatever they were told because that was what they had always done. When they were told to strip, when they were told to hurt themselves, when they were told to drink poison. They were good girls, and that's why they stayed.

I need to sneak downstairs and use the computer to search for Grace but your parents' house is different, set high on the hill, and I can hear everything, hear engines roaring past, so loud it's like they're in the room with me, hear voices, across the river or all the way in Happy Camp, arguing, yelling. But scarier than that are the silences that drop between the sounds, like something far away creeping closer.

Your parents are just down the hall, and the walls are so close, the sounds so easily bent and manipulated that I can hear your mother roll over in bed, hear your father snore. I can't imagine growing up here, in such close quarters. It's no wonder you became fascinated by details, evidence, by defining your world and the motives of the people in it.

I decide to check the computer tomorrow during lunch. I can come back early, while your parents are still working. Tonight I search your room, as quietly as I can. I look under the bed. I lift the mattress. I check behind and inside every book on your shelf. I don't trust a flashlight, so I use the light of the moon.

I find no laptop, no evidence of your podcast. I turn to the files on the floor. I start at the beginning: kindergarten. You have kept every test, every assignment. You wrote your name in all capitals but eventually you learned the lower case, and over time your letters softened, and I can see you taking shape, becoming the person I knew, the person who told me every week, *We are different. We see things others don't.*

I love your homework. I love the story it tells. The cleanness of it. The polish. The perfection. I love it because it tells me everyone was wrong, wrong about you. You are not a liar. You are not a stunt queen or a *falsely accused* or a Gone Girl. You are settled and perfect and good and then you hit high school. I notice a general slackening, a gradual decline, so gradual that I almost don't see it at first. Doodles appear. Flowers with petals shaped like hearts, a Stussy "S," the same carefully calibrated horse head drawn over and over. Your answers are still correct and your tests are still marked A, A+ but your notes become more fluid, messages in the margins:

Do you want to come to my house after school? Y/Y

And then another author: *Will your mom be there?*

Back to you: *She's ALWAYS there.*

Hahaha fuck

I flip through the patterns, the games of MASH, where familiar husbands are listed:

Homer
Moroni 1
Moroni 2

I recognize your games because you skip this section, while your friend (who must be Clementine), somehow ends up with Homer every time.

And then *Where did she go?* Written in pencil in the margins of your fourth-period history notes, then erased but still visible. Then *Flo, Flo, Flo,* again in pencil, again

281

erased. My vision has started to blur but it refocuses now. My eyes zoom in on your notes and they find, hidden inside the section on Reconstruction, the first of your case notes. *I knew she was meeting someone but she wouldn't tell me who. On July 23, August 5, September 19, she told her parents she was staying with me.*

The case notes continue for a time, the details you were so good at exposing. *She was last seen with Rachel Bard and Clementine Atwater and Tasia LeCruce.* My chest zings. You write Florence's age, eye color, hair color, approximate weight, identifying marks. You remind yourself: *Pass details to the police.* Fourteen and you were already in it — you were already trying to solve murders and save people. You were already lost in the details.

I keep flipping through but your class notes thin. They are consumed with notes about Florence. Your style has changed. Your handwriting is looser. You stop paying attention. The doodles breed and multiply. Your grades swing out: B, C, C, D, INCOMPLETE, OFF-TOPIC. You draw girls in the margins, flowers with heart petals in their hair. You draw a speech bubble and write "help" in decadent, loopy script. You make slashes, like cuts along your wrists, in the margins; you press hard as you color in all the gaps.

There is no place for you. There is no place for me. There is no place to put your feelings if you're a woman.

I hate being a girl.

I remember you were asked to leave school. I wonder how you would have stood out on a small campus like Happy Camp. How your attitude might have seemed infectious. I remember the way Tasia acted, like you were a disease that needed to be stamped out.

Florence is dead and no one even cares.

I lie awake in your bed, thinking your thoughts, until the sun comes up. I smell bacon and eggs and I remember that there is no lock on your door and I get dressed quickly.

I have breakfast with your parents. I get to work. I feed the horses. I ride them. I get back early to try to sneak in some Internet time, but your mother is there waiting. She has made me lunch — a sandwich that tastes like its color: beige. She and your father hold me hostage, tell me improbable tales about logging accidents, Bigfoot-hunting expeditions, like I am a guest they are selling their wilderness-family dream to.

I ask where Jed is and your father tells me he's fixing a sink in one of the upper cabins.

After lunch, I head up there to clean the windows. I still have work to do down below but I don't care; I want to talk to Jed. I need to ask him about last night.

I find him in the farthest cabin, collapsed on the bathroom floor. In yellow rubber gloves, greasy tools scattered around him.

"What are you doing here?" He moves to brush his hair back and remembers his gloves. Instead he reaches for a black water bottle, sucks thickly on it so I don't wonder what's in it.

"What was that all about last night?"

"Huh?" His eyes are red. His cheeks are pink. I remember that we slept together and I feel shame spurt through me. Has he always looked this drunk? I feel regret, the way I always do when I sleep with a man. Like even if I wanted to, I was still in some way duped, because it was all a consequence of his being a man.

"You said you did something bad. You said something about Rachel," I remind him.

He peels his gloves off, flips back his hair, revealing a dark purple bruise in a hook around his eye.

"What happened to your face?"

He brushes his cheek, pokes it in a tender

spot and flinches. "Well, Officer, I don't really recall."

He is sitting on a bathroom floor, trashed in the middle of the day, but he still has a cavalier quality. He stinks of whiskey and pheromones. I think if the roles were reversed, if I were the one drunk in the afternoon, how disgusting I would seem. I express legitimate concerns and people think I'm crazy. I am alone and people think there is something wrong with me. Jed is slouched on the floor and he is still sexy. I still feel like *I* need to impress *him*.

He smiles, like he's remembering something I wish I could forget. "I guess I was a li'l drunk last night."

"You seem pretty drunk right now."

He frowns; alcohol makes his reactions abrupt and childlike. "Someone broke into my house. Someone was fucking with my wife's stuff. I got a reason to be upset."

"You're only taking it out on yourself."

He frowns again, and his eyes find focus. He recognizes the sentiment. "You were in my house."

My chest tightens. I can lie, but I know I should have told him all along. "I was looking for you."

He slaps his leg. "Why didn't you just say so?"

"Because I — You cleaned my cabin. I felt bad."

He smiles, like he's proud of knowing he was right about me. "You weren't looking for me." He drops his chin. "You were looking for *evidence.* You can't help yourself." He fiddles with the cap of his bottle, like he's debating whether he should take another drink. "Can't help thinking everyone's no good." He spins the cap. "I'll tell you something, darlin'. You may be a good person, but you're good because you think you're bad, and one day that's gonna catch up with you."

I squat, crouch down on the ground, closer to him. "What were you going to say, about Rachel?"

He holds my gaze for a second, and I can see that he is disappointed, that he wanted something else from me. "Rachel, Rachel, Rachel," he says, and I think he envies you. He shakes his head, slides back against the wall. "Aww, what does it matter what I say to you? You're gonna think what you wanna think." And he pops the bottle cap and takes another drink.

That night I have dinner with your parents. As we are wrapping up, your father makes a sucking sound, pokes his finger beneath his teeth. "That Jed sure is starting to lose it," he says.

There is a finality to his words that matches the sky outside the windows.

"I told you he was bad news." Your mother stands to clear the plates.

"Some people can't take it out here. They start to go *cuckkoo,*" he says in his silly voice. "Cabin fever. We had this guest once — Hey, Addy, remember? She was a drinker too, had a phone installed in her cabin, and one night she calls us up to say there was someone trying to break into her cabin. Remember that, Addy?"

"Oh, yes!" Addy smiles. "You said, 'Can you describe them to me?' And she said, 'Yes, absolutely. It's Bill Clinton.' "

He slaps his knee. "Wearing a tutu!"

"So we went over there with our guns —"

"And found an empty bottle of Jack and prescription pills on the table."

"And we said, 'We don't mean to offend you —' "

" 'But we think you might be just a wee bit intoxicated.' " They both explode in laughter.

I wait a suitable amount of time to say, "But what about Jed?"

Your father mops his brow. "He wasn't there."

"No, I mean, why do you say he's losing it?"

"Oh, right, well, for one thing, he smells like a distillery —"

"Always has," your mother adds.

"And on top of that, he shows up to work this morning with a big ole shiner and says he ran into a wall! You'd think he had a concussion, the way he was stumbling around." He waves a hand. "I just set him up in one of the family cabins. I couldn't do anything with him."

"He needs to go." Your mother sets her hands on her hips. "I told you he needs to go."

"You may be right." Your father clucks, pokes another finger between his teeth. "Don't know how he'd make it on the road though, as loaded as he is. Probably end up in the river."

"It's none of our concern what happens to them when they leave here," your mother says.

My first urge is to defend Jed, but what can I say? He is a drunk and he's probably not a good employee, and even if I can't quite believe he killed his wife, there is something he is keeping from me. But he has been kind to me. I push my fork across the plate. "I think Jed's nice."

288

They both look up at the same time. Their jaws drop, their eyes widen, so they look like brother and sister. They are alarmed that I am voicing an opinion, alarmed that it is different from theirs, possibly alarmed that different opinions exist, on their land, in their kingdom, in their home.

Then your father explodes with laughter. And your mother joins him. They both laugh for a good long time.

He shakes his head, wipes tears from his eyes. "Of course you do! I can't imagine *why*!" And they both chuckle. "Well" — your father presses a hand to his belly and catches his breath — "be satisfied in knowing you're not the first young lady to succumb to his, er, *charms.*"

I think of you. "Did Rachel —"

Your father's eyes widen. Your mother's face goes pale. "Oh, no!" your father says eventually. "Rachel couldn't stand him. She used to call him the Slow Ranger." He taps his temple to make clear what you meant. You also slept with him, if Jed is to be believed.

"But then who did you mean?"

Your father is still catching his breath, so it takes him a moment to say, "Oh, he gets around. You wouldn't think it, to look at the state of him, but I'd bet he's had 'relations' with half the ladies at Happy Camp." I feel disgusted with myself, as if I am responsible for all the women Jed has slept with.

You mother nods. "I'm convinced that's why his wife left."

"Are you sure she left?"

Their heads swivel at once in my direction.

"You think she's still here?" Your father wriggles his eyebrows.

"I just mean, you don't think he did anything to her?" It sounds silly when I say it out loud.

"Jed?"

Your mother shakes her head primly. "The only thing that man could kill is a six-pack."

And they burst out laughing.

After dinner we play the same tile-matching game and I lose and I lose and I lose, but they hold me, with their benign comments, their lame jokes, their inexplicable laughter.

When I finally get upstairs, I am so tired that I can barely keep my eyes open. But I brush my teeth. I splash water on my face and I force myself awake. I go into your room. I shut your door. I search the room again and again I come up empty. Then I wait.

It's three in the morning. I can hear your

father snoring. Your mother has gone quiet. I need to go downstairs. I need to use the computer. I need to find Grace and then I need to look for your case notes. I can't imagine you broadcasting from the living room — you always said you recorded from your yellow house — but maybe you kept your notes on that computer. Your computer-illiterate parents would never find them.

Every second this case is getting colder and colder, every moment you are farther away from me, and I have waited long enough, I have been patient long enough and I need to go, *now.*

I am on my feet again. I approach the door, thinking that if I am careful, I can contain the sound, swallow all the sounds, and sneak downstairs. I press my hand against the knob. Like a spider my hand encircles it, presses it against my palm and turns. I feel the click radiate in my wrist. I convince myself it doesn't make a sound. I walk out into the hall.

Your mother coughs. I freeze. The ground hovers below, down the tilted staircase. I wait for the sound to settle; then I hurry. I can feel the wood grain under my feet as I tiptoe down the stairs. The statue of Christ seems to glow in the dark, holding its hands out as if to say, *Search me.*

And I glide through the kitchen, where your mother's herbs are lined in neat rows, like the bottles in her greenhouse, and I step into the living room, where the computer screen spits rainbows on sleep mode.

I slip into the chair, careful not to let its legs scrape the floor, careful not to make a sound. I shake the mouse.

The screen beams to life, washing me in its electric glow. The Internet browser is open, about thirty tabs running across the top, like your father doesn't know how to exit out of a screen. My heart pounds as I prioritize what's most important: confirming that Grace is still alive.

I click on Facebook. It's already logged in to Homer's account; he must have signed in when he came for dinner. I type *Grace Combs* in the search box, then think she might have switched back to her maiden name, then click SEARCH anyway.

Five results pop up. The first is a picture of a girl with big blond hair and a big blond smile. She hasn't shared her location but I am sure she is Jed's wife; she is Texas personified. Homer is not friends with her, and when I click on her account, it comes up private.

I'm not sure what to do. There are no visible updates. I check if she has an Instagram, or a Twitter, but nothing comes up.

I consider sending a friend request through Homer's account. It makes more sense than logging out and requesting her through my account. She's never met me. She might have met Homer; she would at least be aware of him, and people have accepted friend requests based on less. If I friend her through his account, would that be so strange?

But if she accepts, the update will go to Homer, and he will know someone has been in his account. But maybe he wouldn't care. Maybe he would think he'd requested it and forgotten about it. I hit add friend quickly, like it doesn't count if I do it fast.

Then I minimize the browser and activate a file search. The desktop is piled with photos and files. What search would take me to your files? Your name? The name of your podcast? But your files are probably hidden, so I need to be specific, and, more important, I need to be fast.

I type: *April Atkins.* The name of your last victim on your last podcast. I click RETURN. I almost gasp when a folder pops up, hidden in plain sight on your parents' computer. The folder is titled "84," which leads me to a hidden cache of numbered folders, stored inside an extension, 81134567 — UBC. And I have them. I have found your case files. I want to go through every one, but I don't have time.

So instead of starting at the beginning, I start at the end. I start with your last case. The folder labeled "85," the case you were investigating when you disappeared.

I double-click. I scan your notes; little details pop:

family relocated from West Texas

34yo woman, appx 5'6" /125 lbs, thick blond hair (possibly extensions?)

I know before I find her name exactly who you are talking about:

Grace Annabeth Combs

Grace is never going to accept Homer's friend request. Grace was the case you were looking into when you disappeared.

My first impulse is to go to Jed, not to question him but to comfort him, like he doesn't even know she's gone. But he must know. If she is gone, then he hasn't spoken to her; he has been lying to me. He can't have heard from her in months. But then what was he doing in Abilene? I try to think of what he said, his exact words. He said Grace wouldn't see him, but what about her parents?

My blood runs cold. What if they don't know she's gone? What if they think she's still here? Maybe that is why he is stuck out here, why he says he can never go back, why he doesn't have a choice. I think of Episode 67: *The Murder of Laci Peterson.* I am Amber Frey. Jed knew his wife was missing and he lied to me. It's so obvious and yet I can't believe it, like I am protecting him still, because he is a man, because of the way he looks, because I like him.

And I'm angry. This is not the person I came here to be; this is not the person I want to be, the mistress of a possible murderer. Then I realize, *Is that what I really think? That Jed killed his wife?* It would explain the drinking. It would explain the darkness.

And you were here for months after she left. And then you started investigating her disappearance, and then you disappeared too. I have been wrong, wrong from the beginning. The one person I trusted was the one person I shouldn't have trusted. Maybe you were drawn to him too. Your father says I wasn't the first woman taken in by his charms, his Southern accent and his helplessness, and I slept with him. I slept with a murderer. And the worst part is *I knew.* I told myself I only suspected but didn't I really know? Didn't I want to be part of your story? Didn't I want to be somebody so bad that I did the only thing that would make me somebody? I slept with a man. I slept with a murderer.

I think, oddly, of what Clementine said: *But then, young girls do dumb things.* It turns out old girls do too.

It all feels hazy and surreal and then the pressure mounts; the tension ratchets up. What do I do now? If Jed was involved in your disappearance, how do I prove it? I have listened to enough of your podcasts to know what I need: evidence. And the best, strongest evidence is a body.

I get to my feet, my knees limp, and I walk, off-balance, to the window. I peer through but there is only darkness on the other side. I think about telling your parents about my suspicions, that you were investigating Jed, that Jed is the person you were looking into when you went missing, but the only response I can conjure from them is laughter. Wildly, I think that I could bring them a body, I could show them the murder weapon, and still they would laugh, but that's wrong, that's twisted. That can't be true.

I want to pace, but they might hear me, so I crouch on the chair and I press my fingers into my palm and try to think, try to come up with a solution when I still haven't defined the problem. Are you murdered? Are you missing? Or is this a conspiracy?

I exit out of your files. I open the browser so everything is as your father left it. I get to my feet, careful not to upset the chair. I walk toward the back door.

You have been gone since April. If your notes are accurate, Grace hasn't been seen since December. And Jed is out there.

I think of how he has inserted himself into my investigation. How many times did he tell me to drop it? He's had his eyes on me since the moment he returned from Texas, to "divorce" his missing wife.

I need to catch him. I need to confront him. I can't waste any time. I trip over your father's boot. My breath catches as I steady myself. My head swirls and I think I'm going to throw up.

I remember what Jed said to me that day on Eagle Rock: *You think I'm a murderer, and you rode all the way up out here, to the middle of nowhere, alone with me, and I'm armed, and you ain't. So you could ask me about it?*

What am I trying to do? Am I trying to save you or am I trying to kill myself? Maybe all of this is my way of looking for a way out.

Do I want to find you or do I want to find your killer? Do I want to save you or do I want to be the next victim? Do I want there to be an episode about me?

I turn the knob until it clicks, and the cold air seeps over my bare skin. I don't have a jacket. I'm not wearing shoes. What is my plan, exactly? To confront him? And then what will he do? Deny it? Kill me too? And then no one will be saved, and nothing will be stopped. I have no evidence. I have nothing.

"Sera?" I hear your mother's voice calling me from above. "Is that you?"

I feel it like a rod through me. Like I am the killer. Like I have been caught.

"Sera?" she says again. Your father has stopped snoring.

I let the door click back. I walk out toward the stairwell. "Sorry," I say but my voice shakes. "I was hungry." I think she will like this, that I wanted more of her food. "I — I'm coming up now."

Jed is out there and I am in here, trapped.

Shaking, I return to my room — *your* room. I lie down on your bed. I realize this has gone too far, all of this. I have no reason to believe Jed killed you. No legitimate reason, really, to believe any crime ever happened.

Maybe you left. Maybe Grace left. Why am I still here? All I have is a death wish and this needs to stop. I need to stop. I need to stop digging.

But that's not entirely true. I do have one thing — one real, physical thing. I sit up on the edge of your bed and drag my backpack carefully out from under it. I dig through, searching for the rock, but I can't find it. I rifle through the papers, then empty the entire bag.

The rock is gone. The threat has disappeared. I question my memories — did I put it somewhere else? Did I hide it? Did I leave it behind when I moved? But I know that I didn't. It was in my bag when I left the yellow house that afternoon, when I went back to the staff cabin and found Jed. Did I have it when I moved to your house? I'm not sure. But it's gone now, which means somebody took it. Either Jed or your mother or your father. They are the only ones here. One of them wants me to run. And that's the only reason, the only real, concrete reason, why I can't.

EPISODE 65:
ONCE A RUNAWAY

Her mother reported her disappearance to the police but she made a mistake. She mentioned that Ella had run away before. So the police classed her case as a "runaway." They didn't investigate. Years and years passed and she never came back and the police wouldn't budge. "She's a runaway," they said. "It's not a crime to run away."

I have breakfast with your parents the next morning. I haven't had a good night's sleep in days. I shotgun coffee. My eyes feel stapled open.

"Can I ask you a question?"

"Well, Sera, you just did."

I force myself on. "Jed's wife, Grace. She left."

"That's not a question," your father teases.

"She didn't even last a week," your mother says.

300

"Did you see her go? Did she say good-bye?"

"No —," your father starts.

"She didn't say goodbye or thank you," your mother interrupts. "But none of them do. We've had a lot of crazies out here — that's for sure. Never said goodbye or thank you. Just run off in the middle of the night."

"What did Rachel think about it?"

Your mother's brows drop. "What does Rachel have to do with it?"

I realize my mistake. You are so on my mind, sewn through my brain, that I sometimes forget other people aren't thinking of you. "I just thought she might be curious why she'd left."

Your mother tosses her hands on the table. "Why would she be?"

"I . . . I just noticed in her room all her old school papers. It seemed like she was interested in disappearances."

"Grace didn't disappear; she went home." Your mother huffs in disapproval, crosses her arms. "I don't want you looking through Rachel's things." I think of how they were left, in the middle of the room, in the middle of the floor — how could she expect me not to look at them? "Emmett, we better move those files upstairs. Better yet, throw them out!"

"You don't have to. I won't look at them," I vow stupidly.

"No, no, you've got to be careful. Shouldn't have that stuff around. People are easily influenced out here." She pats my hand. "We wouldn't want Rachel's attitude to bleed into you."

"Well, maybe just a little!" Your father bursts into his inexplicable laughter.

I want to stop them from taking your files, but I don't see how I can. And I know who you are anyway; I don't need your story on paper.

I go out to feed the horses. I plan to avoid Jed as much as possible until I determine my next move, so of course when I hop on an ATV and drive to the barn, I find him leaning heavily against the tack room wall.

I figure he is drunk, so I snap as I pass him, "What are you doing here?"

His face is hidden beneath the rim of his hat, but when he looks up, there is blood caked below his nostril. When he moves away from the wall, he limps.

I temporarily lose track of everything, except this moment. The grass smells raw. The birdsong is piercing, like the sharpening of tiny knives. I rush toward him. "What happened? Are you okay?"

"I think I might have . . ." He sways, darts

a hand out to grab onto something but finds only dead air. I swoop in to steady him. "How d'you know if you have a concussion?"

I check his pupils and they seem dilated, but they're the same size. I think. I walk him to the tack room wall, and he falls against it. I leave him propped there so I can scan the periphery. There is no one around, but I still feel watched.

"Let's go into the tack room." I help him in, find a saddle rack he can lean on. I shut the door behind us. The air is close, thick with dust and mold, the room illuminated only by the thin light between the wood slats.

My first impulse is to pity him, but it is immediately followed by the thought, *Isn't this convenient?* The second I decide it's him I should be investigating, he shows up battered and bruised, playing the victim. But that's crazy. He can't read my thoughts. He doesn't know what I know.

I cross my arms. "What happened?"

"Don't you worry about it, darlin'."

"I'm not."

He scowls in surprise. "Coldhearted woman. You're a coldhearted woman."

"You're trashed."

"I haven't been drinking that much. I've

been slowing down." He is so disoriented that I find that hard to believe.

I find myself scanning his person for some kind of evidence, some kind of mark that says he's a killer, like I believe good and bad can be printed on people. I think of every episode of your podcast, how every answer was the same. *We can never say conclusively; all we have are suspects and verdicts. All we have is evidence.* "Just tell me what happened."

"I was down by the creek —"

"Why?"

"Do you want me to tell you or not?"

"I just don't understand why you would be down there."

"I was murdering someone, Rachel. What do you think?"

"I'm not Rachel."

His eyes unfocus and refocus. "I know that."

"It's the second time you've done that."

"I'm trying to tell you —"

"Were you in love with her?"

"My God. What the hell is this? I'm sorry. I expected a little bit of pity." A button of blood escapes his nostril and he wipes it away.

"I know you did. I know you do, and maybe I'm tired of giving it to you. Maybe it's the last thing you need."

He hacks a throaty cough. "You think I did this to myself?"

"Well, it is kind of your MO."

He shakes his head, fans his face with his hat. "What the hell is going on?"

"When was the last time you talked to Grace?"

"What . . . is this? Are you jealous or something?"

"No, I'm not jealous, Jed. Your wife — did she go back to Texas or not?"

"The hell you talking about?" He shoves himself up, then slides back.

"When did you last speak to her?"

He shrugs. "Couple weeks ago."

"Can you be more specific?"

"Not really. You can look on my Facebook, if you wanna know exactly what I said and when, although I do fail to see how it's any of your fucking business."

"Facebook?" I think of her account, the unanswered friend request. But what if she did accept it? What would that prove? "Have you talked to her on the phone?"

"You know what? Mind your own business, Sera. How about that, for a change?"

He tries to move along, to move past me, but I grab his wrist so hard, he flinches. "You went back to Texas, right? You didn't see her, but has anyone else?"

"My God, you have lost it."

I'm stung, but I don't release his wrist. I'm tired of people telling me I'm unhinged. I know when something is wrong; it's not my fault no one else does. "Was she back in Abilene or not?"

"I don't know."

"But you were there!" I squeeze him so hard that he yips, jumps back and takes his wrist away from me.

He shakes his arm out. He won't meet my eye. "I didn't go."

"What do you mean? If you weren't there, where were you?"

"I was . . ." He clears his throat like that will make it right. "I was at a hotel in Willow Creek. I was too drunk to drive and . . . I guess I just kept getting drunker."

"Then why did you tell me you were in Texas?"

"Because that's what I told Addy and Emmett. They're my employers — what was I supposed to tell them: 'I'm sorry. It's not enough I'm drunk all day at work. I need a vacation so I can be drunk all day in bed'?"

"Have you talked to her family since she left? Have they contacted you?"

"O' course I haven't. You think they wanna talk to me?" I can see the beginning of worry cresting under his eyes, can see the way he swallows it back down. He is so selfish, so slavish to his drinking that his own wife might've been murdered and he never even suspected.

"You need to call them. You need to ask them where she is."

"I know where she is. She's in Abilene. I told you, I talked to her on Facebook, a few times." But his eyes are worried.

"Where? When?"

"I used to go down to the coffee shop to see Tasia." He clears his throat, seeing how that sounds. "They have Wi-Fi there. I messaged her a couple times, offered to send her money. She told me she met someone. I mean, she more or less told me to fuck off."

"How do you know it was her?"

I can feel his frustration as he says, "I told you, it was *her* Facebook."

"Jed, anyone can access a Facebook account. All they need is the password."

I can see the floor drop out from under him and he sways slightly, but still he doesn't want to believe, still he can't let himself. And maybe that is the difference between you and me and everybody else. We never struggle to believe the worst, you and I.

"Where is all this coming from?"

"Rachel was looking for Grace. She was making an episode about her. Right before Rachel disappeared."

He shakes his head, fast. "Rachel's a lunatic." That's what they say about us. That's what they need to think, because the alternative is too much for them to take. We have to be disturbed. We have to be wrong so the world can be right.

"Maybe her family thinks she's out here with you. Maybe whoever's been messaging you has been messaging them too."

He backs away, like I have created the truth just by speaking it. "All right, all right, you're scaring me now."

"You should be scared. You need to wake the hell up."

Jed promises to call Grace's family during his lunch break, so I know he doesn't quite believe me yet. Or else he is involved, and he will spend the next four hours plotting some way to get rid of me. That is the risk I have to take. But if Jed wasn't involved, then who was?

I think of your mysterious gang. I was so distracted by Grace's disappearance, by forcing Jed out of apathy, that I completely forgot about the attack. Jed was attacked, and you were attacked. Who attacked you?

Your parents claim it was the people in this town, but there aren't many to choose from, and I have spent so much time on the ranch, I don't know many. I think of the Moronis in church. They look like they could put the hurt on someone, but why? And then I think, *Homer.* I remember him hovering in the dark when I spoke to Clementine, the way she wouldn't talk about Rachel in front of him. Homer seems like a nice guy, but isn't that a role he has cultivated? By becoming the leader of the church, by flashing those dimples, by preaching forgiveness. You taught me never to trust outward appearances, that sometimes the people who appear to have everything together are the ones who have everything to hide.

And then there are your parents: controlling, manipulative, punishing. They don't like Jed. And they seem strangely untroubled by your disappearance. Your mother claims to believe you're dead and yet she never seems to mourn you. Maybe she wanted you gone.

And I still can't discount Jed as a suspect. I have chosen to trust him, and soon I'll know if that was the right choice. Either he will contact Grace's family, or he won't. And then I will know who he is. And then I will have to decide what to do with that information.

Suddenly I can't stay still; I can't stay here. The trees are closing in. Up until now I have been playing on the edge of something, but if Grace was murdered . . .

My nerves tighten under my skin. *Run.* I am in danger. I should leave. I should get into my car and drive to Eureka, or Yreka, or Trinidad or the Redwoods. I think how close they are but how far they feel, how much longer the drive feels on hairpin turns at twenty miles an hour. My hands feel weak and my stomach shudders and I feel trapped. I feel it building up inside me but with nowhere to go, nothing to do. No way out.

I start across the field, faster and faster, until I am almost running. I reach the pasture and I grab the halter reserved for Belle Star. I halter her up and brush her quickly, check her feet as she dances back and forth, curious, dangerous. I find a saddle and a bridle that will fit her. She hesitates over the bit, but I insert my thumb and get her to open her mouth. She won't hold still long enough for me to mount her, so I make a running leap and she canters off with me on her back.

I rein her in and she dances in place. I

wonder where to go. I look at your parents' house, then up the hill at Eagle Rock, way out to Fountain Creek, and I decide to head across the highway to the beach. My heart pounds as Belle, still surprised to be under saddle, dances unsteadily underneath me. As we trot across the highway, a massive semitruck appears, blowing smoke. Belle half rears. I cling to her mane to keep my balance. My heart is pounding in my ears as the truck passes behind us and we reach the other side.

Belle dives down the steep hill and I lean back, swaying to keep my balance, and then we reach the beach, the long stretch of sand, and I ask her to run. She needs no encouragement and she splits out under me, little hooves pounding frantically in the sand, so fast my throat goes dry and I choke, so reckless I imagine her falling a dozen ways, tripping over a rock, flipping forward on top of me, sliding sideways on the sand, spooking at the birds as they fling themselves up from the river, but she doesn't fall and I hang on to her mane as she runs across the sand, all the way to the end of the beach, where I pull her up at the edge of the water as it rushes by, so heavy and so fast that they don't find the bodies until they hit the ocean.

Belle prances in place, so I follow a little wisp of trail to cool her out. We pass over brush and fallen logs, through a copse of trees. Until we reach one tree, the one tree of many, where everyone has chosen to carve their names and initials, their secret messages and their hearts' desires.

And my fingers go numb and my elbow locks so tight that Belle stops on a dime, as I see plugged deep into the tree inside a roughly carved heart:

HOMER LOVES FLORENCE

Your brother was in love with Florence. You wrote, *I knew she was meeting someone but she wouldn't tell me who. On July 23, August 5, September 19, she told her parents she was staying with me.* Maybe he was the one she was sneaking off to see. And then she slept with Moroni. And then she disappeared.

Belle and I make it back in one piece. I slip off her tack and she races back into the pen, kicking her hindquarters up. I rest the tack on the hitching post and look out after her; then my eyes open up and I look over everything, and I wonder if it's a trick of the light or if things really do look worse.

There is a rotten smell in the air. There is a murkiness, a quality of sinking, as if the land itself is cursed.

This is a place you loved, and I wish I could save it, the way maybe you could have, if only you hadn't disappeared. You never left, not at eighteen, or twenty-one or twenty-five. You stayed here. And I wonder if you were hoping, the way I almost do, that one day all of this would be yours.

I need to confront Homer, but I need to be careful. I will go to Clementine first. I go to the lodge to use the phone, which isn't ringing for once. I pick it up and press it to my ear. I hear only silence but I still dial Homer's number, which is posted on the wall under "Emergency Contacts." Nothing. The line is dead.

This morning I told Jed to call Texas, to make sure his wife was alive, and now the line is dead.

I track your mother down in the garden, where she is on her hands and knees with her red spray bottle, pulling up plant after plant and tossing them in a wheelbarrow. The dogs are heaving on the lawn, ribs popping like bellows. Either I am imagining things, or one is missing, maybe two.

"Dead," she says. "They're all dead! Have you ever seen anything like this?" She motions to the corpselike pile in the wheel-barrow. "We're going to have to start over!"

"The phone line is down."

She sits back on her butt, puts her muddy hands on her knees. There are marks on her skin, all the way up to her elbows, that look like chemical burns. "Do you think I have time for that? Do you think I have time for that *right now*?" It is the first time she has ever been angry at me, and I feel myself recoil. She turns on me, glares with her dark, beady eyes. "Don't you have work to be doing? Instead of chasing after some boy?" I think she means Jed and I want to tell her she's wrong, but I don't want to argue with her. "I think you have better things to do with your time — I'm drown-ing here!" She motions to her dead garden.

"What would you like me to do?" I try to be polite.

"I would like you to do your job."

I don't see Jed all morning. I contrive my tasks to search for him: cleaning the win-dows in the upper-level cabins, cleaning the lower-level bathrooms, driving an ATV up to the far pasture on some phantom errand I am too desperate even to define. I don't see him anywhere. It's possible that your father has stationed him somewhere hidden, knowing he is in no state to work. It's also very possible they sent him home sick. Although I feel safe shooting up and down the ranch looking for him, I don't feel safe going to his house. I'm supposed to be working, and the enforced normality of it, the knowledge that I need to act as if nothing has changed, keeps me tethered to at least the appearance of work.

But I cut off early, just before noon. I drive my ATV to his house. The garage is closed, so I can't see if his truck is inside. I head to the front door and knock, first politely, then in a panic. I ring the doorbell, again and again. I want to call his name. I scan the area for your mother or your father, but they are nowhere to be seen. They are probably back at the house waiting for me and I am so angry, angry with Jed, who for all I know is hiding behind the door, or passed out drunk, or else he is guilty, or else he has made a run for it.

"Jed," I say, too quiet. "Goddamn it, Jed."

I get back on my ATV and drive slowly around the property, looking up and down and into the woods, but he's nowhere to be seen.

Your parents are waiting for me with lunch, another thick, weedy offering. We eat in silence but I am so preoccupied that I don't realize there is something off until your mother says, "You had an exciting morning."

My heart evacuates. My chest is a gaping hole. Jed told them. He told them what I said. They killed Grace and you. And now they're going to kill me.

"Not too exciting."

Your mother stamps her fork and knife down on the table. "I thought I told you not to ride that horse."

My heart returns, peppers in my chest. "I — I'm sorry," I say, but really I am so relieved that I nearly gasp.

"Riding around like a lunatic. You could break your neck." She stabs her salad with her fork.

"I wasn't thinking."

"No. You weren't."

Jed doesn't come find me after lunch. I don't see him all afternoon. I keep my eyes open, but it is becoming clear that I have missed something. I go back to his house that evening, when my shift is over. This time I try the front door. It's locked.

I bang on the door. I call his name, louder than I should. I walk to his garage and I open the door. His truck is in the garage. His motorcycle is in the garage. His ATV is in the garage. My mind takes notes, slips into evidence overdrive. Jed's truck is here. His door is locked. He wasn't at work. Maybe Emmett sent him home early. Maybe he locked the door and passed out drunk. I know I should just go home, maybe alert your parents, but something holds me here, something tells me not to leave.

I walk around the back of the house and try the door there. It's locked too. I tell myself to go home, but instead I try a window. I pull the tabs and the screen snaps as I pop it out. The glass slips under my fingers but I press harder, rock it inside the frame until it judders open.

I take a deep breath and shinny inside, scraping my hip along the frame, slipping through spiderwebs. There is a dryer on the other side and I use it to drag myself inside, climb on top of it so it echoes hollowly through the space, out into the woods behind me. I push myself up, then catch my breath.

The laundry room smells sweetly of alcohol sweat and detergent. The house has a hypnotic quiet; a scrim of gray muddies the air. I stop breathing to listen for his breath, his footsteps, but I hear nothing. Still I keep my voice down.

"Jed? Jed, are you in here?" I hop down to

the floor. "I'm sorry. I broke in. But I was worried about you." I feel protective of the silence, like the house is a chapel. I move toward the front of the house, down the hall, past the guest rooms, where paintings are propped hopefully on the floor, into the kitchen, where the cupboards are open, mostly bare, where empty bottles are lined next to the trash with surprising precision. "Jed? Now you're scaring me," I say like our conversation is continuing without him there. "Jed?"

The gun safe is locked. There is no one here. I try to breathe relief but I can't. There isn't a smell, but there is something stronger, like my body instinctually is tuned to a frequency, a knowing without knowing why. So even though I tell myself I'm being paranoid, letting myself get carried away again, the way Jed warned me I do too often, I know now, in a way I only thought I knew before, that something is wrong.

I cut across the kitchen, to the far hall, toward the bedroom and the Bible and the letter I found folded inside. The hallway is dark. The bedroom door is shut.

"Jed?"

I knock lightly on the door. I shudder and clutch the knob. "Jed, I'm coming in." I expect the door to be locked, so when the knob gives without a fight, I jump back, release it so the door swings open unaided, revealing the whole room in one great gulp.

Episode 73:
Murder on
the Oregon Express

The body was uncovered at the end of the line. Time of death was estimated to be sometime around Medford.

"She only paid up to Ashland," the bus driver said. "I thought I was doing her a favor."

Seeing his body has an unexpected effect on me. Instead of feeling afraid, I feel fearless. I feel more alive than I ever have. I don't scream. I don't run. I think of you. I think: *Evidence.*

I slip my phone out of my pocket and I switch on my camera and I take pictures of his body from every angle. The ragged fingernails on the hand over his heart. The purpling rigor mortis along the stem of his neck. The dried brownish froth in the corner of his open mouth. The outline of his limp dick against the crotch of his Levi's. Then I widen my scope, take in the scene. The half-empty bottle tucked against his hip. The Bible open to Luke 15. Grace's letter, slightly crumpled on the clean floor, as if waiting to be picked up. A glass of whiskey on the table.

All evidence points to alcohol poisoning. The narrative will be easy to define: *He was depressed, he was a drinker, he lost his wife.* Or else: *He killed his wife. He was caught.*

Your father has to use his satellite communicator to contact the police. It takes them ten hours to arrive on the scene. They come from Yreka, and when I complain about the delay, they tell me, "He's dead, inn't he?" Your parents' reaction was similarly blithe.

Your mother said, "I'm not surprised."

Your father said, "Well, that's what happens."

I feel like I am holding on to something heavy, but I don't know what. Ever since I took those pictures, my hearing has gone soft and my vision has gone blurry, as if Jed's death is holding me underwater. I feel guilt, fear I somehow caused this, but I also feel afraid of my own reaction, the way I calibrated everything, all the evidence on my phone, the photos of his dead body. Am

I an animal? Do I have no feelings?

I slept with Jed, I remind myself. I was even a little in love with him, with the broken parts we shared, the life we shared, both of us out here, hiding, quarantining ourselves from the world as if we were the bad thing in it. And now he's gone, and all I can think about is you. What does his death say about *you*?

Jed was right: I have disappeared in your disappearance. I have gone so deep, I am missing from my own life.

I watch your parents for signs that they were in some way involved, but they are as unconcerned as ever: inappropriately light-hearted and determinedly black-and-white.

We are standing in the house, where we have been banished by the police so they can "do their job" without anyone making sure they do it. Your parents are next to the window, peering out across the property, reflections contained in the neat frame.

Your father fans his face with this cowboy hat, a gesture oddly reminiscent of Jed. "Maybe I shouldn't have fired him."

I startle. "You fired him?"

"Well, yes, Sera," he says like he himself didn't just question it.

"He was a terrible worker," your mother says. "If anything, we kept him on too long."

322

She scowls and pinches at a fly, trying to catch it in the air. "You can't blame yourself. He was a drunk. And a liar. I did wonder, all those times he said he went to the Bigfoot Museum in Willow Creek. No one goes to that museum more than once — and even then, it's by mistake."

"It is a lousy museum," your father agrees.

The mortuary van finally breaks the spell, driving past the ranch house to meet the police.

Your mother huffs, steps away from the window like all of this has detained her long enough. "We better get to Ashland."

"Now?" I say.

"It will be good for us to get out. Good for the mind." She taps her head. I have a passing vision of Jed's body being forced into a bag but I push myself past it. "You see what happens, if you don't get out." Like she hasn't been telling me all along, every day, that the only safe place is right here.

"Can I come with you?" I say without thinking. I need to stay here so I can search the ranch alone, but I can't define what I will look for: a signpost, a conclusion, a reason for everything? The truth is, I want to leave. I am anxious and I am clouded and I can't see the forest for the trees.

"No, you better stay here. It's safer. Make

sure you don't go beyond the perimeter,"
she says, like she hasn't warned me half a
dozen times of the impending danger and
death if I dare cross the property lines.

"I won't."

They take ages getting out, moving back
and forth into the house for forgotten
objects, abstract directives.

"Almost forgot my Bible!"

"I would carry. There's a pistol in your
bedside table."

"I would stay inside. It looks like rain." It
doesn't.

My only real concern is the phone line,
which your parents don't have time to
investigate. "Happens all the time. We'll get
Homer down here; he knows how to fix it.
In the meantime, if you need to contact
someone, you can use the Internet." I am
happy I can tweet the police.

On her final revisit, your mother says,
"While you're here, can you clean the
kitchen?"

I do that first, even though it's spotless. I
hear the hum of their SUV turn to a roar as
they reach the highway. I grit my teeth,
imagining your father diving into those
curves, and I am grateful I stayed back.

I finish cleaning the kitchen, but I still
don't feel like they are really gone. I know

that Ashland is hours away but I still feel they could come back at any moment with some gleeful regret. "We forgot the engine!" "Just need to grab another gun!"

I head across the property to ask the police more questions. The mortuary van has gone. I didn't see it leave, and I have the odd feeling that they have stolen Jed from me, taken him when I wasn't looking.

A big black truck is parked sideways out front. I start toward the door and run into Moroni coming out.

"Whoa!" he says, putting his hands up. His knuckles are bruised and busted, like he's been in a fight. He lowers his hands. What exactly is he doing here?

"You're a cop and a vet?"

"Just wanted to make sure he was really dead." He scratches his neck. "You know what it's like out here. Everyone's getting killed but there's no bodies." He's teasing me, and I think he and Tasia must laugh about me.

"I didn't realize you and Jed were close."

"Close?" He spits on the ground and pulls out a cigarette. "That boy was trash. And out here, trash ends up in the trash." His cracked knuckles contract.

He walks toward his truck and I suddenly see his headlights out on the road, hear his voice yelling, *Get the fuck out of this town!* I remember the afternoon I caught Jed driving away from the coffee shop. Your parents said he'd slept with half of Happy Camp. Jed told me he had done something bad. He said he had a death wish.

I follow Moroni to his truck as he climbs in. My cheeks heat up but I catch the door before he shuts it.

"Easy there, girl!"

"Did you kill him?"

"Nope." He slaps a hand on his chest and grins. "But seeing him laid out like that sure does reaffirm my faith in God."

The cops are leaving too. It shouldn't surprise me, but it does. The way nobody cares. The way people just move on.

"How can you be finished already?" I ask, trying to keep my voice level.

The detective claps his hands. "Pretty cut-and-dried: suicide. The Bards told us they'd fired him."

"But what about the bruises? I have reason to believe Moroni assaulted him."

"Ha! If I had Moroni on my case, I'd probably kill myself too." He climbs into his car.

"But what about — what about his wife?"

"More than likely, she just left him. Looks

like he was a drinking man." He pulls down the mirror flap and starts cleaning his teeth.

"But — this is insane!" My voice explodes up my throat, like a choking cough. "A man is dead. Two women are missing."

To his credit, he does stop picking his teeth long enough to say, "Two women?"

"Rachel Bard. She went missing almost two months ago."

"She probably just left," he says, like he hasn't just used almost the exact same phrasing for Grace, like that doesn't strike him as coincidental. He hitches his leg up into the car. "Happens a lot out here, and it shouldn't surprise you. You'd have to be crazy to want to stay in a place like this." He clucks. "Too isolated. The men get drunk and the women get out." He gestures to the woods beyond the ranch. "People come out here to die. If they want to live, they leave."

He shuts the door. I knock on the window. I can see him sigh, but he rolls it down for me.

"This is wrong! You need to do something."

He shakes his head, starts the engine. "You want my advice?"

"I want your help."

He shakes his head, the car rolls forward

and — like he can't help himself — he calls back, "Get out!"

I walk back into Jed's house, knowing it is empty, afraid of its emptiness. There are muddy footprints tracking to the bedroom. Nothing has been preserved or cataloged. The Bible is shut; Grace's note is still under the bed; the glass of whiskey is spilled across the floor. There is no indentation where Jed's body was, just mussed-up sheets. I think about calling Grace's parents. I think they, at least, will care about her disappearance. But I don't have their number, and even if I could find it, the phone line is down and I would have to drive all the way to Happy Camp, and even then, a signal is not guaranteed. And anyway, I'm a stranger, an onlooker, worse — I slept with her husband. I could reach out to Jed's family, tell them I knew him, but I'm a trainspotter; I am not really here. I am only looking for you.

I walk back to your house as the adrenaline drains and a syrupy torpor takes its place. I lie on the sofa in your living room.

Your parents' sofa is floral and smells of the eighties, and the Christ statue is looking down at me, its shoulders hunched as if in a shrug. I shut my eyes and picture myself dying, see your parents coming back tonight — the glint in their canine survivor teeth.

And your father says, "Well, that's what happens."

And your mother says, "I'm not surprised."

Like this is circa eighteen hundred, the true wilderness family, where people die all the time. *The men get drunk and the women get out.* He said a mouthful there. Did I really come here to die?

There are no voices bouncing through the canyon. Occasionally cars pass by on the highway, but I don't hear them so often now. Everything blends and softens.

I picture Jed making the call, then what? Did it hit him, the full consequences of everything he'd done? Did he believe Grace was dead? He must have believed she was dead and it was his fault. She died and he didn't even look for her.

But the phone line is down. Did it go down before or after he made the call? Did someone know? Was someone trying to stop him?

I sit up, back rigid. I remember the discovery I made before Jed died, the name carved deep into the tree. *FLORENCE.* And I can't give up. You kept her spirit alive and you kept looking. You kept the spirits of all these lost women alive.

I'm not perfect. I have made mistakes and compromises, but I have fucking tried. I fucking care. Maybe sometimes I don't care enough about myself; maybe sometimes I care too much about other people. I am not like Jed, or your mother or your father or your brother or Clementine or Tasia. I don't have my head in the sand. I see more. I care more. I'm not perfect, but I'm good enough. I can do things other people can't do. Because I never stop searching.

I don't have the phone, but I have the Internet. I sign in to my Hotmail account and find a message from Clementine, like she read my mind.

Hey, I heard what happened. I can't believe it. She seems like the type who can never believe a bad thing when it happens. I think of Florence; I think of how Homer was in love with her. I wonder what Clementine thinks of that. Please come over! It's probably best not to be alone right now.

I message her back immediately. My fingers are shaking as I type, and I don't quite understand why. Yes! I would love to! Can I come tonight?

I wait, hoping she will get back to me. In the meantime, I toggle through your parents' tabs. I scan the latest toy your father was searching for, a small sailboat to dart through the water. It wouldn't survive the Klamath; I wonder what it's for. I wonder if he plans to build a whole ocean on the ranch, an ocean and a forest and a city and a beach and a whole world, all theirs.

A dark truck crests the drive. I wonder who it could be. I scan the tabs and find the one for Facebook.

I think, *Grace.* I click and the sign-in page appears. Someone has signed out of Homer's account. Instead there is a long row of accounts, all the log-ins for all the people who worked here over the years. I slide through the list, looking for Grace, but other names pop:

Elizabeth Lowe
Leah Townsend
April Atkins

The women you talked about, not in every episode, but scattered throughout your podcast. The women who disappeared. They came here. They disappeared from here.

I find Grace's name. I click on her account. The password is saved, and it signs me in automatically. I hear a car door open, hear heavy footsteps come up the drive.

A click takes me to a Facebook page with

several chats open. I click on the chat with Marybeth Abrams.

I read Grace's message: We're doing well. Jed is finally getting his act together. It's so beautiful out here — like heaven on earth!

The message was sent today.

Footsteps rise up the walk. The doorknob rattles.

EPISODE 78:
A FACE YOU COULD TRUST

He had a face you could trust. That was what everybody said. Even after they found out he was responsible for at least five murders, people still went to pains to say, "He was just so likable. That was the only scary thing about him, to be honest: You just had to like him."

I exit out of the tab in a panic, forgetting to preserve it. It vanishes and I don't know if I can get back in.

Your brother is standing in the doorway. His shoulders sag and his hands are in his pockets. Even his dimples are frowning.

"I'm so sorry," he says, the first normal thing I have heard all day. "I liked Jed." This surprises me; I never saw them interact, but I suppose I don't know everything. I remember Jed said he liked Homer too. That Homer was a good person. And that is what a good person says.

333

I think of all the missing women. I try to contain myself. Where are they? Did they just happen to pass through here? Did you cover them because you knew them? Is it just a coincidence that they all disappeared?

"So did I." I stand up from the desk, move away from the computer so he won't suspect anything. I clear my throat. "I didn't expect to see anyone."

"Clem said I should check on you." His face is hopeful on her name. "And my dad wants me to see about the phone line." He tosses his keys and catches them. "I'm just gonna head up the mountain, have a look. If you want, you can come to our place for dinner. Clem's making chicken pie."

"I'll come up with you." I move toward the door, thinking of his name on the tree. I need to talk to him, alone. He steps back in surprise. "I should probably know where the line is, in case it happens again."

". . . Okay," he says like he doesn't really see the point, which annoys me.

His big black truck is parked out front. He takes your mother's ATV, and rather than climb on the back with him, I follow him up on your father's ATV.

We ride up the hill, above the ranch, close to the shooting range. I see Jed's ATV abandoned on the road and think of that day I found him up here firing his gun, how haunted he looked. I wonder if he's haunted now. Can you be haunted after death? I think of all the women who came here. I wonder where they went.

We stand outside the box and Homer brings out his phone for a flashlight, gets down on his knees and starts tinkering around. I am not paying attention and he doesn't explain what he is doing.

I want to ask him about Florence and the others, but I know better than to jump right in. I need to ease him out, gain his trust. Fast.

"What was it like?" I say, suddenly. "Growing up out here?"

"It was quiet," he says, and I wonder if he is being pointed but I can't tell.

"With your sister?"

"No, not her." He smiles and pulls a new, elaborate multi-tool out of his pocket like he can't wait to use it.

"Why do you think she left?"

"What, Rachel?" He tinkers with something. "She probably just wanted to do her own thing." He winks at me, and I see his dad in him, the slightly loony complacency.

"Then why did she stay so long?"

He sits back. "Can I tell you the truth?" He wipes his multi-tool meticulously with a handkerchief, cleaning off any evidence. I can see why it still looks new. "There was a time when I thought our parents would leave this place to me." He points with the tool down below us, where the ranch sits in the cradle of the mountain. "I thought that made sense, right? I'm the oldest son. They were raising me up to one day take over. But eventually I realized they weren't; they just weren't. They fought hard for this place, and they didn't want anyone to take it from them. That's what it felt like to them, like I was trying to take it." I realize that by "them" he means your mother. "I had to make my own way, find my own life. Maybe Rachel thought, if she stayed . . . She was always the favorite. For a while, maybe she thought it would go to her." I wonder if he thought it would go to you. I think, *Motive.*

"What changed?"

"It was Easter Sunday." He is still cleaning, polishing his multi-tool. "We were there with the girls. Moroni and Tasia were there. Jed was there. Rachel was digging into Jed, right there at the table. Mom was just lapping it up."

"What was she saying?"

"Just . . . I don't know. . . . How clueless he was. Jed had a lot of problems; I really felt for the guy." I think about all the times

I ate into Jed. I think that he deserved it. But it doesn't surprise me that Homer doesn't. "Rachel has a real vendetta against, you know, men."

"Why do you think that is?" I say, and the question sounds pointed. He is her brother. He and her father were the only male specimens for miles around.

"I won't speculate." He stops and I realize I have lost him. That I have to encourage him, make him think we are of the same mind.

"I see" is the best I can manage. "Then what happened?"

"Rachel made a comment. She said something like when this was her place, she wouldn't have any men around. Something like that," he says, and I wonder if you were more colorful.

"And that's when Mom brought out the will. You can imagine it was a pretty exciting Easter dinner."

I lean closer. I can see the ranch in the corner of my eye, darkening like a bowl of blood. "Who did she leave the ranch to?"

He pulls out some electrical tape. "Her dogs."

A gasp bursts from my lips. "What?"

"She willed it to her dogs, and my dad just laughed. My mom likes to do things like that. She likes to play with people." I think of the word Jed used: "punish."

"Can she even do that?" I think of her dogs, think your mother stands a strong chance of outliving them.

"If anyone can . . ." He shrugs. "The two of them went out to talk but the message was clear. That's why Rachel left. She'd been here over thirty years. Never had her own life. Never started her own family. To tell you the truth, I think she was counting on this place. Even if it went to me, she knew she'd always have a place with us," he says like he is the hero of every story.

He stops, frowns suddenly, then looks at me like he's my psychiatrist, like I am the one confessing to *him.* "I'm telling you all this because Clem told me why you came here. She said that you were . . . *fascinated* by Rachel." Your brother has a habit of using the softer word. "I'm hoping, maybe, if I tell you the truth, you'll just go home."

It's weird how much it stings. He's the cute, good boy, and he doesn't want me here. That's what it feels like, in a completely illogical way: Him trying to protect me feels like him rejecting me. And I think: *Why does he want me to leave?* And I think: *What's his motivation?*

"What truth?"

"Rachel just didn't fit in here. She made people uncomfortable." Sweat pops along his brow, like it hurts him to say it. "She could be . . . *too much* for some people." I don't doubt he thinks that, Homer with his perfectly sweet, accommodating wife. And I want to tell him that he has no idea what it's like to be a woman, that there are really only two choices: You can be too much or you can disappear. I want to tell him, even though I know he won't understand me, because some small part of me still wishes he could.

He shuts the door with a clang. "Fixed it."

I come out of my daze. "Really?"

"Yep." He spins his tape. "Easy."

"What was it?"

He frowns. "Wires just split."

"You mean someone cut them?"

"Why would someone do that?" He starts to stand and I realize I have completely forgotten to ask him about Florence. He is walking toward the ATV, and there isn't time to be sneaky.

"Can I ask you a question?"

He stops, turns slowly. "Well, Sera, you just did." He smiles with his father's eyes.

My lips stiffen, and I find I can't form words, can't think — is this because I think he's guilty or because I feel guilty for asking? "Florence Wipler."

"What? What are you talking about?" he says like I am unhinged.

"You were together, right? You were seeing each other, before she disappeared?"

His face closes like a curtain dropping, and I think of all the times I confronted Jed. How I felt safe, even after I accused him of murder. I don't feel safe now. I don't feel like I am looking at the same person I was looking at only a moment ago, and when it speaks — when *he* speaks — it's like something else, like a robot has taken Homer's place.

". . . No," he says like I'm mistaken.

"I thought you were."

"I — Why do you say that? Who told you that? What makes you say that?" His voice is measured but angry. His dimples are on fire.

"I saw your names carved into a tree." I realize my mistake too late.

"Well, Rachel, that's not exactly evidence. Anyone can write someone's name on a tree." He steps closer to me, gripping the multi-tool. "Where did you see it?" he says. "Out of curiosity. Maybe I should just do something about it. Wouldn't want to upset the wife." He smiles like your father, dopey,

340

like this is all a game.

There are at least ten ways he could kill me with his multi-tool. I am alone. Your parents are gone. Jed is gone. And no one would know if I disappeared right now. No one except Clem, who's expecting me. But Homer is her husband. He could say anything to her. He could say I was gone when he arrived. He could bury me in the pet cemetery, hide me under the blackberry bushes. There are a million places out here where he could leave my body and no one would ever, ever find me.

"I can't remember." I want to ask him about the others but I am afraid, afraid of what will happen if he sees, the lines I am drawing, the connections I'm making. Murder. Missing. Conspiracy.

He stays frozen for one, two seconds; then his knee bounces. "Why don't you head down? I'm just going to take a look at something. Then we can go have dinner."

"I'll take my own car," I volunteer. "I don't want you to have to drive me home."

"Suit yourself." He shrugs and heads toward the water cylinders.

I popped a Dramamine while I waited for Homer but I still arrive in Happy Camp with a syrupy ache in my temples, a dizziness that travels all the way to my toes and makes me walk off-balance up the path to their house. It has the same cookie-cutter quality as their house on the ranch, but it's hemmed in by a white picket fence. My eyes drift up to the attic, down to the basement. Is that where he hides the bodies?

Is it Homer? Is it your mother? Is it your father? Is it all of them? Who has access to that computer? Who has been sending messages from Grace's account? Your parents have access, but they barely know how to use it. And the computer is downstairs, next to the back door, and the door is always unlocked. *Everyone* has access to it.

Homer stops at the door and smiles back at me, like Walt Disney on the opening day of Disneyland, and says, "Welcome to our home."

I feel sick but I need to act normal, like every day of the week but worse. In a way I've been preparing for this my whole life. I force a deep breath.

Homer opens the door to the life my parents always wanted for me, the life I was supposed to have. The girls are at the table doing their homework. Clementine is in the kitchen preparing dinner. The house smells like baking and boutique candles, is decorated with homemade goods in pastel patterns.

Homer kisses his wife on her carotid artery and says that dinner smells amazing and did the girls do their homework? The girls explode into a chorus of Disney afternoon-approved complaints.

"But homework is so pointless!"

"We'll never use *any* of this!"

And Homer gives me a significant look like we are all in on this together.

I offer to help Clementine in the kitchen and she is nice enough to say I can, but she doesn't know how to use me and I don't know how to be used, so I end up standing off to the side, feeling more and more ineffectual, feeling a kind of shame blossom on my cheeks, like I am embarrassed not to be Clementine.

I tried the conventional life — the husband and the job and the family — but it didn't take and I left it without ever considering that there was no alternative. I think of Homer in the woods and I look at him here now, and I wonder if when I wished for this life, I was wishing on smoke.

"I can't believe Jed killed himself," Clementine says over the stove, but really she can't believe anyone would. She chose the right life, but, more important, she can be

343

happy in it. Jed couldn't. I can't. You can't. The system that sustains her breaks us.

Then dinner is ready and we put the homework away, shepherd the plates to the table, where Homer sits at the head, with Clem on one side and his daughters on the other, and me on my own at the other end.

They make cooing noises as they eat, like the food has to be placated.

"How are things on the ranch?" Clementine finally asks. "I mean, apart from . . ." She grimaces at her mistake. "How is everything else?"

"It's all right. It's so beautiful there." I think of Grace's message home, the message that was sent after she disappeared, and I shudder.

"Will you stay on?"

"Yes," I say, no pause.

A fork scrapes across a plate. "Really? I'm surprised."

"Why are you surprised?"

"I just thought, with everything that's happened . . ." She wants me to leave. "I think most people would go."

"Really?" I challenge. Asha and Aya both look up, then back down. "Do you ever hear from Grace?"

"Grace?" Clementine says.

"Jed's wife. I just wonder what happened to her."

"I heard she went back to Texas."

"She didn't."

Clementine straightens. "Oh? I always thought she just went back home." It reminds me of when Jed said, *Maybe I just want to believe that Rachel got away. . . . But I do believe it.* When Clem herself said, *I wouldn't worry about Rachel. She always took care of herself.* Because isn't that what we do? Isn't that what we all do? When someone disappears.

"A lot of people struggle out here," Homer points out in his collected preacher voice. "They get cabin fever, like Jed. I hate to say it, but he was starting to get pretty sloppy, I thought." He tugs at his collar, twice.

"I didn't realize you had much interaction," I say.

Clementine's eyes dart to Homer. "Word gets around here," she interjects. "Small town. We were worried about him."

"Hey, we like to check in on everyone." Homer beams like a saint; Clementine smiles.

"Moroni checked in," I say. "After Jed died. Looked like he'd been in a fight. So did Jed."

Homer stretches his back. "Well, the sad

345

truth is, Sera, sometimes people die in the middle of an argument, before we get the chance to repent and ask forgiveness." I think of Florence.

The girls keep their heads down. It's black outside the window. There is not so much as a streetlight for miles around.

My nerves collect in my chest. "Can I ask you a question?"

"You just did," Asha and Aya say in chorus.

I take a deep breath. I think, *This could all end now.* I think, *Don't ask.* It's like the part at the end of a horror film, where the hero is walking slowly down the hallway, clutching a bloody knife, and you're sitting there on the couch with your fingers clenched as they reach for the last door and you want to scream, *Don't look! Whatever you do, don't look!*

"Did you know April Atkins?"

Episode 81:
In the Basement

For nearly six months, they were kept in chains in the basement. He raped and tortured them. They believed it was consensual. They believed he loved them.

Clem's chin rises. The girls duck their heads. "April?"

"Yes."

"At-kins?" she says like it's hard to pronounce.

"I think she worked at the ranch."

"Hmm."

The girls don't meet my eye. Homer blots his brow.

"I think, maybe, there was an April there, at some point." Clementine blows out her lips. "It's hard to remember everybody!"

"What about Elizabeth Lowe? Leah Townsend? Missy Schubert?"

"You'd have to ask Addy." Clementine's fork scrapes across her plate. "She might have records."

The girls stand up at once. "Can we be excused?"

"Clean your plates." They lift them in unison, hurry to the kitchen. And I think: *They know.* And I think: *Clementine knows.*

"Where are you getting all these names from?" Homer says.

"Rachel's podcast."

He rubs his cheeks like he's trying to remove his dimples. "I wouldn't trust everything Rachel says."

"Some of those girls might have come through here, at one time," Clementine says. "But this is kind of a place for lost souls." Homer sets his hand on the table and Clementine takes it, squeezes it, like they are the only two survivors in an apocalyptic world.

I can't shake the feeling, as I leave their house, as I walk toward my car, that they — Homer and Clem — are exactly why I wanted to run, why I came out here in the first place. In their white clapboard house with their white picket fence and their pastel-painted walls, their patterned kitchenware, their jobs and their homework, they know something. They all know something but they're pretending they don't.

I wonder if I should go to the police. I wonder if the Facebook accounts, the missing women, the names on the tree would be enough to convince them to look twice.

I start toward town. I head first to the coffee shop, but it's closed. Then to the grocery store, but it's closed too. The whole town is closed and I head down Main Street, hear the meth rabbits in their hutches and then a voice calls out to me, from too far away, "Did you ever find that ranch?"

I turn and I see, at that same too-far-to-talk distance, the man I saw on my first day in Happy Camp. His cat is gone but he is sitting firm, holding his place outside the Happy Camp Arts Center, calling out when it's too late.

I walk toward him. "Yes. Yes, I did. Thank you for your directions."

He shrinks when I get closer. His eyes are bulbous, yellow. His skin is tough around his lips so they seem not to move when he exhales with a faint, dead puff, like a body wheezing out its last breath. "Why are you still here?"

"I'm looking for Rachel Bard."

"Ha!"

I am not sure how to interpret that, but then I am used to that with him. "She's missing."

He wriggles a finger, beckoning me forward. I step closer, enveloped in his smell, which is overly sweet, like a flower right before it dies. "I saw her."

"What? When?"

He nods, pleased with the effect. "I see her all the time. No one else sees her — no one else is looking. But I see her. *I* see her." I feel a slight chill, wonder if this is how I look, if this is how I seem to other people, a lost soul claiming to see what no one else can.

"Where?"

"In the woods, sometimes. By the river. Out there." He aims his finger at the vanishing point, the end of the road. "Couple days ago, I saw her getting into a big black truck, with that cowboy." I deflate. He hasn't seen you. He's seen me. I am so deep in your disappearance that I have become a clue.

The bell dings overhead as I step into the police station. Officer Hardy sighs, but keeps his eyes trained on his phone.

"I need to report . . . something."

His lips twitch. "How mysterious."

I can't shake the image of that man in front of the Arts Center. I wish Jed were here. I wish you were here. But you're not, and I have to start believing in myself or no one else will.

I put both hands on the counter. "Women have been disappearing, for years, from the Bards' property. Florence Wipler. Elizabeth Lowe. Leah Townsend. April Atkins. And now Grace Combs."

"I —"

"I think Homer Bard is responsible."

"Homer?" He nearly chokes on his tobacco.

"He was seeing Florence, when she disappeared. Did you know that? And then she cheated on him. He acted funny when I asked him about it. And his sister has been investigating him, she's been keeping a record of every disappearance, and now she's disappeared too. I think Homer is responsible. Maybe Addy and Emmett too . . . Clementine. Even Tasia." With every name his eyes grow dimmer.

He sets his phone down and gets to his feet. His hands go to his holster and I think he could shoot me; he could place me under arrest. Maybe he is part of it too. I can't trust him. I can't trust anyone. I step back, analyze exit strategies. "Now, you seem like a nice girl — no — you seem an enthusiastic girl —"

"Woman."

"If you say so." He leans forward on his

elbows. His breath is hot on my cheek. "But I need more than just a crazy story to get out of bed in the morning. What did I tell you? Last time you were here?"

"I need evidence." But we know he doesn't want just any evidence. He wants bodies.

I drive out to the ranch in the soupy, slippery dark. The road seems to have turned against me, slipping and sliding around me in new, precipitous turns, sprinkled with sharp, fallen rocks.

I make a plan. I will call my ex-husband. I will tell him that if he doesn't hear from me in five hours (two and a half hours to drive to Yreka, where there is cell service, which means I have two and a half hours to save you), he should call the police. I will say goodbye to Belle Star. (This is one point I can't find my way around. I have thought about stealing her, stealing your mother's truck and trailer, driving off and saving her, but that would be a crime. Maybe I can come back for her.) And then I will go to the yellow house with a shotgun. I will blow down the door. And I will find my evidence.

My hands are shaking when I get to the ranch. I park my car next to your father's SUV in the lot. Are your parents back already? Or did they take another car?

I hurry inside to use the phone, but it's been ripped from the wall. It is lying, smashed plastic, in the middle of the floor. My heart pounds.

"Hello?"

I rush to the computer. I wiggle the mouse. The screen lights up but the pages have vanished. Someone has been using the computer.

I blink and force myself to open the browser. A white page pops up.

Oops! Something is wrong. You are not connected to the Internet.

I try again.

Oops! Something is wrong. You are not connected to the Internet.

And again.

Oops! Something is wrong. You are not connected to the Internet.

I crouch forward. My stomach churns. I hear a click and all the lights go out at once. The moon ebbs in the window and someone is here. Someone is watching me.

"Hello?" I say again. My voice is a rasp. I

stand but my body is stooped, aching. It's like fear is poisoning me. I take my cell phone from my pocket and use it to light my way across the room. The statue of Jesus flags me down, saying, *Calm, calm, be calm.* But my heart beats faster. I step across the living room, under the curve of the staircase.

I duck into the armory. Your parents keep their four hundred and twenty-seven guns in a room off the kitchen. They don't keep it locked because of course they don't. They want someone to find it. They love chaos. They love brutality. They are a real wilderness family.

The door is already open. I flash the light across the floor and I jump back in surprise. There is a man on the floor in a cowboy hat. At first, I think it's Jed. He is lying on his stomach in a pool of vomit. The smell hits my nostrils the second I see it.

I bend down, knees quivering. I press my fingers against his neck. It is only then, touching his papery, wrinkled skin, that I realize it is your father. Your father is dead. *Merely a flesh wound,* my brain fizzes. And I think that he will pop up and have a good, long laugh about it.

In either hand he clutches a customized silver pistol. If he was going down, he'd want to go down with a set of ostentatious guns. And I have to remind myself that this is real, that this isn't just an object lesson. It looks real and it smells real but my brain is telling me, *Don't worry!* My brain is telling me, *Go nuts! It's safer.*

I press my fingers to your father's wrist, under his chest so I can feel the cave where his heart died and I think, *I don't want to die.*

I came out here to disappear but I don't want to. I want to fucking live. I don't need to live better. I don't need to live right. I just need to fucking survive.

I take the best gun I can find, the one with the laser sight, the one that's so tricked out it will probably aim and fire without my even having to pull the trigger. I check to see it's loaded even though I know it is.

I hold it against my shoulder like I know what I am doing, like I have ever done this before. "I have a gun," I say, but it's almost a whisper. "If you can hear me, I have a gun." I slip back through the kitchen.

I hear a thud on the stairwell and I whirl around, pointing wildly. Two yellow eyes flash. It is one of the cats. I don't know how it got in and it hisses and spreads its mouth in a clown's smile.

"It's okay, kitty." I lower the gun and I run for the door. I am outside and no one is following me; everything is quiet as I pound down the steps toward my car. I open the door, and then I hear a whinny of alarm across the ranch. I recognize it immediately. Belle Star.

I keep hold of the gun and I run across the property. A loud mechanical sound scares me sideways and then the sprinkler system comes on, hissing, firing spinning pumps. I stop in the middle of the dirt path, avoiding the water. It's strangely beautiful, the way the air glistens in the pale outdoor lights, all the way out to the edge of the property. Are they trying to scare me? Are they trying to trap me? I inhale and my nostrils burn.

And then there is a scream, and I can't tell if it's horse or human, and the sprinklers hiss and switch off. I take a shortcut past the greenhouse to get to Belle Star, but pull up short when I reach the garden. Someone has been digging. Your mother's work on the blackberry bushes has left them dried and leached of color. The doll I plucked from beneath the bushes has no face, just an empty plastic cavern. And someone has scraped the bushes back.

My heart is snapping like fingers inside my chest — am I alone? Am I ever really alone, even all the way out here? I start toward it, shoulders crawling with nerves like bugs. I hold the gun against my hip.

The bushes have receded and now I can finally see what's underneath. Episode 33: *There were twenty-two girls buried in the church garden.*

All my plans vanish because there is only one thing to do now. I dig. The water burns my fingers and tingles on my tongue. I have my phone out, flashlight engaged, ready to take a picture, as soon as whatever it is reveals itself — ready to take a picture before I run.

It's hard to dig up a body in real life. Even turned earth is heavy, littered with rocks. I can sense the vultures circling overhead. Sweat drags a cold finger down my back and my lungs are screaming and I keep digging. I dig harder. So hard that when I hit something soft, it feels *like a pillow,* as one Manson Murderer described it; *like butter,* the murderer crowed in Episode 38; *like it was meant to be,* said the killer in the Horoscope Homicide.

I can see her now, coated in moss and rot and smelling of old death. I have my body.

I force the bushes back, ignoring the thorns as they poke my skin, the roots that weigh anchor against me. I dig again. I don't even have to dig that deep. And I have another body, this one flesh clinging to the bone, coated in a mosslike substance. Maggots burrow in an eye socket.

I am sick on the lawn, am so shaken that it radiates through me, and I fall to my knees and I think, *Evidence, evidence, don't leave evidence,* but I can't help myself. I feel like I am dying. I feel like I have been poisoned. I am those bodies. Those bodies are me. I am every woman who has ever disappeared.

I am on my knees, gasping for breath, when I hear footsteps lumbering toward me. I see her feet first, the way they stagger toward me, as if they too are dying.

The gun slips in my fingers and I fumble to adjust it.

"Rachel," she says, and her eyes burn, but they are out of focus; they glare somewhere above me, like Rachel is a spirit floating just over our heads, haunting us. "You destroyed my garden!" There are dark stains on her hands, leaking from her lips, and at first, I think it's mud. I have to remind myself that it's blood.

"There are bodies!" I say. "There are bodies under there!"

"This is all your fault!" But it's not and it never was, and before I can stop her, before I can say anything, she lunges toward me, her arms outstretched, and a gun goes off but it can't be mine. I don't know how to shoot a gun. And that is the last thing I remember.

EPISODE 84:
THE KILLER COMES HOME

The guesthouse was the only place in the derelict thirty-acre ranch that wasn't falling apart. The bar was fully stocked. And the dining room was decorated, with human-sized mannequins in Halloween masks that were dressed and organized so they looked like guests at a grand party. The last party the victims would ever attend.

I wake up on the kitchen floor. I know it's the kitchen because I can see the oven. And I think I'm at home, that my entire life has all been one big "it's all a dream" sequence and I am home with my parents and then the dream dissipates, and I don't know where I am. I am not in Addy's kitchen. Addy, I remind myself, has been shot. I don't know where I am.

I feel a hand on my shoulder. "Hey." I hear the twang of a West Texas accent.

I start, but my head is so thick that I

barely move. I have to drag myself up off the floor piece by piece. The kitchen is similar to Addy's, but like a fun-house version, everything is slightly off. There is a computer and a generator in the opposite corner, jugs of water lined along the floor, and in the far room there are bodies standing upright. I shake my head to clear it and I realize they are mannequins, life-sized dolls in tattered clothing. And the windows are covered, the curtains drawn shut.

"Are you all right?" the blond woman says, helping me up. She is pregnant. Her stomach swells beneath her shirt. She presses me back against the cupboards with gentle hands. There is a cuff around her wrist, a long chain that stretches somewhere invisible.

My head wobbles. "Grace?"

She smiles. "You know who I am." Like nobody would.

"Where are we?"

"We're safe now." She strokes my hair. "She saved us."

My heartbeat fights against whatever force is holding it. I see Addy's cold lips illuminated by the hard light of my flashlight. "What are you talking about?" I slur slightly. I feel like I have been driven through the roads at a breakneck pace. My head is swimming. My thoughts are barely afloat.

"Don't worry." She strokes my back. "It won't be much longer."

"Until what?"

"Until Rachel comes back."

"Rachel?" You're here, and for a moment everything else blurs, all my life refines itself on a single point: I found you. "Where is she?"

"She'll be right back."

My mind swirls as I lean against the cupboard, trying to piece things together. I am in your yellow house. Grace is here too. The door is shut. Your parents are dead. It's like somebody took the world and turned it inside out.

I start to get up, but my balance swings out wildly and I hold myself against the cupboard, waiting for the waves to settle inside me. But they don't. It's like I am driving on that road, someplace far that I can't reach. I am ripping around the edges. I am flying toward the turns.

"Hey, hey, just take it easy." She speaks with Jed's cadence and it spooks me. "It's gonna be all right." She reaches out to quiet me but I bat her hand away. The chain rattles. My head swells.

"How did I get here? Where is Rachel?"

"We just need to be patient." She grasps

at my hand. "She'll tell us when it's safe to leave. We just need to wait quietly."

I walk toward the door, slipping dizzily. I think I have been drugged. A splash of red hits the floor in front of me. I touch my nose and find the source.

"You oughta lie down." Grace follows me, wringing her hands. "You've been poisoned."

"What?" I wipe the liquid on my shirt. It's only peripherally that I realize it is blood. My heart races. I think of Belle Star.

"Homer poisoned the water, up at the ranch."

"Homer?"

"He killed everything. Rachel found you passed out by the blackberry bushes." Poisoned. I think of the sprinklers, the burning in my nostrils. My hands are bright red; my throat stings. I think of Homer, how I left him on the hillside with your mother's ATV, your mother's poison.

"Where is Rachel?"

"She's gone after him."

I reach the front door. I put my hands around the knob. I expect it to fight back, but it comes open in my hand so fast that I stagger onto the porch.

"Sera! Wait! Just wait! Rachel's coming back! Sera, please just wait! You've been poisoned!"

I flail my arms. "Stay away from me."

"You need to calm down."

"I need to go to a hospital."

She can't argue with that, and she has reached the end of her chain.

I don't think I can make it to the hospital, but if I can just get to the turnout south of Happy Camp, the one with the phone signal, I can call the police. I have evidence, more evidence than I ever could have wished for.

I race down the steps. The motion unbalances me, and a cascade of nausea overwhelms me, so one moment I am running and the next I am vomiting violently on the ground so hard, I think I will lose everything inside me. So hard, I think I am dying.

"Just stay here." Grace spreads her arms wide, like she can catch me from twenty feet away. "Just wait!"

But I won't. I need to get my car and I need to drive to the turnout and I need to call the police. I can't wait for you to save me. I need to save myself.

My head swims back into place and I am running. I stumble but I don't stop.

"Don't go up there! It's not safe!" she screams, and I'm reminded of your mother. She told me it wasn't safe to leave, and

Grace says it's not safe to go back, and there is no safe place and I pound up the pathway, up switchbacks in a blaze.

I catch my breath in Jed's thinking spot. I vomit where he spit tobacco. And then I run, farther, faster, longer, along the paths and past the pastures. The horses move like marionettes on jerky, uneven strings, and I think that I am hallucinating, but when I stop to vomit again, I see them staggering, whinnying hollowly, see them snap and fight and take chunks of flesh from one another's necks. One shudders and collapses to the ground, joints stiff, then quivering, legs in the air, pumping wildly, screaming. They're poisoned. They've all been poisoned.

I think about the water supply, how easy it would be. I was just up there with Homer and I told him about Florence and he said, *I'm just gonna head up the mountain, have a look,* and I let him. I let him go off alone.

The entire ranch is contaminated. They're all going to die. *We're* all going to die.

I veer off course, toward the round pen and Belle Star. Part of me doesn't want to see it, but I know that I can't just leave her. I have to try to save her.

I veer around the tack room and the round pen comes into view. Belle is standing in a patch of moonlight illuminating her golden mane. She dips her head softly into the water bucket and I scream.

She tosses her head, then cocks it as if to chastise me. She isn't seizing up or quivering, or biting at her side, and I realize it's her water trough; I filled it myself from the hose days ago. She hasn't been contaminated.

My chest hurts and my teeth are pulsing and I'm going to die. I'm going to die if I don't get out of here.

I reach out to Belle. At first, she shies away but then she wags her chin and drops her head and I run my hand down her face.

"I'll come back for you," I promise, and then I run. The ranch house swims into view.

A wave of nausea overwhelms me again and I stop against a tree. The lawn seems to stretch out in front of me, and phantoms move across it: jerky, haunted, muddy black and burning. It's the cats — all the stray cats have abandoned the petting zoo and are stalking the lawn. I can't tell if they've been poisoned; they seem too clever for it. Bright eyes twitching, tails swishing back and forth. It's as if they know the ranch is theirs now, like whatever was holding them back has gone, and they sit on the porch and they tumble from the rafters and they observe me with their quick, superior expressions and I almost smile. I almost smile because only a cat loves a nightmare, and then I run to my car.

I take my key from my pocket. I jam it in and open the door, collapse into the driver's seat, slam the door shut behind me. My nerves sharpen, tumble into place along the back of my neck and down to my elbows, so I sit up straight, so I realize what I have to do. I have to drive along these winding roads, as fast as I can, without vomiting myself to death.

I grip the steering wheel with one hand. The sweat from my palms seals my fingers to the wheel. I can't catch my breath. I stuff the key into the ignition. I start the car. It crackles, then roars to life. The cats on the lawn all turn at once, all stretch their necks and watch me as I swing the car into reverse, peel back along the bumpy road.

Nausea lifts in a wave, tightens my neck, bulges behind my eyes. I open the window just as I swivel my head, dive sideways and vomit in a stream down the side of my car. I'm going to die.

I put the car into drive and I tumble down the mountain toward the highway. I am picking up speed. I need to slow down but I don't. I can't.

I dive into the corners. I am shocked at how fast I can go and still stay on the road. I can see the turnout up ahead, wide and empty. It blinks in and out like the beam from a lighthouse as I skid through the turns.

And then it's there, right there ahead of me, this wide, beautiful expanse on the other side of the road, clouds swollen with signal, and I speed up.

I remember how Jed used to joke about the highway, how people always showed up at the worst times, and just then his truck rises into view, swinging tight around a turn and barreling toward me. It's going to hit me, I realize. I don't have time to stop.

I relax my knee, ready to smash the brake, but then my nerves twitch, and instead of loosening, I tighten; instead of giving in, I fight back. Instead of worrying about getting out of his way, I force him to accommodate me. I think of your father, how he pulled in front of that other car with no consideration, rode fast into every turn. And I am the asshole. I squeeze my eyes shut. I step on the gas.

The driver blares his horn, amplified in the river valley, with mountains all around us so it tears a hole in my head and I go fast, faster toward the turnout and he honks again. He is not backing down. He is accelerating toward me. And my head aches and my chest opens and my heart zings. He is going to kill me.

I dive into the corner. It's too late to brake. I am over the edge of the mountain. My stomach pops on a breeze. My eyes water. And the trees are all around me, and I'm about to drop, about to hit the ground, but somehow, I never do.

"Take this." I recognize your voice immediately. You sound the same in real life as you do on your podcast.

"No." I press my lips together. I keep my eyes shut.

"Sera, don't you trust me?"

I open my eyes. My first impulse is to be starstruck. You have freckles on your nose; I never knew that. You have your mother's eyes and your father's dark smile. You look put together, even under these circumstances, with a neat flannel button-down. Your hair is brushed.

"Where are we?" It looks like a motel room, but my first thought is that it's a room that's designed to look like a motel room, like I can't trust anything.

"Take this," you repeat. "It's diazepam. For the seizures."

"I'm having seizures?" I shift in the bed. "I'm naked."

"Your clothing was contaminated. We had to remove it."

"Why aren't I in a hospital?"

"We called an ambulance." Your nose crinkles, in a smile or a grimace. "These things take a while out here."

"What have I been poisoned with?"

"We don't know. We think it was something my mother made, to kill the blackberries. The water system at the ranch was contaminated."

"Was it an accident?" You don't answer. Your face is a mask.

The room is quiet. I take in odd things — the red numbers on the bedside clock, the big block television set, the brown mini fridge. I am looking for clues.

"How did I get here?"

"Grace told me you ran away. I'm surprised you could run at all. You certainly couldn't drive. We found your car. We got you out. Don't you remember? You were talking a little."

"What was I saying?" You turn to arrange the bottles on the counter. "Rachel, where were you?"

You smirk, and I can see your father in it, your mother, the disconnect. "Here."

"Where are we?"

"Willow Creek."

"What were you doing here?"

"My mother made me stay here."

"Why?"

"She was trying to protect me."

"Where is Grace? And Florence? And April? And all the other women who disappeared?"

Your eyes flit down. "Maybe you should rest."

"I need to know."

And you're pleased, because you need to tell me. You scoot forward on the chair. Your voice, so familiar, washes over me. "Ever since I was a kid, I suspected. Florence was the first to disappear. Then a woman called Amelia, another called Elizabeth, April. Who knows how many others? Who knows how many got away, how many didn't?

"They came here to disappear, to escape their lives, to start over. They came here because they had nowhere else to go. It always happened the same way. They would befriend us, become like family. We were always sure they would never leave us. Then one day, I would wake up, and they'd be gone. No explanation, just *She disappeared.* It became normal to me, growing up here. The people who came to work at the ranch were searching, impulsive, maybe a little lost. It made sense, on the outside, that they would just leave without saying goodbye. That was how they ended up here in the first place. But I always felt like there was something wrong.

"But I never knew for sure. Or maybe I just didn't want to see until . . ."

"Grace."

You lift a glass of water off the table, offer it to me, but I shake my head. "My parents were always paranoid, 'crazy.' Particularly my mother. The worse things got, the more she tried to control them. You know what I mean." She smiles indulgently. "But she had a reason to be afraid. She didn't trust anyone because her own child was a serial killer. Not that they ever knew for certain. At least I don't think they did. But you can feel it, in your bones, when something is really wrong."

"Serial killer?"

"They killed Florence, April, Elizabeth. They abducted Grace, kept her locked inside that house. When they realized I was looking for her, they tried to scare me off the land, away from the house. But I didn't give up. I stayed close by, looking for an opportunity, a way to help her escape."

"The rock. Was that you in the woods?

Did you throw the rock? Did you want me to run?"

"I wanted to save you from them."

I have more questions for you, but my head is in a fog. I try to swim through, to make sense of everything. "But who killed your cat? Who poisoned Jed?"

"They did." I think of your mysterious gang.

"But who are they?"

"Homer and the Moronis. They've been doing these things for a long time."

"But why didn't you tell someone?"

"I did. I told you." A rush of pleasure like a seizure shivers through me as I think of all the episodes, all the secrets only we knew. "You're the only one who believed me. And they tried to silence me. They threatened me. I went into hiding, but I kept watching. I was watching you." You speak with detached certainty, the way you did on *Murder, She Spoke,* like you have dissected, like you understand everything, like it all makes sense once you get your tongue around it. "Homer poisoned the ranch. He wanted to pin it on you."

"On me?"

"He had been planting seeds that you were crazy all around town." I think of the people in town. Have they treated me like I was crazy? Officer Hardy did. Moroni did.

"Where is he now?"

You shudder through a sigh, unsettled. "He's gone. You're safe now."

"What do you mean?"

"He's deceased."

"What? How?"

You seal your lips, afraid to say, afraid to speak.

"Rachel, you know you can trust me, don't you?"

"He was poisoned."

"Poisoned? Where? When?" I left Homer that night at the house, with his family.

"They found him at the church. He'd been poisoned, with the same poison he used to contaminate the ranch." Your eyes rush over me, looking for clues, evidence that I believe you, evidence that I am on your side.

My nerves simmer like warm coals. I feel myself sinking and I say, "My God."

"There's something else." You brush my hand like you're afraid to touch me. "Do you remember what happened to my mother?"

My senses rock. I remember the blood. I remember her coming toward me. I remember the sound of the shot. I remember pain.

You press your finger bones into mine.

374

"Your secret's safe with me."

There is a knock at the door. You drop my hand. "Come in," you call, and Grace enters the room. Her blond hair spills over her shoulders. Her blue eyes gleam when she smiles.

"You feelin' better?"

"Sorry I ran away." I am not sure why I am apologizing. I feel wrong. I have finally made it to you and it's like the world has done a somersault and, instead of feeling happy, I just feel dizzy.

"That's all right," she says, and her voice is just like Jed's, the same rhythm, and strangely I think I will cry. I feel tears crest my eyes, and I think it has been years since I have let myself cry. "The ambulance is outside. They should be up any minute." Her eyes go to you and your eyes go to me.

"The police are going to want to talk to you."

The words from your lips slightly thrill me. "What should I tell them?"

Your eyes are warm and you smile. "Tell them what happened."

Officer Hardy comes to visit me in the hospital in Yreka. I am surprised that he has driven all this way. I would have expected him to wait longer, or not to come at all.

Instead he sneaks into my room like a kid in trouble. His shoulders sag and his eyes are misty and I wonder why; I thought he hated the Bards.

He sits in the chair beside my bed, where only you have sat. He walks me through that day in particular. I am ready with every detail. It is such a relief finally to have him listen to me that I almost lose track of what I am saying.

"And then I asked him about Florence, and he got very defensive."

"Defensive?" he says, like this is a word I have invented. He lifts his head and the hospital lights illuminate the rugged patterns on his checks, the pockmarks along his jaw.

"He seemed angry."

"What do you mean, 'angry'? What did he *do*?"

". . . Nothing."

He sits back like he thought as much, like I am torturing *him* by answering his questions. He doesn't care about the Bards, not exactly; that's not why he's here. He cares about Homer. And I think how Jed liked Homer, how the town liked Homer, how even I liked Homer. Everyone liked Homer, just like everyone hated your mother, and I think, "He's dead." Only I say it out loud.

And Officer Hardy leans forward. "What makes you say that?"

"I . . ." And then my heart starts to crumble. I realize this is a real investigation. The kind that will be on the record. The kind that will be used as evidence. The kind that will be used to create the narrative of what happened, what really happened, who killed all those people. And I realize I am not supposed to know that Homer died. And if I tell him you told me, the narrative will turn to you, and if I don't, the narrative will stay on me. I found Jed's body. I found your father's body. I was there when your mother was shot. "I just figured, if he poisoned the ranch, he might have poisoned himself by mistake."

"That's a pretty good guess. Do you know how he ended up at the church?"

"I didn't know he was at the church." I always thought that if I was ever involved in an actual police investigation, if I were on the record, I would tell only the truth. But it turns out, I am the same person I am in real life.

"You didn't?"

"How would I know that?"

"I'm sorry. I just thought you knew every-thing." He readjusts himself in his seat. "Clementine said he would go there sometimes to meet members, people who were in trouble, late at night. Any idea who he might have been meeting?"

"Why don't you check his phone records?" I am not surprised I am telling him how to do his job.

"We did. Guess where the call came from — you'll like this."

"Where?"

"His own house."

"Maybe he called himself."

"Looks like he did."

I try to get him back on track, back on Homer. "Anyway, we talked about Florence, and then we separated. I went back to my car. And he walked toward the water system."

"Did he tell you what he was doing?"

"He said he was going to go look at something."

"Did he say what?"

"No."

"And was he carrying anything on him, anything unusual?"

"No. But he was using Addy's ATV. She kept the poison in the basket."

"Did you see it?"

I didn't see it, but maybe I did. "I don't remember."

"*You* don't remember?"

I press my fingers to my temples, imagining a headache before it's really there. "I feel sick."

Officer Hardy shifts. "Mrs. Fleece —"

"Miss."

"Whatever. *Real* people are dead."

"Maybe they were real to you," I say without thinking, and then I am appalled. I cover my mouth with my own hand. Were your parents never real to me? Was your brother? Was Jed? Or was this all just some game, some escape, that got away from me? "No, that's not what I mean. I mean, you never cared until it affected *you,* until it affected someone you cared about. I cared." Did I? Or am I really that much of a monster? Am I really that lost? Am I really so alienated from the world that I can't even feel a mass murder — not on a podcast, not on a *Dateline* episode, but in real life?

Officer Hardy sits back. "I'm surprised you haven't mentioned her."

"Mentioned who?" I say, like I don't know he means you.

"Mentioned Rachel. That woman you were so hard searching for. She's back, you'll be glad to know. With another wild story." Something knocks loose in my brain. It's the words "that woman." He has used those words before to indicate your mother,

I thought, but now I realize he might have been indicating you. You were the one with the "crazy stories." The one who used to bother him. "According to that woman, he's been plotting to get the ranch for years."

"Maybe he has. He told me he wanted it to go to him." Was that what he said?

"Then it wasn't very smart of him to contaminate it."

"Maybe he wanted to destroy the evidence."

"It wasn't very smart of him to poison himself."

"Maybe he felt bad for what he'd done. Maybe he wanted forgiveness. He was in a church."

Officer Hardy puts down his pencil. He stretches forward. He traces a finger down the edge of my pillow so close to my face that I feel my cheek sinking, smell the tobacco in his finger pads. "See, I don't think he did." I can hardly breathe all of a sudden; I think that poison is still affecting me, contaminating me. I can't think straight. I can't see clearly. "I don't think he had anything to do with this."

"Of course you don't."

His features pinch. "Oh, come on, now. I've never been anything but nice to you."

I laugh. "Is that what passes for 'nice' with you?"

"Homer is a good man. He wouldn't do a thing like this."

"It's easy for a man to be good, just like it's easy for a woman to be crazy." I lean in. "You can believe whatever you want, but you need proof. Something beyond whatever nefarious ideas you have twitching up in your head. Right?"

He sighs. Sits back. "Clementine said you were a writer. You sure know how to tell yourself a story."

"Right back at you."

THREE MONTHS LATER

Every morning I wake up early to feed the horses. They are new horses, replacing the old ones, but we take better care of them. We have moved to the yellow house, which was kept safe by its lack of a water hookup, while we wait for the main property to become decontaminated.

We plan to turn the ranch into a safe haven for women who need to disappear. All day we work clearing trails, rebuilding, and all night we work our cases. We take care of the animals and we take care of each other and nobody bothers us. We can look however we want, act however we want, be whoever we want. We are not disappearing. We are multiplying. Every weekend, more and more guests participate in our retreat. They are brought here sometimes by the podcast, sometimes by the website and the Instagram photos and the promise that this is a place where we can just be. This is a place where we are safe.

The police keep looking into what happened at the ranch. They have counted the bones in your mother's garden. There are thirteen women. Florence is one of them. Most have been identified, but some never will be. They won't accept Homer as the villain. Moroni has skipped town, even though they never accused him, probably never would have. You say the police won't stop, because of course they won't.

Grace has her baby, and it's a girl. Grace names her Hope, because that's something a woman with a name like "Grace" would do. She doesn't even consider going back to Abilene, to the family who never even realized she was gone. She says, *Jed would have wanted me to stay here,* and I can't correct her, even if I suspect it is the last thing he would want. We all help her with the baby. We all take turns looking after her, like she's our baby, so sometimes we forget who she belongs to.

You talk about growing up on the ranch, how trapped you felt. How free we are now. You say it over and over, the way your parents used to say, *We're so happy you're here.* You say, *I'm so happy I'm free.*

And the sun sets the same way each day. The trees rest in their piles. The creek is loud and fast and so close to us that I can feel it pounding in my chest after a heavy rain. And I think how lucky we are to be here, and I try not to think too much about the why, or the how, how we became so lucky.

But not everyone is happy about it.

Almost every morning I see it sitting at the end of the drive: the big black truck. Sometimes it's Tasia; sometimes it's Clementine. And it irks me. It makes me feel dirty. It's like they are waiting for something to go wrong.

And I ask you, "Is this what they did to you? Homer and Moroni, when they ran off the road, when they attacked you? Were they following you, all the time? Were they watching you? Was that why you ran?" And you say, "You're the only one who understands."

Early one morning, a nightmare wakes me up and I walk out alone. Belle Star is in the pasture. She nickers at me as I pass. We put her in with our new horses and she has become the alpha mare. Now they are the ones that wind up wounded and I am proud and scared at the same time.

I walk down the river. Up close it sounds like an orchestra tumbling down a hill. The walls of the valley are green but there is a smell that hovers in the air, especially in the early morning, of death from above, a constant reminder that we are living in the fold of something bigger.

I can see the truck — Clementine; I recognize the plates — waiting at the end of the drive. I try to ignore her, to shake it off, but the headlights flash. She's signaling me. She's calling me in and I think, *I should confront her. Someone needs to.* You say to let them watch. "They think they're so scary."

I walk toward the truck. I hesitate when I see Tasia scowling in the front seat, but I won't back down. I am stronger than I thought. I am not crazy. I was right.

The window rolls down and Clementine stretches over Tasia's lap. Her hair is askew and her face is pale but she almost smiles, like it's been a rough few weeks but we're all together now.

"Will you come with us? We want to talk to you."

"I —" My fingers slide toward my gun. I carry now, all the time. I don't know why or when I started, but I can't stop.

"We're not going to kill you," Tasia says, and the emphasis dances in my mind. *"We're"* — or was it *"you"*?

"I don't know if I should."

385

Tasia scowls. "What, *now* you're scared?"

"None of this is your fault." Clementine puts a hand on Tasia's shoulder. "We just want to talk to you, woman to woman."

My eyes dart toward the house. I know you wouldn't want me to go, but maybe I can fix this. Maybe I can convince them that everything is solved now. We solved it. I would like to have Clementine and Tasia and Asha and Aya here with us. I would like not to see that big black truck waiting at the end of the road every single morning.

I open the door and climb into the back of the truck.

We are quiet all the way to Happy Camp. We pull up outside the coffee shop and Tasia unlocks the door and leads us inside. She doesn't bother with the lights. Doesn't offer tea. We sit in a circle of chairs next to the window. I choose the one closest to the door. My gun pokes into my back and I shift to get comfortable.

They say nothing. Tasia glares at the floor and Clementine gazes wistfully out the window. It's as if they expect me to lead their conversation though I don't even know what it's about.

I shift in my seat. "Rachel wants you to know that she doesn't have any bad feelings toward you —"

Tasia groans

"Tas," Clementine warns.

Tasia's knee bounces. "You realize what she did to you, right? You're finally putting it together. The great detective!"

"Be nice."

"Be nice? That's exactly what got us here in the first place!" Tasia jumps forward in her seat, a sudden live wire. "Your best friend is evil."

"We don't know that!"

"Oh my God, Clementine, get real!" She cracks her knuckles so fast, it's like a smattering of sparks. She turns to me. "Remember Florence, our good friend Florence? Who do you think was the *last person seen with her*? Who do you think ran off after her, after we fought?" But I'm not falling for it. It doesn't even affect me, encased in stone as I am.

I cross my arms. "If you really thought Rachel killed her, why didn't you do something?"

"Because Homer told us not to. He said that even if something *did* happen, it was an accident, and we should forgive her. He wanted to protect her."

"Or himself." I sniff.

"No! That's not — You don't get to choose

who the criminal is!"

"I could say the same to you."

Her eyes go flat but she continues. "Florence disappeared. It was suspicious but life went on. Rachel became *obsessed* by it. Back then it made us believe she was innocent, but not anymore.

"The way I see it, Florence was her first kill. Maybe it was an accident. But that's what got her started. She wanted to kill again, but she knew she would have to be more careful. She would have to find victims that no one was looking for. And she was lucky, because at her parents' ranch, she had a constant source.

"Clem and I were the only ones who noticed how women came in and out." She stops for a second, hovering over some uncertainty. "We tried to talk about it but it was 'What do you expect? It's a seasonal job' and 'It's not a crime to disappear.' So we started watching."

My eyes expand. "You were the ones harassing her." In the big black trucks. In their husbands' trucks.

"I'd hardly call it harassment." Tasia frowns. "And we didn't wear masks. I can't believe Addy told you that. She had to make sure nothing pointed back to Rachel."

"We used to listen to her podcast," Clementine volunteers.

"You're kidding," I say.

"For research," Tasia says, like she wants it to be clear she's not a fan. "We chased a couple of leads but they didn't go anywhere. The women she picked, nobody really cared about, y'know? And it was hard to believe — it was hard to keep believing — when everyone acted like there was nothing wrong." Her eyes flit to Clementine, who nods. "Even with Jed, I asked him about Grace and he said that they talked, that she was back in Texas. We didn't think Rachel would touch her. She never touched a woman with a man. We had no idea Grace was in that house." She sits back, stunned. "And now talking to Grace is like talking to a jukebox in a country bar."

"You talked to Grace?"

"Tried to. One minute she's telling us how she met Jed in a church. The next he's coming home drunk with lipstick on his collar. Do you know she thought he was dead?"

"He is dead."

"No. I mean, before that. She had her believing Jed was murdered and she was in danger."

"Jed was murdered and Grace was in danger."

"Do you know how Grace ended up in

389

that house? Because neither does she. She woke up chained to the wall. And then Rachel appeared, said she was just sneaking in to help her. Told her these wild stories about murder and mayhem. Had her believing everyone was out to get her, that Rachel was the only person she could trust.

"We sat Grace down. We tried to talk to her. We tried to convince her to leave. But she thinks we're the bad guys, because Homer was the bad guy. Because Rachel is the only one who understands." But you're the only one who understands *me.*

"This is crazy." I push deeper into my chair. Outside the window, Happy Camp is a portrait in pink morning light. The streets are deserted. Everything is deserted and I wonder how I got here, like it was all an accident.

"You don't believe us," Clementine says. In some ways, this whole thing seems to have breezed right by her. She still sits with the same passive rigidity, and I realize she will probably marry again; she will probably find someone else. She is too perfect not to be someone's wife. Thirteen bodies were unearthed, an entire ranch was decimated, her own husband poisoned himself, and she still sits there like she's waiting for the oven timer to go off. She is exactly the wife every man wants.

I shake my head. "If all this is true, why didn't you just tell me? Why didn't you tell me that Rachel was a murderer?"

"Because we thought she was dead," Tasia says.

"Not dead," Clementine corrects.

"Whatever. We thought she'd been dealt with. We went to Addy. It was almost summer, which meant they were about to start hiring again, and Rachel would have a new pool of applicants. And we said that all these women were disappearing and it couldn't be a coincidence and we were going to the police. Addy said she would take care of it."

Clementine clasps her hands. "We never should have done that."

"No, we should have killed the bitch ourselves." I cringe at the word.

"I don't think Addy believed us," Clementine says.

"Really? Because I don't think she cared. Rachel's been in Willow Creek this entire time." Tasia turns to me. "Isn't that true? You told me you were in Willow Creek. "Don't try to tell me Addy didn't know that."

"Why go to Addy at all? Why not go straight to the police?" I don't think the police would have had any qualms about putting you behind bars.

"We did." Tasia exhales slowly. "Addy didn't know that, but we did." Tasia worries her fist. "We didn't have proof. Officer Hardy thought we were crazy." I shiver. Our stories intersect so much, it's like Tasia and Clementine are mirroring me and I feel tricked and seen at the same time.

"And even if we did have something, Rachel would have found a way to turn it all around. She was good at that. And she had that podcast, that stupid podcast, to paint her as a hero, to explain why she kept *everything.* That stinky house you live in was where she kept her evidence. That's why she sealed all the windows and keeps the doors locked. It used to be filled with all this creepy stuff." I think of your posts: *This is where I go to find peace. I'm so lucky to have this little corner of heaven!* "She probably still has it somewhere." You do. You kept it in a shed in the woods behind the house, but recently you moved it to a room upstairs. You tell me not to go in there because you don't want anything compromised.

"I'm sorry," I say, and then I hate myself for apologizing. "It just doesn't make sense. If Rachel hates men, like you all claim she does, why does she kill women?"

"Who told you she hated men?" Tasia arches an eyebrow. "A man?"

"Your husband."

"I don't know how much time you've spent with Moroni, but he's about as clueless as they come." And I like her more, and I wish I knew her better. I wish I hadn't jumped to conclusions. Just because she married an ass doesn't mean she didn't know it.

"Rachel doesn't hate men," she continues. "When Florence slept with Moroni, it wasn't Moroni she was angry with. It was Florence. We think she targets women because she sees them as inferior. The patriarchy is a hell of a drug."

I think of the notes in your homework. You said you hated being a girl, that there was no place for you. Killing women might have been a way for you to feel that you were better than them. Not like other girls, in the sickest sense of the phrase.

And it's not just that. You knew if you wanted to kill, if you wanted to keep killing, that you should choose as your victims the people who had already disappeared — the lost, the disenfranchised, the women with nowhere else to go.

I can't help but feel a small thrill in dissecting this — whether it's true or not — in examining the psychology. What *could* make you the killer. In a way this is what I wanted all along. To sit down with a group of women and talk about a crime.

"All these women who came to the ranch, all these kind, lost women. Rachel despised them and she wanted to control them and she . . ." She blinks at her train of thought, like she still can't take it to its conclusion, not when it's about something real. Maybe that is why she can't convince me. Maybe that's why she can't be right. Because I can think it and I can say it: *Murder.* "I mean, she locked Grace up in some death house while she incubated her child, and what did she do to Jed? She fucked him." I remember how Homer said you ate into Jed at Easter dinner; your father said you called him the Slow Ranger. Did it get you off? Did it make you feel important? Did it make you feel *here* to sleep with a man whose wife you had made disappear?

The gun is digging into my back and I feel slightly dizzy. Everything is turning over in my head and I am trying to keep hold of it, trying to hang on to the thread of your narrative as it flips from under me.

"Didn't Rachel poison him too?" I say. "I mean, in this narrative reconstruction, who killed Jed?" Tasia won't meet my eyes and I wonder if she thinks Moroni did. It could have been Moroni. It could have been suicide. It could have been you.

So, let's pretend. Let's make it a podcast episode. Let's build a narrative, all of the evidence against *you*. Let's talk about what *might* have happened.

"I told him to call her family. He said he would call during lunch, but they fired him."

"Maybe he told them what you said about Grace." Tasia glances at Clementine, bringing her in. "Maybe Addy told Rachel."

I think of what the man outside the Arts Center told me, how he saw you with Jed. What if he wasn't mistaken? "Or else Jed told Rachel."

"And Rachel killed Jed?" Clementine scoots forward.

"Addy told me she was going to Ashland," I say. "About an hour before Homer came over. So how did she get to the ranch before I got back from dinner?"

"She didn't go to Ashland," Tasia says.

"She went to Willow Creek," Clementine adds.

"To find Rachel." We all pause for a moment, trying to catch the threads of the story.

"But Rachel wasn't there?" Tasia suggests.

"Someone cut the phone line," I add.

"What if Rachel was already at the ranch?" I remember seeing Jed's ATV abandoned at the shooting range. At the time I didn't even think of it, but there was no reason for it to be there, no reason he would have abandoned it and walked down. "Then Homer and I went up to repair the line." Maybe Homer noticed the ATV too. What if that was why he stayed behind? What if he was looking for you? "Did Homer mention seeing her? After I left?"

"No," Clementine says. "But he got a call about half an hour later, before he went to the church. He wouldn't tell me who it was, and that usually meant it was Rachel. He knew I didn't like him talking to her. Homer believed in forgiveness, for everything. It was probably the thing we fought most about." Her voice chips and I feel a wave of guilt and don't know why.

"So Rachel was at the ranch," Tasia continued. "And she poisoned the water." The poison was in the back of Homer's ATV. What if you took it?

"Emmett was poisoned, like all the other men," Clementine says. "But Addy was shot."

"That's the key!" Tasia jumps in. "The problem is, all the evidence was contaminated, but there must be some way someone can prove Rachel shot Addy." My back goes rigid. "Even if we can just lay one crime on her." She turns to me, and fear slithers like an eel down my throat. "What happened when you got there?"

"It was just . . . chaos."

Clementine reaches over and squeezes my hand. "You don't have to talk about it if you don't want to." Tasia shoots her a look.

"It's all kind of a blur."

I found Emmett in the armory. I found Addy in the garden. And then you found me.

I always thought it was strange how you left me in the house with Grace, how there was no sign of you at the ranch when I ran to my car. Where did you go? Grace said you went to stop Homer, but he was with Clementine. Maybe you called Homer from Jed's house, from Homer's house *on the ranch,* and asked him to meet you at the church. Then you poisoned him too. And then you drove back to me.

Or worse, I think with a jolt, that was Jed's truck I saw barreling toward me before the accident.

In this made-up series of events, you left me in the yellow house with Grace and drove Jed's truck to Happy Camp to pin the murder on Homer, then accidentally caught me on the way back. You were in a rush; you were trying to get back before I woke up. We were playing a game of chicken, and you ran me off the road.

And then I think, *That's not all. That's not the end of the evidence, the case against you.* Because Jed spent almost every weekend in Willow Creek. He spent a whole week there when he was supposed to be in Texas. Jed said he liked any bad thing; what if you were a bad thing? What if he came home with your lipstick on his collar a week after he and Grace moved here?

The eyewitness claimed he saw you all the time, claimed he saw you *with* Jed. And Addy used to hate Jed, but did she also know, or at least suspect, that you were sleeping with him? While you were supposed to be in hiding, not seen by or known to anyone, but still close enough to visit the ranch, to take the journal and throw the rock and use your parents' computer to message Grace's friends through her account, assuring them that she was fine.

And close enough to look after Grace. You told her she was in danger. You told her a story of murder and madness where you were the savior, where you were the hero of the heroless stories, the only one who understood what it is to be a woman in a world that wants you to disappear.

You kept Grace alive because she was pregnant, and maybe you had scruples or you wanted her baby, or Jed's baby, or you were afraid of what might happen if you murdered one more person. Maybe you knew you would lose the ranch. And then you would have to get rid of everyone, everyone who had shielded you, your mother and your father and your brother.

That burn book I found in my cabin — it could have been about you.

The headlights I saw outside your yellow house could have been you pulling away.

You could have thrown the rock. You could have told me to *run,* because then you could chase me.

The reason Grace didn't make a sound when I pounded on the door.

The reason Jed kept such a close eye on my investigation.

The reason his dog died, a week after he moved here, because she would have known where to find Grace.

The reason Addy told me not to leave the ranch, why she tried to control me, keep an eye on me. She was protecting me from you.

The reason I felt watched. *You* were watching. It could all point back to you.

Isn't that a crazy story? Isn't it fun? To

connect a narrative, to build a case, to investigate a murder without the burden of ever having to solve it?

I don't offer Tasia and Clementine this version of events. After all, I don't really know, not for sure. How can I? It's all just a story I put together, a mental game, an exercise in "true" crime.

"It's fun to speculate." My tone and my words sound off. They sit heavy in the air. There is something off about me. And it was crazy to think, even for a moment, that we could be friends. "But I'm sorry. I just don't buy it."

"But you might be in danger," Clementine says, still unwilling to commit.

"So what?" Tasia says. "It's what she deserves."

"Excuse me, but this is the first time I'm hearing any of this. You should have told me when I asked you, instead of treating me like some crazy loner." But didn't I treat them like suspects? I questioned Tasia until she refused to talk to me. And I looked down on Clementine because she chose a life I rejected. How many times did I forgive Jed? And I couldn't even forgive Clementine for being a good wife. I underestimated them. We underestimated each other.

"We never intended to treat you that way,"

Clementine says. "I think we felt guilty, both of us. We felt like it was our fault."

Tasia glowers. "It was never any of your business. Did you ever consider that? None of this was ever any of your business. And now all those women who come to your little sanctuary are in danger, all the time. All because you *know* Rachel is innocent."

I turn to Clementine, the safer of the two. "If she killed all these women, why did she never kill you?"

But it's Tasia who answers me, and her eyes swell with significance. "Because someone would care if we were gone."

They leave me at the end of the drive. I expect you to meet me there, to confront me. To ask me what happened. I am surprised when you don't. You are everywhere, and suddenly you're gone.

As I approach the house, I hear Hope crying. She is really wailing, her voice dry, like she has been left for a long time, and my heart skips a beat. I rush up the porch and up the stairs, where we keep jugs of water stockpiled on every single step.

I sweep into Hope's bedroom and the window is open; the curtains feather with a breeze off the creek but the crib is empty.

"Hello?" I shout. "Hello? Is anyone here?"

I follow the sounds of her wails out into the hall, toward your bedroom. I try not to think about what Tasia and Clementine said. Or that this is the first time I've let you out of my sight.

I step gingerly into your bedroom. I recognize the cross on your wall from Jed's house, and I wonder how it got there. Hope is crying herself hoarse in the evidence room.

"Hello?" I say. "I'm coming in to get the baby." I feel the comforting dig of the gun on my back.

What if I was set up by Clementine and Tasia? What if they wanted to get me out of the house so someone could take care of you? Moroni? The police? We are running out of suspects.

My palm closes around the knob and I twist, but it's locked. The door of the evidence room is locked with the baby inside. I scan your room, panicked now, heartbeat ratcheting up my chest. Where are you? Where is Grace?

I pull the gun out of my holster. *I could shoot the door down,* I think crazily. I try to calm myself and then, without thinking, without even knowing where it is coming from, I am kicking the door, harder and harder, again and again, like I can make something true if I hurt myself bad enough.

The door cracks. You built this house yourself and it splinters and breaks. Hope cries louder and then I shove, I force myself against the door and I am inside your evidence room.

The baby is on the floor like a discarded doll and I pick her up, inspect her for wounds as my heartbeat scatters like applause. I hold her against me, with the gun still in my hands, and she stops crying, that easy.

"Rachel," I say, but my voice is a whisper. My leg aches all the way to my groin. I feel the beginnings of a cramp. I am inside your evidence room and I am surprised at how many things I recognize: the rock you threw at me, the red glass bottle still half full of poison, the journal from the staff cabin, Bumby's collar, the gun I used to shoot your mother, Jed's pale blue boxer briefs. And then there are the things I don't recognize, as I hold Hope tight against me, bouncing inanely: the dirty, tangled friendship bracelets, the used lipsticks, the tampons, and, spattered with dried blood, two tickets headed south on the Murder Line.

You would have to be stupid to keep these things. You would have to be crazy with confidence, but why wouldn't you be? You were being watched, you were being followed all the time and you didn't stop. Nothing and no one could stop you out here, where there were so few people, and the people you knew were protecting you, or afraid of you, or didn't care.

I hold Hope close to my heart. She has fallen asleep now, relaxed by the race of my heartbeat. I suppose she is used to it, a baby in the womb in this house.

Your voice sends a shock wave up my spine. You sound exactly like yourself, the voice I heard every night, every day, for a year. I press Hope against my chest and I follow your voice down the stairs, into the room off the kitchen, where you record your episodes.

You are seated at the desk. Your back is to me and your words wash over me, the way they always did, like an incantation, like a secret only we knew.

". . . She was kept chained in an abandoned house below the main ranch. . . ."

I walk toward you, the sleeping baby and the gun in my hands.

I think, *What would happen if I killed you? Would I go to jail?* Would your evidence room be enough to convict you, to exonerate me? Or has the evidence been compromised? Are you smart enough to make sure none of it points back to you? That it all lines up, with your podcast, with your sick obsession, with doing the right thing, with making the world a better, safer place?

And I think of the gun I used to shoot your mother. I could hide it. I could bury it. I could bury you.

". . . While her husband lived above her, six hundred yards away and he had no idea . . ."

I set the baby down and she starts to fuss. You hit PAUSE and turn toward her.

Your face has been peppered with a fine spritz of blood. A line appears between your brows. "I wish it was a boy," you say. "Girls cry so much."

And I think about all the men I have known. How my ex collapsed at the first sign of *my* struggle, how Jed was a victim of his appetites, how your father and Homer lived in their little bubbles, so sure of everything. And then I think about the women. I think about Tasia and Clementine, I think about your mother, I think about you and I think about me.

And I think I can survive anything, even you.

ACKNOWLEDGMENTS

This book would not exist were it not for the tireless work of Sarah Bedingfield, who took it to the next level, then harnessed all her agenting powers to find an editor as excited about it as we were. That editor was Jen Monroe, who was pure magic to work with. It is every author's dream to work with a team like this — intelligent, passionate and always going above and beyond.

Thank you to the team at LGR, especially Melissa Rowland and Cristela Henriquez, and to the team at Berkley — Loren Jaggers and Stephanie Felty for publicity, Fareeda Bullert and Natalie Sellers for marketing, Allison Prince and Jamie Mendola-Hobbie for promotional material, and Emily Osborne for the jaw-dropping cover design.

Thank you to all the people in the Siskiyou Forest who opened their homes and hearts to me.

Thank you to the true-crime podcast community, especially Brit and Ashley, Karen and Georgia, for creating a safe space for women in a scary world.

Thank you to Chris Nicholson and the ponies at PRC for making me smile.

Thank you to my mom for watching *Dateline* and my dad for watching Hallmark and to my family — Brazier and Wass — and to my ghost husband for infecting me with his strength, confidence and joy for living.

ABOUT THE AUTHOR

Eliza Jane Brazier is an author, screenwriter and journalist. This is her adult debut. She currently lives in Los Angeles where she is developing *If I Disappear* for television.

The employees of Thorndike Press hope you have enjoyed this Large Print book. All our Thorndike, Wheeler, and Kennebec Large Print titles are designed for easy reading, and all our books are made to last. Other Thorndike Press Large Print books are available at your library, through selected bookstores, or directly from us.

For information about titles, please call:
   (800) 223-1244

or visit our website at:
   gale.com/thorndike

To share your comments, please write:
   Publisher
   Thorndike Press
   10 Water St., Suite 310
   Waterville, ME 04901